D1029757

THE GLANCE
OF COUNTESS
HAHN-HAHN

(Down the Danube)

THE GLANCE
OF COUNTESS
HAHN-HAHN

(Down the Danube)

PÉTER ESTERHÁZY

Translated from the Hungarian
by Richard Aczel

WEIDENFELD & NICOLSON
London

First published in Great Britain in 1994 by Weidenfeld and Nicolson
Orion House, 5 Upper St Martin's Lane, London WC2H 9EA

First published in Hungary in 1991 by Magvetö

ISBN 0 297 84053 3

A catalogue record for this book
is available from the British Library

Filmset by Selwood Systems, Midsomer Norton
Printed and bound in Great Britain by
Butler & Tanner Ltd, Frome and London

The Danube

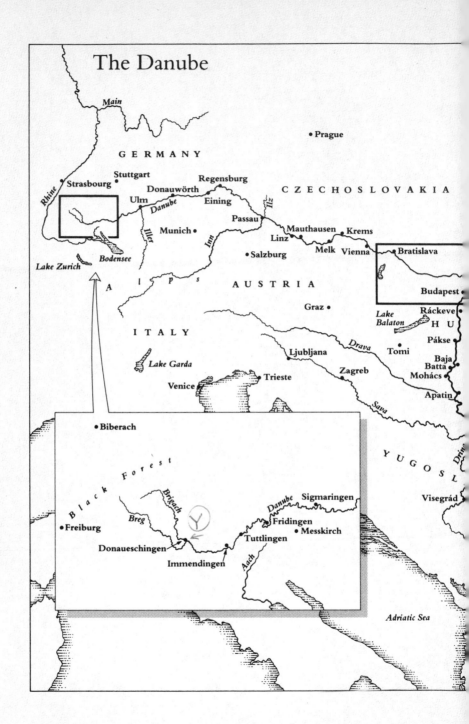

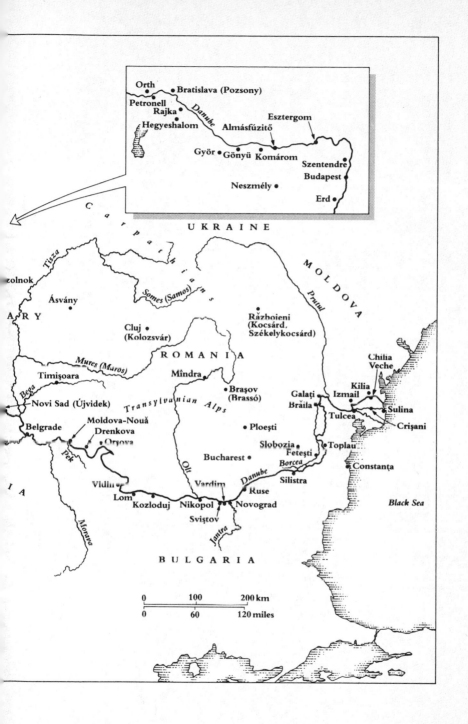

Orth
Bratislava (Pozsony)
Petronell
Rajka
Esztergom
Hegyeshalom
Almásfúzitő
Danube

Győr • Gönyü Komárom
Szentendre
Budapest
Neszmély •
Erd •

UKRAINE

Carpathians

Tisza
zolnok
Ásvány
Somes (Samos)
MOLDOVA
Prutul
A R Y
Cluj •
(Kolozsvár)
Războieni
(Kocsárd,
Székelykocsárd)
ROMANIA
Chilia
Veche
Mures (Maros)
Mîndra
Timişoara
Brașov
(Brassó)
Kilia
Galați
Izmail
Bega
Novi Sad (Újvidek)
Transylvanian Alps
Brăila
Sulina
Tulcea
Belgrade
Moldova-Nouă
Drenkova
Ploești
Crișani
Orșova
Slobozia
Toplau
Pek
Oltu
Bucharest •
Fetești
Borcea
Constanța
Vidin
Vardim
Danube
Silistra
I A
Lom
Ruse
Black Sea
Kozloduj Nikopol Novograd
Svistov
Morava
Jantra

BULGARIA

0   100   200 km
0   60   120 miles

1

'Don't prattle.
You're adding to the chaos.'

I once had this mysterious, distant uncle, whom everyone simply called Roberto, as if he were some Italian gigolo. Everyone, that is, except my father, who didn't call him anything at all: the man's name 'never so much as passed his lips'. He wasn't a blood relation. It was as the husband of a kind of aunt that he briefly became part of the family, joining it at precisely the point where the two sides, maternal and paternal, playfully and fatefully joined hands. A river is always the same river, however many arms it has.

There was something essentially festive about Roberto. Whenever he arrived, or simply dropped in out of the blue, suddenly it was Sunday. His wife, Aunt Irna (a picture of whom my mother and I once discovered in the attic, an oil painting depicting her naked, for which she won our greatest respect), suddenly left for Brazil in '49. Roberto stayed behind. Apparently, the only benefit he ever reaped from his marriage was that, in the summer of '51, he too was 'resettled' – an honour to which he was not, strictly speaking, entitled. He ended up on the Great Hungarian Plain in Russian-style *exile*, which is, of course, to forget that our country doesn't lend itself to internal exile, because if someone has a sweetheart in, say, Eger, he can do *that*, there and back, in a day.

Every now and then he'd look in on us in the small North

Hungarian village where we'd been resettled, and would even bring us presents, as if he were some rich relation from the West, and not just a common nobody like us. My mother became younger by his side. They giggled like children, like brother and sister, at least that was how it seemed to me as I watched them longingly, a make-believe sister with her make-believe brother, obviously because I never had a sister and would have loved to have had one (or two).

I remember my mother turning to my father one evening, with a whole day's Roberto-fest glowing on her face, and saying with a chuckle: 'That's how I would love to have been, just like that.' My father grumbled in reply: 'Don't prattle. You're adding to the chaos.'

You're adding to the chaos – that was my father's favourite turn of phrase, and the one and only sentence he ever directed towards Roberto. I remember the exact date, 28 June 1963. It was the day before I went on holiday to Vienna, or, more exactly, to get my relatives to help me with my homework, 'Summer Holidays in the Country with a Pseudo-Rustic Cousin'. They always stuffed me with Maggi-cube soups, which to this day make me feel sick. I forced them down with bread dumplings, or, when no one was looking, secretly watered the plants – then whoosh, they packed me off to a charity-camp somewhere in the Salz-kammergut. I didn't know just how good this was for me at the time.

'Hello, Noodle,' said a smiling young man on the train, the following day. In those days I addressed even my parents in the polite form. Roberto was the only adult I addressed informally.

'Of all the ...' I leaped to my feet and immediately went bright red.

'I suppose you know the whole story?' he asked. I did, or at least pretended to. My father had thrown him out of the house the night before. I woke up to the sounds of a scuffle. My father shoving Roberto towards the door, the latter hardly resisting, only repeating the words: come off it, come off it! My mother was silent. She stood back and watched it all, as I did. 'You're adding to the chaos!' Roberto always laughed. And he was laughing now as he asked my father what the difference was between chaos and an as yet unrecognized, complex order. 'Out!' I have a remarkable memory for sentences. Winking at the No-Smoking sign, Roberto lit a cigarette. Without waiting for my potential answer, he told me how, the previous evening, he and my father had decided what I must surely already know: that we were to be travelling companions, travellers, that we were to sail the whole length of the Danube, etc., etc., that I must be sick to the teeth of the sober solicitude of my aunts, etc., etc.

'Well, Noodle?'

'Fine,' I nodded, as if I myself had reached the same conclusion. I said nothing of what I had seen through the crack in the door.

2

Nelly Backwater

I could never remember his name, Franz, Joseph or Thomas, but he was waiting for me at the Westbahnhof in his grey chauffeur's uniform, turning his flat service cap in his hands. Knowing it was futile to protest, I handed him my bags at once. He was never in a particularly good mood, but neither was he *moody*; he was simply like a machine. Had their lordships had a comfortable journey? Indeed they had. And was the Count looking forward to his well-earned holiday? The Count was me, and in those days, when I was thirteen years old, I thought nothing odd of this form of address. I drew on what I'd read. No, the chauffeur was somehow devoid of mood; he simply manifested a kind of tension. A centuries-old tension, that is how I'd put it now. We glided down Mariahilfer Strasse in a large, dark blue Citroën. My eyes, accustomed to greyness, simply couldn't get enough of all the colourful advertisements. Roberto didn't speak to either of us.

A few years ago I had, as they say, some business in the family's ancient eyrie (name not important). In the castle a precious library lay hidden away, inaccessible to the general public, and I hoped to find something I needed there. (I found nothing, unless this not-finding-anything was actually *it*.) I received permission from my relatives and, on the agreed morning, I 'reported' at the castle office. I parked illegally outside the castle, but as I glanced up at the building I saw my own name before the word 'Platz', and, disregarding the spirit of the French Revolution, I mistakenly reached the conclusion that whoever would dream of fining me on such a spot would have to be some kind of sorcerer. (The sorcerer, in the form of a young policeman, calculated the price of European emancipation at 150 schillings.)

The *Kanzlei* looked as if it had just stepped out of a novel about the Austro-Hungarian Empire. Four grey and boring, ageless men leaned haughtily over their tables wearing elbow-pads, as is right and proper. They did not stir at my greeting, only barked some kind of command under their breath. I told them I was looking for Nabucco, the Master of Hounds. The youngest of the men looked me up and down. Nabucco, indeed! The Master of Hounds, no less! No one else will do, eh? That is roughly how he looked at me. (An optician would have had his work cut out.) I announced, in the friendliest of voices, that I didn't wish to keep the Master of Hounds waiting. The young man pounced on the word 'waiting'.

'Wait!' he shouted.

'Fine,' I nodded. I felt I was swanning about in a kind of Kafka novel where the publisher has guaranteed a happy end: that is to say, a *pretty* desperate novel. After a while I gave a polite cough and cleared my throat. This time another of the men looked up. Dust sifted from his face. He said nothing, just raised his eye-brows. He must have been older than the first man, but younger than me. (Until the age of thirty-five I always looked at people in this way: older, younger, and if younger then as old as which of my brothers . . .)

'As I was saying . . .'

'From the beginning!' he suddenly bawled.

'I beg your pardon?' Officials are so arrogant and cowardly. This one was particularly the former. For what or whom was it that I was kindly waiting? I was already sick and tired of their agile paraphrastics, but they were only just beginning to get into their stride. They tossed their threats and insinuations this way

5

and that with a weary whimsicality. And they seemed even a little grateful for the opportunity to amuse themselves thus.

'Would you be so kind as to announce me.' They looked at me disappointedly.

'Whom, pray tell? Whom should we have the honour to announce? My dear fellow, whom in the name of God?!' They made it quite plain to me that I did not exist, for in order to exist, something had to be named, named by them, and we hadn't got as far at that just yet. I detested their wordy Austrian dialect. (There had been a time when I couldn't stand German German, because my father had always ridiculed and parodied it. *Meer-retich-tunke* and so on, which is why I felt Austrian German to be more *human*. But later, when I heard it spoken by politicians, it sounded so *schlampig*, and at such times I'd say: they speak the best German in Prague. As if I were really in any position to judge. I have quite a few of these Father-sentences. Cast-offs from the old aristocracy.)

Then I quietly uttered my name.

I'd never seen anything quite like it. All three of them sprang to attention as if possessed, clicking their heels like in some film and staring at me with their chins slightly raised. Their faces could not quite keep pace with events and for a moment preserved their earlier mimicry, vexation, boredom and arrogance. But an expression of embittered servility soon took control, yes, that same centuries-old tension. In order to suppress my laughter, I quickly turned to the youngest and said something like : my dear boy, calm down for fuck's sake, I'm not here on official business. But he was already scurrying to and fro, as were his colleagues who thrust me into a chair, while the most senior among them kept repeating, with tears in his eyes : 'Your Excellency, Your dear, dear, Excellency.' And he stroked the top of my head.

It was Tante Nelly who had sent the chauffeur to meet us. Nelly

schlampig: slovenly, sloppy

was a princess, an old maid of a princess, and very clever. I'm as old as the century, she always liked to say. She was unbeatable at chess. Even last year, more or less on her deathbed after having suffered a stroke, unable to speak and dribbling continually, she still managed to wipe the board with me. In principle, I was pretty smart too, at least such was my reputation as a boy, and this brought us together, a couple of cripples, made for each other. 'Let me have a look at you,' she said when we first met, as if she had been waiting for me, waiting for my mind. Hardly something worth waiting for.

When she was as old as I was then, she regularly played chess with Katarina Schratt, the infamous actress, Franz Josef's confidante. *Die Schratt!*

'She was a shrewd player,' Tante Nelly told me. 'Believe me, as shrewd as they come. She had no culture, and wasn't in the least familiar with the specialist literature, but she played sensually.'

'Sensually?' I grinned.

'I mean with feeling. And she often played chess with His Majesty too. He, on the other hand, was a great bungler. She showed me a couple of their games. Laughable. Boredom and opportunism. We'd sit for hours in the Volksgarten.' She both did and did not want to continue. 'The sun shone into our eyes and made us squint. She pulled her hat down over her face so as not to be recognized, but naturally everyone, absolutely everyone, recognized her, although they all behaved with great tact, as if all they'd seen was a beautiful woman sitting with her daughter. We balanced my little ivory chess set on her knees and played like that. Check, I said, aha, said she, the king is in trouble. And the Emporer, I retorted, at which we both laughed. The Volksgarten ... ah yes, the Volksgarten.'

Nelly came from one of the Empire's most illustrious families. Her ancestors had made all kinds of trouble for Hungary, sometimes arm in arm with my ancestors. For me everything is a matter of family history. Nelly herself resembled the Empire in so far as she too was made up of diverse, internally contradictory elements: she was a large, hefty woman, as big as a wardrobe, but had small, fine hands with a light silken touch, and bushy, almost manly eyebrows which leaped up and down like brushes, or like a pair of misplaced moustaches, *spruce* moustaches, and she had wild blue eyes, like those of a spaghetti-western star, and her sharp, penetrating gaze shone with intelligence, an intelligence which – apart from chess – had no object, because her life had no object either, or if it had, she herself was most certainly not it. And I believe she must have had a goitre too, for a straight path, a path of flesh, led from her chin to her massive, but totally unfeminine, breasts. She wore sinfully expensive and utterly tasteless clothes.

She had never worked in her life, had never desired anything, and wasn't even a coward, or if she was, only in so far as she didn't even desire to become a nun. I thought I understood *the whole thing.*

Nelly was the only person in the world who took more pleasure in me than in Roberto. In Roberto there was indeed much pleasure to be taken. The Maggi soup was already on the table. Retching, bread, flowerpot. Eyebrows ready to leap, but Nelly goes on spooning calmly.

'Has the harvest begun?' She never neglected to ask this. She wanted to know all that was happening in the country, disciplined patriot that she was. 'How is your father?' she asked, turning to me. I nodded. Fine. Adding to the chaos. The maid came in with a tray, Nelly signalled that she should set it down. We went on eating. Roberto and I pulled faces at each other. He talked about our plans for a Danube tour.

'Your parents might have told me,' she grumbled, then cast a penetrating glance at the young man. Roberto was particularly handsome just then, his long, bushy eyelashes like those of an Italian bella donna, his tanned skin giving an oily glow in the warmth, and his black hair smoothed tightly back over his head.

It was as if he had just climbed out of the bath. His elegance encompassed a certain untidiness. 'Say, Roberto, is there something you're not telling me ?'

'Who, me, my dear aunt ?'

'Splendid,' replied the old woman, before ringing for the Gugelhupf, which we all knew would taste like sawdust. My God, I thought to myself later – many years and many cooks later – how much sweat and toil it must take to produce such consistently, regularly, dependably shitty cooking.

3

Ein Wintermärchen

The problem of problems is, above all else, the problem of its existence, of its existence or nonexistence, that is to say, we are in no position to recognize it, we don't know if we're walking on thin ice while the offended river grumbles discontentedly beneath our feet. The missing questions – these are the meta-problem. That is why the brave Wittgenstein is right – although he always twists words, always *uses* them in such a way that, if anyone is to be right at all, it has to be him, and if there is still a problem, and there still is a problem, he falls silent, and we, deeply moved, read even this silence as further proof of his being right – in saying that there are no riddles, for if a question can be posed at all, it must be *possible* to answer it. Scepticism (ergo) is not irrefutable, but simply and quite obviously nonsensical, because it seeks to doubt where there can be no doubt. For doubts can only emerge where there is some kind of question, and questions can only emerge where there are answers, and the latter only where something *can be said*. We sense that even if we have answered all the *possible* questions of science, we have still not begun, in so doing, to touch on the problems of our lives. Then, of course, we are left without any further questions, and precisely this is the answer. The solution to the problem of life is synonymous with the disappearance of the problem.

★

But we've not got that far yet (and besides, *that* Wittgenstein had quite different things to say later on).

Heine, that 'unpleasant mind' (in Engels' caustic, and not altogether unenvious, phrase), having passed through Aachen, then Cologne, suddenly headed north, and with good reason, as he was on his way to see good old Hoffmann in Hamburg. Why then should we speak of an account of Donaueschingen as 'lacking'? That which does not exist is not lacking. Why *should* there be a question? The poet clearly didn't visit Donaueschingen, just as he never visited New York, nor made a significant contribution to the development of artificial fertilizer, and so on. One thing is, another isn't.

Chance is the god of fools, my father would boldly pronounce, if we, having broken one of the last, worthless pieces of the family china, held the 'garish mask of chance' up to our faces as an excuse. 'Pure clumsiness,' is what fathers would like to hear at such times before shooting us on the spot by way of a pardon. Which is what they always do.

I once got hold of a superbly annotated edition of Heine's epochal *Deutschland (Ein Wintermärchen)*, with woodcuts by the Soviet G. Echeistov. It was published by the National Peace Council in February 1956, as part of the Pocket Library series of the Peace Committee. I didn't think much of it at the time, but I did notice that Heine spent – as I would now say, in retrospect – a *suspiciously* long time between Aachen and Cologne, first at the beginning of October 1843 (from the 4th to the 10th), then on the way back (from Hamburg to Paris) in December (from the 8th to the 10th), and again in the summer of 1844 (about a week). *By chance* I just happened to leaf through Miklós Várhegyi's little philological masterpiece which places two Heine-sentences (?), aphorisms (?), under the microscope. (For my part, I'm terrified of aphorisms, along with all those other sentences that openly seek to encapsulate the Truth.) Várhegyi came across this Heine-refuse in the *Ehe bei Tageslicht*.

And it was this which caught my eye. For this short-lived but adventurous periodical contained Wolfgang Menzel's literary excursion – or leapfrog – to Donaueschingen (three numbers, dated 1827 and 1828)! Who could fail to be surprised at finding Heine – who really wasn't 'a grave man' (*Romeo and Juliet*, Act III) – in Menzel's journal, the very same Menzel (whom one can call, without exaggeration, reactionary) who turned against Goethe, then vehemently attacked the political and literary aspirations of the Young Germany movement and the 'French influence' it was said to embody, singling out in particular Ludwig Börne and Heine himself. Heine, who preferred to be indebted to his uncle than to a stranger, attacked Menzel in a pamphlet of 1837: 'Über den Denunzianten'.

As it happened, the rat I had smelled turned out to be a mere field mouse beside the real discovery. Two young men together, then each on his own. (How many such cases do we witness in this country today, now that the external power that forced people together has finally disappeared? We thought they were our friends, when in truth they were only refugees. As for the heavy breathing on our necks, we were simply mistaken.)

Várhegyi comments quite sensibly that to become something is purely a matter of *decision*. We can catch *this* decision red-handed on the bridge that arches between two discovered sentences. What is actually at stake here is a choice between the Danube and the Rhine, and it is here that Heine proves himself to be: German. Exclusively German. Which is – that is to say, being anything whatsoever is – after all, a kind of parody. (See the letter to Marx.) But then, who would have had greater need of Paris than a German? For Paris, that which is French and not German, can only have meaning and significance if that which is German, and not French, has meaning and significance too! The more he damns his damnable nation, the more he loves it! While we do not reproach him for this, we cannot fail to point out the narrowness of his horizons, and, however strange it may sound, bearing in mind that Heine has the reputation of a man of courage, we can see in him the traces of intimidation by his own nation, even though these traces suggest intimidation of the highest quality and of the most generous kind. In attempting to account for our sense of something lacking, it might lead to misunderstanding were we to allude to Hölderlin (who closes his poem, 'Der Gott', with the words : *Doch was er tut, der Storm, niemand weiss es*), so we may as well throw in Goethe too, the author of the *Farbenlehre*, a Lehre which, as it stands, is nonsense, in that it seeks to enlarge what cannot be enlarged, namely : Goethe himself.

When we listen to Heine's Deutschland-music, however, we hear the voice of a great patriot :

> I am breathing the air of home again !
> My cheeks glow and understand.
> And all this dirt on the road, it is
> the filth of my fatherland.

> Like a welcome from old acquaintances
> were the waving tails of our dapples,
> and their steaming dung seemed as beautiful
> as Atalanta's apples.

But let us return to our investigation.

Várhegyi's first discovery (on the very first page) is as follows : '*Between Donaueschingen and Brăila: that is the only meaningful definition of the present moment in time.*' This is the beginning ! The breathlessness of a young man, but also his faith, openness, undecidedness. How much more resigned he sounds some six months later (from about page three), armed with all the melancholy of knowledge and, not to exaggerate, with the horrified realization of the necessity of decision : '*What would the Rhine*

'*Doch was er tut . . .*': But what the storm does, no one knows

(*Danube*) *be without the Danube* (*Rhine*)? – *Or is it precisely questions of this nature that are making me feel nauseous?*'

No! No! It isn't nausea we feel, rather let our sails be swollen by the wind! Could it be that the whole question of the German orientation of Central Europe stems from this *choice* between the Danube and the Rhine? For what does it matter that the Danube is German (among other things) at its source? An Ulmer can only see as far as Regensburg, a Regensburger only as far as Passau, and as for the good people of Passau: they're blind. Doesn't this hydrograph tell the history of the last hundred years? (Give or take a little digression to the Don and the Spree, leaving a few million dead ...).

WWII

That all this isn't simply idle gossip is borne out by a letter published by Walter Victor in his book *Marx und Heine* (Berlin, Henschel, 1953). Although the letter speaks pretty much for itself, it is worth emphasizing in advance the staggering to and fro that characterizes Heine at the source of the Brigach: that all-European irresolution which is not so much a dilemma, as a kind of ambivalence, the ambivalence signified by Heine's tiny steps before such a watershed (even if we disregard Marx's current loss of prestige). We have omitted from the letter the sideswipe at Engels (for reasons already touched upon), and have elected to leave the epithet 'Liebster Marx!' in the original German, as the rather elevated form 'dearest' is alien to Hungarian letter-writing style. Heine knew only too well what was at stake, and it is no accident that, even from a distance of some seventeen years, the experience has remained so poignant and vivid. This was the moment of Heine's essential evolution into manhood, the great defeat! Anyway, the letter:

Liebster Marx!
Once again I'm struggling with my fatal eye trouble. I pour in eyedrops every morning – it is rather like taking a shower, but I do hope at least something gets into my dim-sighted eyes. I beg your forgiveness for my untidy scribble. Even I can't read what I've written, but then we two need very few signs in order to understand each other.

My young friend! I shall not say that you reproach me without cause, nor shall I beg your pardon. But you should know that I am who I am, and consequently I go which way I can. (Herr Goethe goes which way he pleases ...) In vain do you *want* something of me. Everyone wants something. I allow you to choose among me, and if you cannot, you must simply shrug your shoulders.

Your remarks concerning the Danube are far-reaching and at times even frightening. But now you are speaking to one who has, over the last seventeen years, with humiliating frequency, walked the hills of Brigl (by which I do not mean wandering casually up and down), not so much in search of, as surveying, the river's sources. Had God created this obscurity for me alone? Maybe. But you must not forget, I am not nor ever have been a cynical man. I am an old poet, blind as a bat. Oh, how pitiful to be something! And I am, that I know.

Thus the confusion concerning the river's source does not *interest* me, it simply concerns me ; and it is not in the least surprising that this confusion follows the river all the way – you need only think of the Jews.

But I do not want to think of such things. It is all too much for me. Clearly it would be easy to adhere to the thesis that there is no Danube at all, only Breg and Brigach! Thus the Danube becomes a fiction. Poetry. If I walk one hundred metres higher up, I already find the little Elz making its way to the Rhine, Old Father Rhine. The Danube is a sonnet, a mode of speech, a discourse. I have to confess to you now that I'm looking at the Elz.

Whenever I can I come here among all the puddles and whisper wicked little sentences into the wind. Do not think that I am sentimental. Where is the man who could see all this *in one*? We are all bound by the fishing regulations. I no longer even remember who it was who mentions on page 28 of the German edition of his book that Dielhelm speaks of a tavern on the road to Freiburg from whose gutters the water flows on the one hand into the Rhine, and on the other into the Danube. Well, I am not that gutter.

I am glad to be getting out of here. I sent my wife on ahead to France, to her mother, who is dying.

May God go with you, my dear friend.

With all my heart,

H. HEINE

15

PS. If the Danube, as a great integrator, does not exist, then where are the Habsburgs? Nowhere. But I don't dare say that Europe is nowhere either. Nor do I accept the notion that history has come to an end. Or is dead.

Do not forget: the difference between water and a river is that the latter has a memory, a past, a history. There is no such thing as progress. Nor history. But there is fate.

Write to Hess. Campe will send the offprints. Do not be impatient. Grow a little older. Gradually I shall become like a woman novelist. Do you know what I mean? One eye glued to the paper, the other always glued to a man. With the exception of Countess Hahn-Hahn, who has only one eye.

Yours, H.H.

What can we add to this sandbank? Let us close with Várhegyi's poignant supplication: The most vain and laughable of all endeavours is the attempt of creation to create chaos ... God – *pars pro toto* ...

4

'Oh Roberto,
these are harsh words indeed!'

I could see that what Roberto was saying was not in the least to our host's liking. My uncle was explaining how he'd been up to the source of the Breg that afternoon (not a word of which was true; he had been asleep in our room, next to me, who didn't dare so much as bat an eyelid, while he, from time to time, would let out a snore, and seemed so tired that it frightened me), no, honestly, he, Roberto, had been talking to the *very* woman from whose dark, rank kitchen the Danube – how shall we put it? – *rises*, although it is not altogether impossible that the water trickling from her low gutter feeds the source from which the water in the gutter itself derives, which is to say that we have at once an endless cycle, which comes in very handy to the fine ambition and forbidden attraction towards chaos which characterizes the German spirit (see the expression coined by the elder Mann: '*Verzweifelt Deutsch*'), honestly, the woman was a *witch*, although he was loath to dwell on that subject right now, for obvious reasons, and here, with a smile, he pointed at me.

At that moment Roberto looked very much like my father, discounting the moustache, which was actually impossible to discount, a full, thick tuft, the most characteristic feature of his face, a conspicuousness that was immediately disconcerting, as if one were to declare of a mask that it represented the *sine qua non* of the face. It was just like János Megyik's moustache – if the name means anything to anyone. It always exuded a particularly delightful smell: a mixture of tobacco and perfume. It was a foreign smell. I say that because there is also a distinctive Hungarian smell. It would be both vulgar and ungrateful to say that Hungarians stink, although in our present confusion we might willingly accept this – stink? you bet! and if what for us, for our poor little nation that has suffered so much, is a kind of consolation, is for others simply a kind of stench, then there are reasons for this, for it surely has something to do with the quality of the soaps and sprays, and with the percentage of nylon in the shirts we can buy here, and such factors are never independent of international politics. Wash with Viennese soap each day/You'll have to fight the boys away.

Walking down Mariahilfer Strasse one can see from afar who hails from where. A crippled shoe sole, a concertina-like trouser leg, a shining Red October Clothing Factory label, a fresh denim suit: these are all important tell-tale sign, just like Megyik's moustache or the gutters of the Breg. But in the last analysis it is the *whole* impression that counts, the overall disposition, the atmosphere, the spirit of place, the dramatic and slovenly, worn and aggressive, weary and pushy style of dress which immediately strikes the eye. And for me it is enough to look at a shop window, that is, at my own reflection.

While still in Vienna we went to the tailor's. 'Well, Noodle! What are we? We're travellers, that's what we are. So what is it we do?'

'We travel.'

'Exactly. So we're going to need special *travelling uniforms*. And what does that mean? It means it's time to go and see the great Gigi.'

Gigi was like Truth personified: 'Only those who knew him could find him.' And Roberto knew everyone. I had the feeling he knew everything, and could organize absolutely anything. I thought the same of my father, only in his case I was ultimately forced to recognize that he couldn't quite organize everything, which is to say he was more like me, stood closer to me, while Roberto stood closer to my father.

Sometimes I took his hand, then let it go again, and he took mine, and then we'd start laughing. When we turned off from the Hoher Markt, I suddenly pressed him up against the wall, then stood back against it beside him, in fun, as if we were being chased. I was about to go on again, grinning merrily, but Roberto's brown face had turned snow-white. Had it made any sense to do so, I might have imagined that he'd taken fright. Had I seen someone, he asked. Who should I have seen? Just answer the question. And then I thought, he's playing, he's *playing back* at me.

A modest brass plate indicated that a gentlemen's tailor with an Italian name could be found on the second floor of the building. A tall, attractive woman wearing nylon stockings and pungent perfume received us. She shrieked and blushed when she saw Roberto and it was clear to me at once that she was in love with him.

'*Nicht vor dem Kind*,' I said quickly to avert the impending theatrics. Then the white folding doors opened and a tiny old-maid-like figure with shrivelled skin stepped out, wearing trousers and a waistcoat, thick lipstick and light eye makeup. This was Gigi. Roberto and the tailor embraced. I noticed that the beautiful woman was no longer smiling. The two men disappeared into the back room. For some reason the woman felt she had to keep me company and chattered a lot of nonsense.

My head was spinning when we once again stepped out into the street – Juden Gasse, it has just come back to me. The whole fitting session had seemed like some kind of ritual dance, and I didn't even know what we were looking for or trying on. At times the *Meister* groped my thigh. He had an unexpectedly deep and growling voice, rather like that of István Kormos – if the

'*Nicht vor dem Kind*': 'Not in front of the children'

19

name means anything to anyone. Bits of material flew through the room, socks, butterflies 100 per cent wool, and at times they called out: catch! Mmmm, what fine material. It was the sheer abundance of it all that made me dizzy. In the meantime the secretary came in and laughed with the men. They drank too. Now you're going to have a nice tweed jacket, the *Meister* told me, but don't go growing out of it, will you. At this they all whinnied with laughter, especially the woman. But I didn't really mind. Oh, I'm so embarrassed, the woman kept repeating, or I've got a terrible headache. She always said these two things together: Oh, I'm so embarrassed, or I've got a terrible headache, and she didn't seem in the least embarrassed, but perhaps she really did have a headache, poor thing. Her face changed continually: from a woman of the world to a little girl, then an austere employee. Everything about her kept changing, even her body, which at times also became austere, then at other times simply twitched or receded into the background, or rather, pressed itself into the background. Only her eyes remained perpetually the same, two enigmatic precious stones, strange cat's eyes with a certain tigerish gaze. I had never looked so closely at a woman before. I had never thought that there could be so much of anyone to look at.

The three of us went on, plunging deeper into this newfangled stupor, which by now had become the stupor of shopping. Ties and tiepins, cashmere scarves, I'd never done anything like it before. I didn't know then, and have since forgotten, that one can get drunk from shopping, just as one can from gambling, sinking ever deeper, increasingly unable to see one's way out, losing all sense of any valid, *external* logic, propelled by the laws of intoxication alone, the rules of the dance, a tottering that turns into spinning, and . . . don't let me go!

Nor did we let one another go – shoes to go with the dinner jackets, socks to go with the shoes, trousers to go with the socks, a shirt to go with the trousers, a jacket to go with the shirt, an overcoat to go with the jacket, a briefcase to go with the overcoat,

a suitcase to go with the briefcase, and to go with the suitcase
. . . a dinner jacket, a white one this time, which meant another
pair of shoes, stop ! . . . ice creams on Schwedenplatz, a stroll by
the Danube canal, see, Noodle, there it is !, but on again at once,
back to the Kärtner Strasse, a cosmetic bag to go with the scissors,
then various types of razors, but I'm not even stubbly ! Oh,
young man, but how time flies ! . . . deodorants, lotions and
potions, hand cream, body cream, face cream, eau-de-cologne,
shaving foam, to this very day I still have a little bottle of Azzaro
perfume which they threw in as a gift, on the house, and a nice
little butterfly strass with open wings, I remember, it had the
number 99 on it, which, as I realized later, meant dollars, not
schillings, and in those days there were twenty-five schillings to
the dollar.

Then, just as we were coming out of Steffl (where, needless
to say, we hadn't bought anything), my uncle suddenly said :
'Now I'll just have to pop in here,' and he hung his head. The
woman stopped short, almost underneath Roberto, underneath
him with her breasts, supporting his head, which she then took
in her hands, in a way that was not so much coarse as impassive,
holding it like a watermelon. Then, as if both to confirm and
contradict the preceding impression, she suddenly launched into
the following entreaty :

'No, don't, Roberto, please don't !' They spoke in German,
which irritated me, because I hadn't the slightest idea of what
they were or were not saying. (Once, much later, on the 1st of
August 1976, when the Reichsbrücke in Vienna collapsed, and
we had been hearing all morning that the Reichsbrücke had
collapsed, and I, as someone who had often gone bathing with
Roberto in a backwater of the Danube at Gansehaufel, happened
to know that the Reichsbrücke wasn't the kind of construction
to just collapse like that, I found myself left wondering in
total exasperation what on earth it could have been that these
Viennese had been saying which had led me to understand that
the Reichsbrücke had collapsed. When, on the very same day, I

heard that Niki Lauda had been badly burned, I simply nodded, saying to myself: this is just one of those days; that is how German works today – in me.) *Sie wissen, dass ich das besser kenne. Du weisst . . . Gehen Sie nicht dorthin.*

We stood outside the Vienna branch of the Hungarian state travel company, IBUSZ. Roberto went inside. The woman, for her part, mumbled the following sentence under her breath: 'Oh, Roberto, these are harsh words indeed.' Then she looked up at me, and I thought to myself, I'd never forget that gaze, but forget it I did. It is only sentences that I can be counted on never to forget: Oh, Roberto, these are harsh words indeed.

'*Sie wissen* . . .': 'You know that I understand these things better than you do. You know . . . Don't go in there.'

5

Supplication for a sentence

Drafting down, says Pilinszky. Writing is born on the page, not in the head. Just as travelling is born *en route*. Thus I was unable to avoid measuring the object, step by step in pedantic detail, bend by bend, puddle by puddle, over eddy and marsh, over bar and dam, from the 'narrow vale of the winding Danube' to the spit of Sulina and the thousand *piccole tole*. I changed, I would say, were this a matter of public concern.

Twice I missed the turning, but then, after all, Donaueschingen is not the kind of place one can fail to find. I was tired, the air had suddenly cooled; shivering and frustrated, I looked at the town to see if it had anything to 'say'. But the small town, like all small towns, kept silence. As always, I asked myself what it would be like to live here – and shuddered at the thought. Even Ludwigshafen would be better than this, I shouted out loud. (Why Ludwigshafen, of all places, I have no idea.)

   I felt duty-bound, even on the way out here, to follow the path of the river. Looking at the map I had been seized with excitement. And that excitement remained the only real experience between Budapest and Donaueschingen. Even though all that had happened was what could happen : the road had followed the Danube, but followed it like a good detective, in secret. What had been a millimetre on the map was some kilometres in reality.

If road and river crossed, it simply meant that I clattered across a bridge, and could catch a fleeting glance, nodding: aha, so you're the one they call '*Fürst aller europaeischen Flüsse*' (see: *Eine genaue Darstellung aller um und an der Donau gelegenen Königreiche ... An das Tagelicht gegeben von einem Liebhaber*, Nurenberg, 1688, Johan Hofman), and with that we parted company (Liebhaber apart).

Thus I jiggled and juggled around the river, unable to worm my way close. Nevertheless, when I did finally get up here, I was at last forced to concede that the Danube: exists. No great discovery, but let's begin modestly.

'The Danube does not exist, that is as clear as day. The Danube is not something, not the water, not the molecules, not the dangerous currents, but the *totality*: the Danube is the form. The form is not some mantle beneath which something still more important and serious lies hidden. (*In concreto*: the water ...) What does it mean to say that the form of a book is the Danube? Is this a form in the same sense that a sonnet is a form? Where are the fourteen lines here? Or not so much a sonnet as a novel? There you don't even have the fourteen lines; so what is a novel? Each individual novel provides its own answer to that question these days, which means that all the definitions turn back in upon themselves, from the source to the gutter and vice versa; they are simultaneous, they neither have been, nor will be: they simply *are*. To be – it is a bit late for that. Is the novel identical with its own death? I don't claim that the novel is dead if, and only if, God is dead. Nor do I claim that if God is dead, the novel must also be dead. And neither do I claim that if the novel is dead, God must be dead too. But to the question of whether the novel is or isn't dead etc., I have a very resolute and concrete answer: I DON'T KNOW.'

I wrote this in my notebook at the point where the two little

---

'*Fürst aller europaeischen Flusse*': 'Prince among the rivers of Europe'
Eine genaue Darstellung . . . : An Exact Description of All Kingdoms Lying on or by the Danube . . . Brought into the Light of Day by a Lover

Amateur
Dilettante

24

rivers converge, and whereafter the *thing* is referred to as the Danube. I decided to come out here first, before calling on Baron von C., with whom I was going to stay, just as I had done with Roberto all those years earlier. I clambered down the steep bank and walked out to the Y. I sat down and stared at the converging waters, trying to distinguish between them, or, to exaggerate a little, trying to distinguish the molecules, this one belongs to the Breg, this one to the Brigach, and over there, that is already the Danube! They say – although I no longer remember where I read this – that to find the source of the Danube, you have to find a river that could reasonably be the Danube and stroll up and down its banks mumbling continually: this is the Danube, this is the Danube.

'How will I recognize it? How does one *approach* it? Is there a given method? Evidently general questions. Questions of love? – As for death, I'll return to that later.'

Now and then I threw a leaf into the water, in the hope that it would float all the way down to the Black Sea. I attempted to calculate the speed of the current. I chose a section of riverbank about 3.5 metres long, threw a leaf as far into the middle of the river as I could (mainstream!) and measured the time. Ten seconds, that is about, say, twenty metres per minute, which must work out at 1.2 kilometres per hour. Now, if the river is 2850 kilometres long, that must be about 2400 hours, which is one hundred days. Jackass.

I watched this slender, graceful, silver ribbon innocently wind its way across the Eschingen plain. Who could say what lay in store for it? In a bright yellow frock woven of golden thread, the ball of the sun sank lower and lower as it changed into its violet evening negligée. It was then I knew that this river would give me everything: orography, hydrography, history, ethnography, tourist information, complete with anecdotes, hopes and corpses, everything, past, present and future, flood and drought, maelstrom and fish soup, and people too . . . There was only one thing it would not provide, the one thing I needed most of all, for I simply couldn't see how, how on earth, it could possibly give me sentences. 'And with true tears, Oh Lord, I pray . . .'

6

Roberto narrates

'Ignorance does not protect innocence,' crowed Roberto, deciding not to make allowances for me after all and launching into the story of the witch who dwells up by the Danube-Breg source, where, in her fury and her boredom, she keeps switching on her cassette recorder to recite the great and true story of the Danube, the smallest and briefest of smiles only flickering across her otherwise dark face when she hears the word Tulcea played back in her own voice. This woman, so the story went, would give birth to horrible monstrosities and sell them at a very good price. It had all begun during the boiling hot days of haymaking when she was still a girl. They'd gone and got her pregnant, and to keep it hidden she covered herself up tight, her stomach, so tight that the kid got squashed, and the circus offered her good money for it. And that's what gave her the idea. Later she could plop out the required shape almost to order. Our host, the Baron, shook his head in disapproval. He was busy waltzing to 'The Blue Danube' with the gardener.

Uncle Adalbert was a peculiar little man, short and fidgety, like a ladies' hairdresser. He counted as one of the richest men in Germany, or rather, he owned one of the largest estates, woodlands in particular. We were somehow related, at least in so far as we addressed each other in the '*du*' form in German. When I asked at home exactly how we were related, my father, who took only a marginal interest in genealogy (and under-standably, too, for people are usually related *to* him, although it should be added that he exhibits in all this a genuine modesty, which this sentence is unable to suggest), answered, with the indifference such questions always elicited from him, that 'one' was usually related to us through the Lichtensteins, and he watched me slyly to see whether I took him seriously or not.

The Baron was only eighteen years old when he took up his duties, so to speak, his parents having died in a car accident on their annual trip to see the Bayreuth *Ring*. (In those days I didn't know what the *Ring* was, and I confused Bayreuth with Beirut. Accordingly, I posed a few politely interested, gentlemanly ques-tions, which must have created a rather bizarre impression.) Uncle Adalbert started out as a highly talented atomic physicist, Dirac's prize pupil ('the brightest of the bunch') and it was not his great estates which put an end to his scientific career, but a tick bite from which he got melangitis, just like Sarolta Monspart – if the name means anything to anyone. For weeks he hovered between life and death with tiny muscular spasms running all the way down his body, just like a peaceful Danube bay ruffled by an evening breeze. His heartbeat slowed almost to a standstill. (Incidentally, there are two types of tick (*Ixodes ricinus*), Eastern and Western, with the Alps constituting a kind of border in between. The consequences of Eastern bloodsucking can be more severe, although the reasons for this have not as yet been scientifically explained. In Hungary, in spite of the fact that it is on the eastern side of the Alps, one finds both this kind, and the other.) When he recovered, his brain no longer functioned in its former, reliable fashion. It was rather like a beautiful Brussels lace shawl in which moth-eaten, burnt and mouldy patches alternate with the perfect, unblemished squares. And one could never tell just how much he knew about all this, which made him very difficult to get on with. But not, of course, for a child, who could see at once that he was dealing with an idiot who was much cleverer than everyone else. Since his illness, his days

28

had been filled with two activities : hunting and dancing.

'Slow waltz !' he called out to someone in the room, who was meant to jump up and dance with him at once as the music miraculously began to play. 'Cha-cha-cha !' our host cried out anew in the middle of the dance, and the music immediately changed. (How, I never knew.) Uncle Adalbert danced with ease and devotion, his face radiating a sublime, contented glow. Whenever he stumbled they thrust an armchair beneath him, into which he would collapse. In the silence Tante Maria immediately opened a bottle of champagne. There was something decidely grand about the whole madness. Perhaps because here it seemed authentic and valid.

That it was champagne we drank on these long, late afternoons – there was no breakfast, we each took lunch in our own rooms, and only met in the afternoon, in the downstairs drawing room, neighbours, guests, always some ten to twelve people dressed in suits, while in the evening we met in the drawing room, or rather, inner garden, upstairs, in dinner jackets – that it was champagne we drank I had no idea at the time. To myself I called it 'fizzy wine', which wasn't good as wine at all, it tickled and scratched, but this tickling was quite nice. Sekt, they called it, and I'd have only understood a word like champagne.

'Don't even think of praying,' Roberto threatened at bedtime. Our bedrooms opened into each other. We swaggered about in our new night garb, pirouetting like a couple of angels. I laughed at Roberto – in those days I found it impossible not to pray. I think he had the whole thing planned, because he stroked my head, we got into bed, and he turned out the light. We said nothing. I waited. Silence. I gave up.

'No story today ?' He did not reply. I ran over to his bed and climbed in beside him. It was nice and warm. (My father's bed was always cold, my mother's always warm. No value judgement intended.) He still said nothing. He lay on his back staring up at the ceiling, his hands folded on his chest like a corpse. I turned on my side and, resting my head on his shoulder, nestled against him. Everything had grown too serious, and this frightened me, because I didn't understand.

'Why don't you say something?' he asked suddenly. 'You can see that I can't speak. Why don't you help me?' This frightened me all the more. You just don't say such things to a child. 'What kind of man do you think I am?' His gaze on the ceiling. Helpfully, terror-sticken, I said:

'Roberto, you're an idiot.'

We woke up too early for lunch, and without the appropriate slovenliness. We squinted at each other to check who was awake and who unable to meet the minimal requirements of leisurely life – that is to say, to wait for the sun to shine on one's belly before even contemplating climbing out of bed. My head was still on his shoulder. He always told me a story, every day, whether at bedtime or in the morning or in the middle of the afternoon, during one of our excursions, or even in the company of others he'd whisper a sentence in my ear, if only a line of poetry, or a weighty, merry secret, but there was always a story. This isn't a story – I bristled at once – after all it's about us, because it's about a traveller who's sailing up the Danube, who 'throws yet another sleepy glance towards Donaueschingen'. What did I mean about us? he said with a dismissive wave of the hand, more disappointed than angry, anybody! anybody! about us? what's that supposed to mean? And if I look back at all those stories now it isn't myself I see, nor even my wonderful scoundrel of an uncle, but someone I know, not a relative, not even a Hungarian, nor a Serb, nor a Czech, not anyone, but that isn't true either, rather, sometimes this, sometimes that, neither likable nor unpleasant, but someone who simply *is* – although I agree with Várhegyi's observation that it is an unforgivable arrogance on the part of a human being if he *sees* that everything is okay – and above all that someone who created this *is*, someone (more exaltedly: the someone) who created this rotten twentieth century *is* in his own image, yes indeed, that much-questioned and highly-questionable someone. They were like my mother's

30

old stories, there too one could always see (*the mother allowed her son to see*) that the story was born of the events of that day, and there too I had always wanted to ask who was who, and which one was I, Porky the pig or Suzy the Sow, or was I the crocodile, or the air, or the river? And mother, just like Roberto, would simply nod huffily, it would seem that *they* didn't like this who's who.

THE TRAVELLER INTRODUCES HIMSELF

The traveller began travelling. He cast a sleepy glance at Donaueschingen. He was a professional traveller; travelling was his occupation. In his younger days he had concocted great literary plans, and had with his literary efforts in his homeland, which is called Hungary, and where Hungarians live, who speak Hungarian, or, more accurately, throw Hungarian words in one another's faces, eat Hungarian, chomping Hungarian meat between their Hungarian teeth, make Hungarian love, with their Hungarian heads resting on Hungarian thighs, are born Hungarian, and die Hungarian, with Hungarian light falling on their cradles and Hungarian soil falling on their coffins, on their velvety or, as the case may be, wasted Hungarian bodies, and they live Hungarian, in his homeland, that treasure chest which lay like a treasure chest in the lap of the Carpathians, he, with his literary efforts had even made a name for himself, but then, when it became clear that even God had created him to be a traveller, he became a traveller.

★

He travelled on commission. He would be hired by this or that illustrious gentleman or shabby country, and then he would set off on his travels.

★

Just between ourselves, he hated travelling, and loved nothing more than to sit around in his study. No, that's not true. His soul was the soul of a traveller, in so far as he had several souls, and in his more ambitious moments he felt he had as many as he liked. It is always possible that 'one' is more than 'several', but he didn't give this much thought. To put it bluntly, he didn't give death much thought. Although, as far as death was concerned, he was no virgin. He had stood beside the grave before, sobbing, silent, numb, he knew what it meant to lose a parent, to cry, to feel pain, he knew what black stood for, but his life did not stand in the shadow of death, even though life does stand in the shadow of death. All this may well be called paradoxical, or, better still, comical, because it was for precisely this reason that Contractors (Hirers) engaged him, for in essence they sent him out into death. The traveller was immortal, in so far as he thought of himself as such.

APPENDIX TO THE TRAVELLER INTRODUCES HIMSELF

'It is Christmas-time as I write these lines, and the Christmas of '89 in Central Europe is not a festival of peace and love. To put it nicely, I'd say it was a festival of freedom. But for days now I've sat glued to the television, watching the formation of my own destiny, just as the Americans once followed the Second World War ; Schwarzwaldklinik. Weeping faces and the crackle of gunfire in the background. Broadcast live. A man of about my age from Temesvár says that he was just walking by the banks of the Bega, his child on his shoulders, when he heard shooting. I simply couldn't believe it had anything to do with us, he says in tears. His son shook slightly, then fell. By this time the Securitate-murderers were already beside them. They threw the child into the river like a cat, and handcuffed the man. But they forgot to shoot him. – It is Christmas, but again and again I have to wrestle

Schwarzwaldklinik : A popular German soap-opera

32

with my hatred. At least to reach the point where I feel ashamed. But I am motionless.

'I simply couldn't believe that all that was happening had anything to do with me.'

TRAVELLER'S FATHER HELPS OUT

When he received his first commission – to prepare 'a travelogue about the Danube, in his own very individual style, spiced with ironical reflections, from, shall we say, the Black Forest to the Black Sea' – and it suddenly occurred to him that, once upon a time, it had been with precisely such a Danube tour that his father had rewarded him for passing his matriculation, he decided to pay the old man a visit. He waited for it to get dark, to avoid arousing the suspicion of the neighbours, then with base but agile movements, tied the ageing man to one of the three trees his mother had planted some thirty years before the three birches, which had grown aslant in the constant north wind, like three hardy travellers pressing on against a headwind (south wind!). When the old man was so tightly bound that he could not move an inch, the traveller began, coolly, full of love and gratitude, and with blows that were not so much hard as agile, yet brutal all the same, to beat every last Danube story out of his father.

His father did not give in easily, for he had little faith in his son, who, for his part carried on with his beating regardless. Then he wiped his father down with a flannel, washed and dried him, and they both sat down at the garden table and drank whatever kind of alcohol they could find in the house, wine, beer, schnapps, Unicum, eggnog, aftershave.

DESCRIPTION OF TRAVELLER'S DUTIES

The Traveller could be hired for longer or shorter voyages, groups or individuals, in principle or in practice. There were special offers too, for voyages in time, for example ('Check out the Peace of Karlowitz!') – the latter being the so-called Orlan-do-Step-Package. All this he posted on a small, modest plaque outside his house. He even prepared fliers.

Do you wish to travel? Do you suffer from the illusion that you can simply head off? You think you just have to find a travel agent and basta? You are mistaken. This century does not favour the traveller. This is the century of the tourist. The Tourist does not travel: he simply changes places. He goes somewhere. (Where? Where? Oh where shall we go?) He is the century's degenerate traveller, who timidly flees into the future. When he has unpacked his bags in one of those hotels which are the same the world over, and lies down on the beach that comes with such hotels, he pronounces haughtily: 'We'll come back next year too,' and 'Let's make a note of this, this bodega!'

Is this enough for you?
For me it would be the end of the world.
The hired traveller brings the whole world to your doorstep. In all its splendour. The traveller will uplift and ennoble. Identity problems? Hire a traveller. A hired traveller is not a solution, but a possibility. Your tragic existence will know no bounds. At the centre of it all you will – in Van Cha's words – still not find the One who dissolves all contradictions, but will confront chaos, lack, the abyss, the unfulfilled, the tension between coming into being and passing away. Everything depends on what you do with the 'I'. You will remain unable to view as a superfluous burden that which is better forgotten; on the contrary, you will drag your 'I' behind you wherever you go, be it to heaven or to hell. The Westerner will be astonished to discover that the two are not so very different after all. The hired traveller will put an end to this astonishment. You will be like a pilgrim who carries a pianino on his back and finds the world a little uncomfortable ... The traveller is always himself, and as such is infinite. Hire a traveller and you hire infinity! A promenade in the soft lap of Nature, among other things! Fare-stage concessions! Timeplay–spaceplay! Gather personal experiences! Be traditional and up-to-date.

In fact he was only and exclusively a Danube-traveller. He simply couldn't count the times he'd stood at Donaueschingen. He was well known there. Look, there's that Hungarian, they would whisper. They awaited his arrival, as if waiting for spring after a long winter.

Being a Danube-traveller was in no way a limitation. The contract would always contain a sub-clause (generally 8/y) in which the traveller stated: *What constitutes the Danube is for me to decide.* He had little patience for those contractors who dragged their feet (or simply pulled faces) when they received a bill from Los Angeles. 'I'm here on the hills of Pacific Palisades. Looking for the agreed river. Good news: I can't find it. STOP.' Surely that was more reassuring than if he were to scurry up and down the hills and finally find a way into the Pacific Ocean. It is the traveller's duty to be vigilant, attentive and tactful – vis-à-vis the river. Anyone might be the Danube! (Beuys).

It is also true, as it soon became clear, that if anything (etc.) might be the Danube, then the best thing of all would be if the Danube were the Danube. The acceptance of a refined, sub-jective (indeed subjectivistic), provisional and sophisticated con-sensus would afford particular pleasure to ... Well? To whom? As if, instead of taking one right turn, we'd taken three to the left. To the subject. Every journey is an inner journey. That is to say, the traveller goes off in search of himself. Not as if there were actually someone to search for. The traveller is under obligation *not* to be an individual; that is, he must stagger between being somebody and nobody. He is to be the infinite, or, with more false-modesty, to be being itself, to be pure form, a carrel, a creel, a cell, full of books, full of fish, full of chains.

7

Duke Bluebeard's Castle

But – as Balzac was fond of saying in female company – let's get back to reality.

This sitting around by the confluence of the two little rivers was more romantic than I could ever have imagined. They were already waiting for me at Uncle Adalbert's. The Brussels lace had become still more rotten and moth-eaten, and my uncle did not speak at all. But he recognized me all the same. When I came in he was sitting in his armchair with his chin on his chest, but the moment he saw me he looked up and smiled. He had grown still smaller, thinner and more pale ; almost everywhere you could see the veins beneath his skin. (He looked a little like Leslie Howard.) He stood up, tottered towards me, and we began to waltz.

I gradually became aware of the new contradiction which filled the whole house, just as the 1970 Danube flood had filled the boathouses in Rómaifürdő, north of Budapest. Uncle Adalbert really didn't utter a single word. Sometimes he opened his mouth, then gave a discouraged wave of the hand, not angrily, quite cheerfully in fact, but his total silence was scary all the same. Tante Maria, on the other hand, simply couldn't stop talking, about my uncle, his condition, uninterruptedly, like a sports commentator, explaining what her husband was thinking at that moment, how he felt, what he saw and heard. And she offered her account of everything in the same elevated, lofty style as, say, György Szepesi or Mór Jókai – if these names mean anything to anyone. This stormy, dreamlike speech of hers served to remind her (or both of them) of the one last thing that continued to exist: their past. To be precise, something else existed too. In stark contrast to this actual, factual, rapidly gaining jadedness, stood the equally manifest and ubiquitous presence of: their wealth. It wasn't an obtrusive presence – it simply couldn't help being there. But it was exactly the same things that both withered and blossomed; and it was absolutely impossible to separate my aunt's unbearable, mechanical euphoria from the swarm of butlers, cooks, chambermaids, valets and chauffeurs, or my uncle's pitiable silence from the truffled 'boeuf' or even the lack of our presence from the exasperatingly natural presence of a world whose sole purpose seemed to be to enhance the brilliance of our presence.

Maria chattered on to the helpless old man as if talking to a child. I knew this was a mistake, even when I'd been there with Roberto I knew it. For it was clear that the old man knew everything. Or even more than that, as it soon turned out. My aunt winked at me: 'I'll just put him to bed, then I'm all yours.' I shook hands with Uncle Adalbert, to whom I felt no special attachment, but as I held his fine, silken, childlike hand, I was overcome by a feeling of warmth – perhaps the same sentimentality I'd felt out at the Breg–Brigach Y – and suddenly embraced him. My uncle immediately began to dance, but Maria, like a football referee with a particularly quarrelsome player, irritably tore us apart saying: 'All right, all right, that's quite enough of that.'

I waited in the upstairs drawing room. The drinks cabinet was so discreetly hidden away that I had trouble finding it. But find it I did. With a glass of cognac in my hand, I walked out onto the terrace, a large indoor garden with pine trees, bushes and an internal stream which was simply made for picturesque description. As usual, I began to envy painters and musicians.

Travelling is travelling. Both more and less than words about words. I went away and came back again, and a little period of time passed in between – i.e. water flowed down the Danube. I went here and there, experienced this and that, although I cannot claim that I was one thing or another then, and am one thing or another now! I picked up the in-house telephone directory. A finished novella, just as it was! All it needed was a good title. The Unbearable Difficulty of Being. The Structure of Wealth. Liberty, Equality and Fraternity. Heine Attempts to Make a Phone Call from his Uncle's.

Telephone Directory (in-house)

Basement

Garage Corridor	51
Garage	52
Wine Cellar	53
Air-Raid Shelter	54
Emergency Exit	55

Ground Floor

Swimming Pool	44
Corridor	45
Guestroom 1	41
Guestroom 2	42
Guestroom 3	43
Butler	46
Cook	47
Valet	48
Chambermaid	49
Telephone Exchange	77
Ping-Pong Room	78
Wash House	79

Mezzanine

First Floor

Second Floor

'He's gone bye-byes,' Maria smiled. I detested her for that sentence. She was always playing the accomplice, which probably didn't mean exactly what I thought it did (that is: petty treason). We had a drink together, and she began to speak more naturally, her face growing increasingly weary and grey, making her altogether more likeable.

Then suddenly the dining-room door flew open, and there stood a haggard-looking Uncle Adalbert. We both leaped to our feet, thinking something terrible had happened. But not for long. In turn he looked us scornfully up and down, then spat a single word in our faces, with such wild, tempestuous hatred that I had to shut my eyes.

The following morning I left without saying goodbye, even though, the previous evening, Maria's grey face had reminded me that I wanted to look at Holbein's *sogenannte graue Passion*. Twaddle. The hated word which had broken Uncle Adalbert's long silence was : Roberto.

sogenannte graue Passion : so-called 'Grey Passion'

8

What was wrong

'Come on, Noodle!' Roberto stood beside my bed, fully dressed in the dawn twilight. He was wearing his travelling uniform. 'I've already packed your things. Quickly, get dressed,' he whispered.

'Is something wrong?' I asked in my mother's anxious voice. Roberto raised his eyebrows.

'Why should anything be wrong?'

TRAVELLER'S OBLIGATIONS

The Traveller is obliged to provide the Contractor (Hirer) with a regular account of his travels in the form of a written Report. This Report should be factual, but lively. That is, it should be both instructive and provide a genuine experience. (This latter clause was later omitted from the contract.)

The writing of the Report did not present the tecny-weenyest of problems to the Traveller. As for the travelling itself, this did, once in a while, here and there, present him with the odd difficulty. It happened, for example, that he was simply unable to go on, to go on travelling. He came to a complete standstill, like the old Kádár régime, or like a backwater of the Danube. He simply got stuck in one place.

The Traveller is obliged to satisfy the Contractor's (Hirer's) every whim. Nothing that is remotely human should be an anathema to the Traveller. Even in a pool of bloody phlegm he must find a thing of beauty. The Traveller is obliged to be an experienced old fox, a real man of the world. He must understand the nature of money and must recognize that his position is extremely precarious and ambiguous, for he travels as a master and serves as a servant, and even though he might, by way of compensation and secret revenge, plunge the poisoned dagger of his irony into his Contractor's (Hirer's) back, what, he will have to ask himself, would then become of 'the spaciousness, the dignified independence, the fateful adventurousness of travelling'?

Regarding the financial management of the gratification of his desires, the Contractor (Hirer) must exhibit generosity (to the same degree that the Traveller exhibits willingness to serve) and he may not, even in an 'emergency' (the exact word used in the contract) fail to meet this obligation, or if so, then under pain of punishment. The following telegram will serve to illustrate such an occurrence, while also demonstrating the frequency with which the Traveller is forced to reformulate his report (which, as mentioned earlier, he can do standing on his head, what's Hecuba to him . . . !).

TELEGRAM

Once more! With more feeling! I want to know what I felt at the source! And anyway: do hurry up and get started! Enough of all this insolent nonsense about the Danube rising from the gutters or a bucket of rainwater! I'm simply not interested!!! Go and stand by the marble slab in the Fürstenberg park and be deeply moved, then put it all down in words. Throw ten Pfennigs into the pond and wish yourself all the best. I know I'm not supposed to remind you – and I've sent a cheque with this telegram as a forfeit – but I'll remind you all the same: I'm the one who's paying you, and not, most certainly not, for whipping cream! Contractor (Hirer)

Forgive me for getting so carried away. But perhaps it is a good sign. For you too. The role of the woman you mentioned is not clear. Is she really important, or just thrown in to spice things up? And what is all this about breasts? Good thing it's not all bum and arse and stuff. Look, I can take a joke, you know! Has she something to do with old Holbein's grey stations of the cross? If you stumble on secrets, that I can accept, but please don't go all enigmatic on me. Contractor (Hirer)

Like my country under the Russians, the gravel beneath my feet moaned and groaned and ... remained where it was. You are this and that, and I build upon this gravel etcetera. The Fürstenberg Castle is like an offended, twilight face. By the source my gaze slowly ventured its way towards the solemn slab; *Hier entspringt die Donau*. In other words, here rises the Danube! What a moment! The beginnings, the origin! All beginnings are pure? Or – but I don't even dare go on. Well, what did I care if it looked like water in a stagnant bowl, a provincial Trevi Fountain where, when throwing in one's money, one doesn't think of one's desires, nor of the Earth, nor of the Heavens, but simply of how the Deutschmark stands right now against the dollar ...

Yes, Baar sends her daughter Danube on her way. (Only further down does the river become Don Au, the Prince of Pain – as Berinkey Farkas remarks wittily, and not without self-irony in his fastidiously researched *Investigation of Fish Nutrients in the Soroksár Arm of the Danube*, Budapest, Academy Press, 1956, ah, what times!)

Then the castle gates flew open with a horrific yawn and a woman in a filthy grey cloak leaped out and began charging – as if she had set off simultaneously with the Danube – directly towards me! After a while two men suddenly appeared beside her, two elegant gentlemen, although I wouldn't wish to presume, or hope, or suggest that it was the old Prince and his son, nor even, it is true, that they were the Rosenberg couple fleeing from the agents of the CIA. But whoever they were, the Prince, Mr Rosenberg, or the Queen of England looking remarkably like my mother, they stopped short as soon as they saw me and nodded affably in my general direction. Then, with elegant arching movements, like a swan bending over backwards, or like a pair of highly experienced valets, they closed the folding gates of the castle which then sank back into solitude; but the twilight face that I used earlier as a metaphor blushed from all the excitement and scandal (while the similarly metaphorical swans sailed elegantly down the Brigach).

I'd hardly call myself *au fait* in matters of repeating weapons, but I'm pretty certain that the hundreds of flying stones whipped up by the running woman could best be compared with the crackle of pistol fire. Her cloak and broad-brimmed hat suggested all the radicalism of a woman of the 1920s. That was about the time when women rejected the roles assigned to them by the centuries and became beautified by enthusiasm, anger and the prospect of certain defeat. Her blouse flashed coral-red, a flesh wound. Her fashionably long legs leaped comically up and down on one side in her narrow skirt. When she drew level with me I said:

'My starry-eyed, tousled little orphan girl!'

The woman hissed to a halt, like a cat in a Walt Disney film.

'Are you out of your mind?' she asked indifferently.

'Don't be so childish,' I said to calm her down. 'You know full well that I'm going to talk to you and you're going to talk to me. I like you like this, my little miss!'

The wings of the woman's nose trembled violently. Then she

slowly ran her hand along the hard, blood-red –

Stop taking me for a fool! Is this some kind of VEIL-
ED ENTWICKLUNGSROMAN? A STRUGGLE
AGAINST FORGETTING? A HANDBOOK OF TOL-
ERANCE? Or is it supposed to be an ANARCHIST
GUIDEBOOK? Don't go making me throw quotations at
you: TRAVELLING IS LYING! How are you going to
demystify the self-admiration of postmodernism? How do you
intend to display the stubborn zest for life that is born of
the beyond of sympathy sharing in pain? Reply optional.
Contractor (Hirer)

TELEGRAM

My angel, my little one! Find out something about this Hindemith character. Bug his telephone, steam open his letters,
infiltrate him, distract him, arouse his sordid passions and point
them out to him. But don't do anything distasteful! Correction:
do not be restrained by good taste. If he proves to be beyond
reproach, make sure he is reproachable; if he is reproachable, let
it be provable, if provable, then exploitable, if exploitable, exploit
him ... Allegedly a string quartet or something? Contractor
(Hirer)

TELEGRAM

You are postmodern!

REPLY

Up yours.

9

Hindemith's great love

Just like a murderous – exaggeration – a prowling thief – still too much – I discourteously slipped out of the house; it seemed to be the kind of house from which one could only ever steal away without saying goodbye.

I cut across the park and turned left into Prinz Fritzi Allee. I was hungry, and I missed Hungarian coffee. I simply can't get used to the coffee they serve here, and have to drink three or four every time just to remember this fact. I should probably never have started.

I initially mistook the old woman who turned into the Allee in front of me for a little girl. Everything about her was so thin and white, translucent, incorporeal. It was frightening, and I was frightened. Her feet were pounding the ground, her face was heavy with powder, her short silken hair fluttered like a veil, but the dark furrows beneath her eyes made one think of a skull. Her expression was now that of a child, now that of a madwoman. She gave me a friendly nod of the head.

'Hello, darling.' She went on by. I was rooted to the ground. 'My God, it's been a long time.' At this she stopped and took a long hard look at me. She was dragging a box behind her on a piece of string. 'I've never seen your ears stick out so much before. So sweet, so bizarre, so lonesome. Never.' At that moment her face lit up. 'You too are dying! No doubt about it! Not just me.'

'Enough!' snapped the hotdog vendor wearily from his nearby stall. The old woman gave another refined nod, like a little bird, greeted him, then toddled off on her way.

'Don't mind her,' said the red-faced man, squeezing out a revolting worm of mustard ('*scharf*'), 'she *had* a hard life. Hard, but interesting. Harpsichord Barbara, if the gentleman has heard the name ...'

I had heard the name all right, the famous Barbara-letters, Hindemith's notorious correspondence, a bit like the letters of our Kelemen Mikes, that is, letters written to a fictitious 'aunt', letters that Hindemith wrote from Ankara, in 1935, I think. So there really was such an aunt? Her? There was a time they thought he had written them to Rebner, his one-time violin teacher, perhaps the only person whom Hindemith ever really respected.

The hotdog vendor was obviously keen to share his knowledge with me, which was the last thing I wanted. He launched into a mini-lecture on how Hindemith's art, as I surely knew, was characterized by formidable technical brilliance and craftsmanship. And how they had been playing music in the castle park ever since 1921, when – as the locals, including the hotdog vendor himself, were always proud to point out – the park witnessed the premiere of Hindemith's Second String Quartet, with the composer himself playing the viola part.

'He owed a lot to Bach,' I said, so as not to appear impolite. The man shrugged.

'My dear sir! It was then that this truly significant individual, at a truly significant moment in time, standing on that little platform by the wall, bow in hand,' and here the man's voice faltered, 'made a gesture, a vile and abominable gesture, I might even say a gesture which comprised the filth of several centuries, the shadow of Europe, the other Europe, that dreadful Europe, which just so happens to be inseparable from this one ... he made a gesture, a blustering gesture, as the young have a habit of doing, beyond all valid values, yet this side of tonality, beyond

47

childhood, yet this side of manhood, wallowing up to his ears in triumph. All of which could not have passed unnoticed nor been considered in the least ambiguous, after all, just think about it, this is a small town, a small German town, what else do we have? We have the Danube, and we have Hindemith. So everyone fell silent. With one exception.'

'Borbála,' I whispered in Hungarian.

'Precisely! The girl, who was hardly thirteen years old at the time, was one of the star pupils of the Municipal Music School of Freiburg. Utterly possessed, she stood up in the front row, not far from the Prince, whose stipend she enjoyed, she stood up, and with all the sensibility and innocence, etcetera, of a child, she took the whole outrage, the whole metaphysical burden, on her own two shoulders, which was something the local community had proved utterly incapable of doing (do not forget that this is Germany). The Germans are a people of the middle way. By the time she had staggered over to the musicians, her hair was like, well, sir, you saw her a moment ago, like needle-grass, she stumbled over to him, resolute even in this stumbling, over to Hindemith and said ... well you already know, don't you: 'Hello darling ... My God it's been a long time ...'

He fell silent. A red mark crawled across his forehead, as if Gorbachev's birthmark had taken a tumble.

'The whole town knows about this. We never speak of it. I do, of course, but I'm the exception. But everybody knows. Hello darling. My God it's been a long time. I've never seen your ears stick out so much before. So sweet, so bizarre, so lonesome. Never. You too are dying. No doubt about it. Not just me.'

He minced out the sentences like a machine. Even so, he seemed to be addressing them to me.

'This, sir, happened in 1921. You can calculate exactly how old Hitler was then.'

I didn't even begin to calculate. I ordered a coffee and asked him what was in the box the unfortunate woman dragged along behind her.

'Her harpsichord. She was studying the harpsichord in Freiburg. She'll never part with the thing. A harpsichord! Not a harp,' he stressed. We clearly didn't like each other. But I asked him all the same:

'What makes you an exception? Why did you tell me Barbara's story?'

'No one has ever asked me that before.'

'Well, I'm asking you now!' I shouted, staring at the shifting crimson island on his forehead. He replied impassively:

'Why me, you ask?' I dunked the dry bread in the mustard and suddenly my eyes filled with tears. The mustard had gone up my nose. He shrugged:

'She was my mother.'

Without saying goodbye, I headed back to the car. I thought of Canetti: When travelling one is more lenient. We tend to leave our indignation back at home. We look, we listen, and even the outrageous can fill us with enthusiasm, just because it is new. Good travellers are heartless. 'Where's your father?' I shouted back at him. 'None of your business!' he replied with hatred in his voice. I shrugged, turned away again, and waited. I didn't have to wait for long. It hit me like a stone on the back of my neck, a meek, almost apologetic stone:

'You know full well. I'm sixty-eight this year.' That was in 1990.

———

PRACTICAL JOKE FROM DONAEUSCHINGEN

TRAVELLER: Name your sources!
DANUBE: (shrugs)

49

10

'Nature to back ...'

To say our boat *glided* downstream is not quite an exaggeration, for if we tone the exaggeration down slightly, we do arrive at some kind of *reality*. As if reeling from gunshot wounds, up to our knees in water, pooling our last, hopeless physical and spiritual resources, we bobbed along perhaps the most beautiful, most spectacular stretch of the Danube in our little tub-like skiff. At least, that's how people usually talk about the 'breach' between Immendingen and Sigmaringen, about the young Danube's 'first ordeal', and the 'castles that have defied the centuries' (the ruins of Entenburg, Kallenberg and Bronnen, Heidenschloss). Roberto rowed in silence, occasionally gesturing with his eyes, rock, castle, wooden bridge, ancient tree.

I have always found Nature rather boring, ever since my childhood, as they say. I never understood, and thus never accepted, its privileged status. Peaks and plateaus, rocks and deserts, the hairpin bends of rivers all leave me cold. I was never one for excursions, and I always skipped over the descriptions of nature in novels (see: Verne, *The Danube Pilot*). I can't see why a hidden breeze at the Iron Gate should be any more self-explanatory than a five o'clock literary tea, or *Jause*, in Vienna. And why should the powdery face of an aunt be any more ridiculous than a woodland lane (a *horribile dictu* Holzweg), or why should malicious gossip be any more humiliating than a

also: dead end in arguments

50

rising wind that rustles the leaves of the poplars casting a silken, silver light over the surrounding green? When I find myself in a place where there are no people, nor hardly any trace of humankind (and this is what I call nature), and therefore nothing for me to remember, no past, no sentences, I enter into a remarkably immediate, indeed crude, relationship with my surroundings. Because I have no words for this, no words of my own, I primitively anthropomorphize my relationship, which is what I generally do with my relationships anyway. My crazy voyage with Roberto only changed this to the extent that I now compare everything to the Danube, even the Danube itself, in so far as I am standing at the point where the bank splits in two, between, say Erd and Batta, from where you can see the upper bank covered with Pannonian loess.

We put in at Sigmaringen, directly beside the Hohenzollern Castle. Two women were watching us.

'Ah, these green trees!' sighed one of them wistfully. To which the other, a young creature, replied with baffled naïvety: 'Tell me, mother, what have those green trees ever done to you?'

Roberto tied up with considerable expertise. I staggered about in the boat like a city boy should. Roberto radiated a certain confidence that had nothing to do with anything concrete, or rather, derived from the relationship between concrete things, whose order I could sense, but not fully recognize. I asked him why we had left Donaueschingen in such a hurry. Later, it was only ever from lovers (women, men, myself, others) that I heard such outbursts of sincerity, the aim of which was invariably to forget. We blurted out truths like the Danube throws out those alluvial deposits from which sandbanks are formed; around Rajka it isn't uncommon to find 'pebbles' as large as children's heads, while at Ásvány they are about the size of hen's eggs, at Gönyü the size of pigeon's eggs, and at Pakse they are hardly bigger than peas, and still farther down you come to the alluvial deposits themselves.

51

Roberto laughed. Again it was as if I saw my father. An unburdened father, and thus a nonexistent one.

'Noodle! Of course we were in a hurry! Not even just in a hurry, we were running for our lives. Helter-skelter. The telephone caught up with us. You see, I've kidnapped you. Your parents have just found out that you're with me. I hope *we* haven't caused them any consternation.' We?! 'It's more authentic like this, don't you think? We hit the Danube and *che será será*.'

I didn't really understand what he was saying, but I liked what I heard. With a single leap he was on the bank. The river was rising, its colour a probably nonexistent shade of brown, that crazy brown you only ever see on Trabants — if that means anything to anyone. Branches were swept along by the current, thick with yellowing foam.

'Noodle, wait for me here!' he called out as he took the two women by the arm and, muttering, laughing, tittering, floating, waltzed off towards the Prince's game reserve where the delightfully situated *Josefslust* hunting lodge stood.

11

Watching TV in Biberach

It was raining. I had got lost at Tuttlingen, and instead of following the adolescent river as I had planned – visiting the wise fathers of the Beuron Monastery who deciphered the secrets of ancient parchments, of writing that had long since been scratched or washed away (which is also, if you like, the glance of Countess Hahn-Hahn's blind eye), or looking up at the commanding sight of Wildenstein Castle, or simply getting on with the task in hand, for example, standing around beside the cowering Knopfmacherfelsen, or reluctantly *doing* the so-called beautiful sights, the 'counter-trees' of the riverbank reflected in the mirror of the waveless stream, the eternal stillness, the ancient tree-trunks slanting into the water, the sea of yellow water-lilies, the water sedge with its lancing leaves and mauve flowers, the various greens, the yellowy, silvery, angry, oily, blackish, whitish greens, and the almost kitschy *spaciousness* of the landscape – I suddenly found myself in Messkirch. (You suddenly find yourself in Messkirch, or so the Schwabian anecdote begins, according to which it was here that the Good Lord tried to halt the Danube, to stop it flowing altogether and send it back up the other way. Why, no one knows. And once He was here, according to the narrator, he more than likely called in on the Heideggers.

'Evening, Martin.'

the rock of the button makers

Martin Heidegger German existentialist philosopher, pro-Nazi

53

[Heidegger remains silent.]

'All right?'

[Heidegger remains silent.]

'On the way to the absolute, are we?'

'Hm.'

'Absolute wisdom without intelligence, absolute truth without facts, absolute happiness without pleasure ... Am I a Jew, you ask?'

[Heidegger remains silent.]

'Only on my mother's side. Just a trifle. I know you don't ask because ...'

[Heidegger remains silent. Fetches meat. Begins to eat alone.]

'You want to get straight onto language, eh?'

[Heidegger eats.]

'You're so depressing, Martin. I'm worried about you ... You know what your problem is? That you want to answer too.'

[Heidegger remains silent.]

'You pose all those nice questions, then come up with tyr-annical answers. For answers *are* tyrannical.'

[Heidegger remains silent.]

'You ought to know that, Martin.'

[Heidegger remains silent.]

And so they went on talking, bored out of their minds, neither able to get anything out of the other, which is where the anecdote ends.)

I was furious. What annoyed me most was that I was sure I'd come the right way. That I was on the right road. I tried to remember signposts, even got out the map. This, however, only got me into still more of a muddle, as map, reality, plans and memories became entangled in my mind. I seethed with rage. But there was no one there for me to be angry with, besides myself. I wasn't going to get very far if, on the very first stretch of river, I was already so full of hatred.

I decided to hurry *onwards* until sunset (onwards? what was that supposed to mean? I had clearly failed to meet even the minimal conditions of being a traveller). I turned off the Ulm road, because I knew a Landhotel on the Iller which kept a good table ('a matter I take very seriously'), but then my windscreen wipers broke down, that is to say, stopped, then gave the odd, unaccountable jerk, like a torn-off spider's leg, all of which I found so tiring that I decided to stay in Biberach, because I liked the name and mother used to call us all her little biberachs, after the famous intriguer.

So I gave up the idea of culinary delights in Illereichen, 'the culinary concert of many a sweet tone' (as the specialist literature puts it), electing to stop as soon as possible, anywhere with a television in the room, because there was a football match *soccer* on that night (Holland v. FRG), and I'm simply incapable of not watching a match. That is my weakness. I might add, somewhat conceitedly, that I am a veritable storehouse of weaknesses.

The buxom, rosy receptionist only shrugged her shoulders at the mention of a television. But then the owner arrived – a crocheted patchwork of clichés, a 'strong woman' who could 'stand on her own two feet' and 'always got what she wanted', but a well-crocheted patchwork all the same – and she began issuing instructions at once. 'Anni, move the travelling salesmen to the verandah room !' She yelled like a sergeant-major, banging on doors, barking out orders. The whole hotel suddenly came alive. 'You sir, in here! This room has a lovely view. And we'll have the new gentleman in here. Anni! Sheets! Pillowcases! Frau Cevapci! Bathroom! On the double !' It was as if she were flinging cats around a soft drawing-room, from one ornamental cushion to another.

Little pussy Hahn-Hahn sat on one such ornamental cushion watching Van Basten with one eye, while reading Georges Tim Aar's seminal *The Secrets of the Danube* with the other. His account of the Danube source is just like a good whodunnit, the way the river suddenly disappears at Immendingen, leaving its karstic bed *chalk* completely dry. Now you see it, now you don't, he writes, and

55

the same thing happens at Fridingen too. Well now, said the locals, racking their brains, what on earth could have happened? Who was the thief, they asked, and they each began to look askance at everyone else. Perhaps it was you? Or you? Hard times these. In 1719 a prelate by the name of Brauninger suggested that the scoundrel might have escaped underground towards the Bodensee. The proof only turned up a good hundred and fifty years later. At four o'clock in the afternoon, under the direction of the geologist A. Knop, they poured 1,200 kilograms of slate-tar oil into the bed from which the cowardly river had disappeared. And they waited. Sixty hours later it was reported that the Aach source, some twenty-five kilometres away, reeked of oil. The Aach, for its part, flows into the Rhine! No comment, including Heine! At any rate, in 1971 they directed the irresponsible water into a new bed. And there are dozens of equally interesting things to read in *The Secrets of the Danube*: for example, that the Danube is more likely to go into hiding in vintage years (1921, 1947, 1959), whereas in the years when the wine is bad it hardly disappears at all (1922, 1965). That in terms of length it comes twenty-first, in terms of catchment area twenty-sixth, and in terms of water output twenty-fifth. That the Nile and the Huangho are longer, but the former has a smaller water output and the latter a smaller catchment area. That, therefore, the Danube is quite a giant. And that one ell equals 1.14 metres. And that this region is inhabited by a cunning, priggish, reticent people, rather like Normandy. And that heavy clouds gather towards the Baltic. And whoever drinks turpentine will pass fragrant water.

On this day important events were taking place in Hungary. The surreal, ten-ton bubble of socialism finally burst – and we have had dirty, soapy water on our faces ever since. (All those metaphors, including the one I've just used, which treat this so-called socialism as something separate from the country and its people, and then look at it, for the most part with disgust, as if it were some plague or ulcer: all such metaphors are fundamentally misleading, forgetful, and ignore their own responsibility, however small . . . for socialism, as the poet says, was never simply a quantity of water which society shook off its back like a dog; after all, one can never tell for sure exactly where the water ends and the dog begins . . .)

During the thirty-minute news bulletin they must have played the Hungarian national anthem at least six times. At first I thought they were being ironical and making fun of my poor, defenceless homeland. But, as the grey Biberach rain went on desolately falling and I kept hearing noises from the next room where Anni (?) seemed to be packing or cleaning, I gradually and ponderously reached the conclusion that these six helpings of national anthem were actually signs of matter-of-fact report-age. For in our country something personal, or even sentimental, always has a way of creeping into even the most important questions of national existence. Ah yes, the constitution, of course, of course, but first the national anthem, dignity, deport-ment. Oh and justice, of course, of course, all in good time. (I remember once, during a nice little supper, a young Austrian journalist asked us on which constitution ours was based. We leading intellectuals could hardly understand the question. Was our constitution really based on someone else's? We looked at one another, utterly perplexed. As is my custom, I fled in the general direction of the crème caramel.)

To sum up: a West European speaks about an object, there *is* an object, and he examines it, sometimes, albeit, in a very subjective manner; an *East* or *Central* or kind of *in-between* European, on the other hand, speaks about himself, there *is* this thing himself, and he speaks about it, albeit through an object.

Question: is this true, and if so, is it in my interest to disclose it? Answer: it is true, and must be vehemently denied.

———————

57

TELEGRAM

Darling, I miss you terribly. Your little face, everything. So much so it gives me the shits. Stop. Contractor (Hirer)

REPLY

I beg your pardon? Traveller

AN OLD TELEGRAM

That evening the Traveller felt himself to be in a state of utmost security and calm. Perhaps because a half-litre bottle of Chablis stood on the table before him, and this counted as something of an occasion. The Traveller had had rather a lot to eat and his stomach grumbled. Now and then, the woman with whom he dined leaned down to his stomach, listened, and drew music-historical parallels. The clock had almost struck midnight when the telegram arrived. When he read it, he was so surprised that it gave him the shits. Later he would regularly receive such instructions, and in time he grew used to them. Usually it was in Ulm that such telegrams caught up with him. 'Traveller! Repeat the events of yesterday!' The first time this happened he had sat trembling for several hours on the foreign W C.

TRAVELLER AND THE WHO'S WHO

The first years passed quite poetically. He desired, at all costs, to personify the Danube. A woman to melt into. Old mother Volga, etcetera. (He disregarded Heine's objection: old father Rhine.) He made it his goal to get to know this woman. Note the enormous ambition of this plan: neither to conquer her, nor to be conquered by her, but to get to know her. *I shall satisfy all clichés*, he promised. Or to treat the river as history, the wise river, the stream of time, indeed: life itself. The metaphors swirled like dirty Budapest water after passing the pillars of Margit Bridge.

★

The Traveller seldom travelled alone. What was the point? The traveller *is* alone in any case. Why should this make him feel lonely? (Unless, of course, it was the express wish of the Contractor [Hirer]. You must be an absolute outsider. Be soured by solitude. Roam aimlessly in Ulm. Don't even feel inclined to change your underwear.) He shared his solitude above all with so-called Travelling-Ladies. The truth is, however, that they would usually end up offended. 'I'll make a note of all this and when we meet on Saturday I'll be offended.' Not that the individual in question was jealous. She simply took out a revolver with an elegant mother-of-pearl handle (handmade craftsmanship from Regensburg) and threatened to commit suicide. Or, wearing thick lipstick and promising to desert the Traveller just as St Paul deserted the Wallachians, she would finally up sticks, after all, there were limits to everything, and she wasn't going to be taken for granted, nor work herself to the bone for someone else to reap all the benefits in Novi Sad. She even wrote him a letter, the usual short letter announcing the endless farewell: 'Traveller! I want to be your each and every Mrs Traveller! Signed: Mrs Traveller.' The Traveller shrugged and bowed to his own better judgement. Women have a tendency to disappear, he had read somewhere, just like the lost city of Atlantis.

★

Among the most fashionable, and hence exacting, of his special offers was the 'Bluebeard-Construction'. Starting out from a statement by the great Széchenyi – WATER IS LINEAR – he divided the river into eleven sections from top to bottom and

59

travelled the length of each section on the arm of a different lady
(Ira, Dóra, Elvira, Eleonóra, Flóra, Mira, Teodóra, Petra, Imre,
Barbara, Sára). Beside the quoted price – which, exceptionally,
did not include any special concessions – stood nothing but a
poem, a poem by Ferenc Szijj, entitled 'A Longer Fragment':

> *A woman carries me beneath her veil and feeds*
> *me daily with her spittle, whatever of which I can*
> *no longer take trickles down onto her shoulder and dries*
> *– it already reaches my ankles. Through the eyes*
> *of the veil I see all, wherever we may pass,*
> *but here inside it is too dark to recognize*
> *the woman's face, and I can only guess that she must feed*
> *another on her other shoulder. While I count numbers*
> *he must surely give things names.*

To *Ira* belonged the section stretching from the source to Schwa-
bischwörth, or, as it is now called, Donauwörth. One morning
the Traveller told her: You do not have to go to such great
lengths in perfecting your mimicry. I'm not wearing my glasses.
Dóra lasted until Passau. Already at the Deggendorfer shipyard
the woman rolled towards him; just like that, no questions asked,
only because there had been word of such rolling once, many
years ago. The great, shared moment of desire and desirelessness.
Elvira's boundary was the Tulla plain, 'where, according to the
Niebelungenlied, Attila, Prince of the Huns, kept his betrothed
Krimhilda waiting' (Georges Tim Aar). 'Could you ever love
me?' asked the Traveller. Elvira shrugged: 'Discuss it with my
husband.' *Eleonóra* accompanied him as far as Komárom, or,
more precisely, to the Conco brook. He met her while playing
Capitály (our *Monopoly*) with the children of a friend. He was
enormously fond of the game and found himself once again in
a very favourable position, with a hotel on Váci Street, a whole
row of houses on Andrássy Avenue and so on. Just then a girl
came into the room with freckles, red hair and spectacles, a
classmate of one of the children. You could see that she would

only remain ugly for a moment or two longer, before suddenly growing quite beautiful. And when the Traveller looked at her, he knew at once he could lose everything, his hotel on Váci Street, his houses on Andrássy Avenue and so on. He got to know *Flóra* (forester's lodge for the water meadow at Gemenc) when he touched her breast and asked: Budapest? The woman shook her head impetuously. Budapest? the Traveller asked again, trying to draw closer to her personality. Why do you keep going on about Budapest? she shouted in exasperation, but then smiled. The man touched every last part of her body, inch by inch, going through the whole of Europe as he did – Prague? The hills of Tuscany? Stockholm? The Danube delta? The hottest part was Naples, or rather the part which passed for Naples *there*. Until the Castle of Galambóc his companion was *Mira*, who cooked for him. As if my mother had risen from the grave, uttered the Traveller after the second day of goulash. With *Teodóra* too he dined at several different locations. Once, at the last moment, that is, in Vidin, not far from the Kossuth memorial, in a shady interior garden, during the asparagus season, he ate veal kidneys and said: I need that other kind of knowledge which is yours. The way you know cheeses, literature, the human body, Goethe, the Greek Islands, wine (the dangers of a taste of cork!), computers, banks – or rather bankers, children, your father, the coast of Yugoslavia, the North Sea, Lake Aral, the Danube, the Karst Caves, the Judas-eared mushroom, Joseph Roth, your crotch, my crotch. And they might have said more too, had they not been swept away by the torrents of desire, whipping up enormous waves on the Danube, as if it were the sea, which was actually a long, long way away. *Petra* stayed until Nikopol, but in the last few days they only met in the library, because her eyes were failing rapidly and the Traveller was afraid she was going blind, and that one day he'd return to the news that she had indeed gone blind, and he would go looking for her, and he would find her with ease, for she'd either be by the Betov memorial after Lom or farther down by the ruins of Ulpius Escus, yes, he'd find her, sit down at her feet and read aloud to her heart's content and never ever go away. By the end he didn't dare venture into the library at all. The girl no longer worked there anyway. Apparently, she'd taken up with some man from the Dobrudzha and helped him on the farm. *Imre*'s territorial waters reached all the way to the frontier, more or less as far as Silistra. From here on yes meant yes and no meant no, at least as far as the nodding of heads was concerned. Perhaps this too was a cause of certain misunderstandings(?). At any event, when he saw Imre's name on a postcard lying on a foreign table – the postcard depicted the dome of a Danish church at sunrise (Kitte Fennestad/Marmorkirken) – the dark cloud of jealousy (or its shadow perhaps ?) lay heavy on his heart. That is, the dark cloud of jealousy cast its shadow over his heart. And his shadowy heart was wracked with pain. He didn't often feel this way. Right then, that was that, he'd run straight up to this *personage* and drag him out from his ... from wherever he happened to be, from before his easel, from behind his writing desk, out of bed, out of the kitchen, why, he'd simply drag him out and rub the postcard into his face, without even stopping to read it, no, he'd read it all right, he'd read it from that dark, evil, convulsing swamp of a face, as he screwed the postcard into it, here you are, you ?! what on earth are you doing here ? what ? how ? what ? and the thick postcard would tear, not crumple, the Danish dome curling away, and with it a torn piece of the rising sun. *Barbara* was already on her deathbed, but she was his until Galaţi. She asks the Traveller to stand beside her bed at pillow height. The Traveller obliges. Barbara gasps for air, feverish, perspiring. In September she would be sixty-four years old. She gathers her strength. She reaches out for the man's trousers. The Traveller shuts his eyes. Barbara takes the man in her mouth, sucks a little, like a baby on a dummy, then puts everything back, neat and tidy. The horn of an ocean liner can be heard. The Traveller sits on the edge of the bed and they hold hands. *Sára* : Sulina. I don't trust you. I haven't trusted you ever since Ismail ... You were not honest in Tulcea. All the way up the St George arm you were totally insincere. And at the bar you weren't even honest with yourself. I don't like the twilight, you'd better remember that for once and for all. As they couldn't find the Sun, they both looked at the lighthouse. The Traveller remembered a famous actress from his youth. She's probably dead too by now, he thought, but what enormous boobs she had.

★

'Who am I?' This is the question the Traveller never asks. 'Where am I going?' Nor does he ask this. 'What is the Danube?' Not even that. The Traveller doesn't *think* at all. The Danube is the foremost river of Central Europe, Black Forest, Black Sea, facts, done. But this has nothing whatsoever to do with indifference. The Traveller fulfilled his tasks with pleasure, it was just that definitions had somehow melted away from him, like the meagre, late March snow from the Regensburg hills. The Traveller is a traveller, travelling is travelling (a rose is . . . something that could do us a favour). The Traveller had a leaning towards Pascal, that is, towards some kind of empirical metaphysics which, contrary to widespread belief, is not the same as the nice idea that God dwells in details. Because Satan dwells there too, as do Truth and Love. One can read all about this. So the four of them dwell in the Details, a bit like living in a crowded co-op in Moscow, God, Satan, Truth and Love, sharing one television set that is on all day long. Love wants to watch a debate on channel one (he's a Yeltsin supporter) and Satan wants to watch the ice hockey on channel two. One hell of a fight ensues. Justice goes through the motions of administering justice, while, ignoring the futile entreaties of all three, the Lord simply turns his nose up at the satellite dish. Just to get to the next tree, declared the Traveller, no longer even knowing *after* whom.

He had little time for all the pathos that surrounded the Danube, but nor could he pretend it did not exist, or that he was not aware of it, especially as he was forced to establish that behind all this confusion, billowing self-importance and fashionable prattle : there was *something*. The Danube as memory. The rediscovery of lost moments of unity. A highway that linked whole peoples together. Danube and Olt, sharing the same voice. The Danube as the *sine qua non* of Europe. The fluent code of cultural multiplicity. The artery of the continent. River of history. River of time. River of culture. River of love. A yoke connecting peoples. Freedom-yoke.

It was all rather hard for him.

But seeing, or at least supposing, that there was something which connected Ulm with Vienna, and Vienna with Belgrade, and not wanting to call this something the Danube, that metaphysical, imaginary, hotch-potch of a river, he would arrive at the conclusion that it was he himself who connected Ulm with Belgrade, he the traveller. His ornate vessel glided between the rows of people on the bank. But the boat was carried by the Danube, and the Danube by the *weight* of lived-out lives, that unbearable weight we carry with us, we travellers. That is why the Danube comes before he does. And that is why he sits on the bottom step of the quayside, watching the melon rind float away downstream – if that means anything to anyone.

12

The bar and eddy of Ulm

We got held up in Ulm. I thought it was because of the two women from Sigmaringen, who had come with us. According to Roberto, however, we were simply tired. 'This tiredness, Noodle, is part and parcel of travelling. Tiredness, torment, disillusion – they all count among our many privileges. A tourist is fit, a traveller lives. And life is like the Danube, sometimes blue, sometimes grey, sometimes brown, sometimes rises, sometimes falls, meeting of tugboats forbidden.'

I adored this frivolous fellow. (I adhere to the rules of the Danube, to Széchenyi's notion of linearity – but I simply have to pause at this sentence, there is so very much at stake. However, it is still only six months since I learnt what people would probably call 'the truth' about Roberto, which was so awful, so terrible, so *difficult* that it is not quite so hard after all to keep image and reality distinct, just as one can distinguish the river Inn for some time before Passau. It should be noted here that, below Passau, the river is constrained by mountains on both sides, and as one continues down this beautiful, mountainous stretch, one catches a glimpse of the ruins of Krämpelstein Castle, the 'Tailor's Castle', just above a bend. These ruins are said to be, on the one hand, those of a haunted castle – haunted above all by Ruprecht Moosheim, the one time dean of Passau cathedral, who, found guilty of heresy in 1556, died a bloody death in the castle dungeon. According to a different legend, however, a tailor had once attempted, in his anger, to throw his goat down into the Danube – on account of a conflict whose details I cannot enter into here – but the tailor was such a frail and puny little man that the goat pulled the unworthy Austrian Dugovics into the water with him.)

I adored Roberto.

It is not entirely certain that we got held up. To get held up while travelling is not the same as the pause between moving from one place to another. To sit down somewhere and not go on – that is not at all the meaning of getting held up. That can always happen. Waiting, looking around, contemplating and so on. Getting held up, on the other hand, is simply nothing, nothingness itself. Getting held up means merely waiting for the hold up to pass. On such occasions, time oozes from the Traveller like the blood squirting from a chicken's neck on the dirty chopping block in the dark kitchen of a smoky little Belgrade inn. For example. Anyway, I shan't grumble; usually it only becomes clear after the event that one *has been* held up, instead, that is, of going on ahead.

I loathed the two women – the way they had simply latched on to us. Besides, I found them vulgar, and couldn't stand their smell, that continually sweet smell of perspiration. 'Noodle, stop that sniffing!' said Roberto now and then, because I kept nosing about like a little Sherlock Holmes, my nose twitching like a rabbit's. 'What's that smell?' Roberto, for the most part, couldn't answer, either because he couldn't smell it himself, or because he didn't know what to compare it to. 'Ulm smell,' he said, and shrugged.

I was a well-brought-up and rather stern little boy. Or austere? Puritan, more like. I had no qualms about despising a cousin for skinny-dipping with a girl from the German Democratic Republic (which still existed in those days). It almost froze my balls off – I remember the sentence. Don't make excuses, it's so pathetic.

Roberto and I rented a room for a month in the Fischerviertel, while mother and daughter stayed in the *Ulmer Spatz*. One was called Brigitte, the other Barbara, although I could never work out which was which. Roberto called them Breg and Brigach, leaving him with no choice but to be the Danube, at which they giggled. Again, this irritated me. Roberto's vulgarity was somehow different, which I found disturbing. At that time I thought (because the little I knew I thoroughly analysed!) it must be because he wasn't after anything. But I was mistaken – vulgarity is always *after* something, and, what is more, the reverse is probably equally true.

I hated it when they treated me as a child, and I hated it when they treated me as a grown-up. The former bored and offended me; the latter made me feel embarrassed and ashamed, because I understood more than I understood, no, that's confusing, I understood more than I was able to analyse, which is to say that there was an obscure, grey area, a catchment area with mosquitoes as big as your fist and trees that collapsed like tents in the wind and continually oozed rainwater, like in a primeval forest, or in Gemenc, a grey area that I grasped, but didn't understand.

Adults usually make decisions, saying either this or that. Roberto and the two women were exceptions. Roberto never made any decisions at all, and I think it was by calling me Noodle that he achieved that certain rainbow quality which characterized our relationship: he saw me as a kind of grown-up child, with neither of us really knowing quite what that meant, and this somehow simplified matters. To the same degree that I loved Roberto's indecision, I detested that of the two women, who considered me now one thing, now another, and were thus continually mistaken. Roberto took me playfully seriously, while the women either played with me or waxed serious.

They were testing me. Once, when we were waiting for Roberto in the *Ulmer Spatz*, the girl suddenly said: 'Lie on top of me.' I shrugged, why not. 'Oh, you're nice and light, my little one.' At this her mother began to scream: 'Me too! Me too!' She jumped up and down, clapping her hands. This sickened me, and I gave them such a look that they seemed altogether to lose interest. They wore the same big yellow earrings, the sort that gypsies wear back home. When I told Roberto that I had seen plenty of earrings like that, he replied with a laugh: 'I very much doubt it. For the price of those earrings they could buy half of Budapest.' At that time we hadn't had any money for two days, and I could see that the women paid for everything. 'Are they really so rich?' I asked. 'No. They have simply got a lot of money.' Roberto never said anything bad about them, but he did allow me to scheme against them, and as if he cheerfully agreed with me, too.

Our sudden, and to me incomprehensible, lack of money didn't seem to trouble us, even though we lived in ever worsening conditions, wandering around the Fischerviertel and moving into ever higher and smaller rooms. We ended up in some hole beneath an attic. The obliging Turkish cleaning woman had to climb two flights of stairs to reach us. We took breakfast on the ground floor, where the old stagecoach drivers had rested in times gone by.

No, we didn't worry about our lack of money, but something else seemed to be troubling Roberto. He kept disappearing for half the day. At first I thought he had gone to see the two women, Breg and Brigach (ha-ha-ha), but it turned out that they were waiting for him too. Sometimes we all waited together. I learnt a lot of German from them. They knew masses of poems by heart, mostly Heine, plus a little Rilke, but there were just too many new, unfamiliar words. Rilke made me moody, offended and ashamed – just as when they treated me like an adult.

Mysterious things kept happening, but in those days I wasn't afraid of mystery, just as I wasn't afraid of parts that didn't seem to make a whole, or of the dark. It was because of Roberto that I was never frightened. I could see that he would always complete the fragments, or rather that all the obscurity and darkness gathered together within him, while he himself would go on beaming and sparkling.

In spite of all his recent wanderings, we always had breakfast together. When, for the third day running, we were given slices of garlic sausage filled with cheese to go with our crispy rolls (in Hungary the problem of crispiness had seemed irresolvable in those days, and even now the results of the struggle vary), Roberto asked if this would always be the case. 'What do you mean, always?' My uncle said nothing. The landlady smiled and patted him on the head, as if she had mistaken it for mine.

'"Always" is for those who only stay here one day ...' We exchanged concerned glances. 'No one, you understand?! No one stays *this* long in Ulm! Not like you!'

'Then I shan't stay either,' said Roberto softly, as if replying to a schoolmistress.

'Sure,' said the woman with a dismissive wave of the hand as she passed Roberto a letter, or rather a folded piece of paper. Roberto opened it. It read: 'Effi Briest is sorry, but she will be unable to make lunch on Thursday. She'll be in touch.' He screwed up the paper. 'It was delivered by your secretary,' said the woman.

'I don't have a secretary!' Roberto shouted.

'Then someone belonging to that Effi Briest,' shrugged the landlady. 'She wore a pretty blonde bun.'

'What did she look like?'

'What do you mean, what did she look like? They all look the same. Pelerine, that kind of thing ...' Roberto knocked over the chair as he leaped to his feet. The blonde woman recoiled, her mouth twitching in disdain. At that moment a man in a leather coat walked into the room. Roberto fell silent.

'Don't do anything foolish,' whispered the woman. 'I'll bring more garlic sausage. For you too, my little one.' This time I was not annoyed by her deceitful caress. I could see we were in danger.

Roberto climbed the stairs three at a time. By the time I caught up with him, he was already busy clearing up the room. It was a room which preserved the trace of strange, rummaging hands, the empty wardrobe, the unmade bed, clothes strewn all over the floor – it was like a badly beaten face, the nose pummelled to a pulp, or more defenceless still: a pockmarked face, a *fresh* infection, a purulent wound, an oozing scab. I threw myself at Roberto, sobbing.

'There's no time for that,' he said coldly. 'You hide in there,' and he span me into the wardrobe. I could just about catch a glimpse of the man in the leather coat coming through the door. Where had I heard that voice before? Then the wardrobe door slammed shut in my face, almost against my lips, as if I were kissing the wood from the inside.

'Pleased to meet you. In fact we've already met in passing. At Donaueschingen.'

'I don't recall,' said Roberto sternly.

'*In passing . . .*'

'I don't recall.'

'My starry-eyed, tousled little orphan girl?'

'What?'

'I like you like this, my sweet little miss.'

'What do you want?'

'Why are you so brusque? Or are you tired? In a bit of a bad mood?'

'Please, just get to the point. We're not children. I would emphatically remind you that we, myself and my nephew, who at this very moment is visiting the Fugger Castle in Weissenhorn with our dear travelling companion, are doing a tour of the entire Danube in order to turn our subjective experiences into a genuinely objective picture, this throbbing . . .'

'That's enough, Roberto!' Before losing consciousness, I

heard a woman's voice. Same as before? 'Don't prattle so much
...'

TELEGRAM

1 GO TO 1

TELEGRAM

If you're exhausted, take a break. Discipline makes good sense.
Wander about a bit in Ulm. Do you really need me to remind
you that the Danube is not some tiny, gushing mountain stream?
Rent yourself an attic room for a month. Get a – shall we say –
helpful Turkish lady to do the cleaning. You're bound to get
some breakfast downstairs with the stagecoach drivers. The garlic
sausage filled with cheese is superb. Stop. Contractor (Hirer)

13

The heart

In a film, someone claims that New York is the heart of the world, to which someone else angrily replies that the world has no heart (and also that he shouldn't have come in before his number was called, because all this takes place in a famous Turkish bath in Budapest).

The heart of the Danube is Ulm.

Or so Engineer Neweklowsky maintains in his painfully painstaking book, *The Hegel of the Upper Danube*. He refers, above all, to a central point, a centre that conceals its emotions. In one place he describes – and here one might suspect a printing error – a 'gigantic centre of gravity', and, in his own punctilious manner, he provides interesting calculations to support this theory ('nothing is more practical than a good theory'), which are not only utterly convincing, but also offer a nice, quiet example of the not unusual marriage between German pedantry and leisurely madness.

In his intellectual experiments, Neweklowsky simply stands the Danube on its head. That is to say, he inverts the real distribution of water volume. His calculations demonstrate that the centre of gravity of the figure weighed in this fashion is Ulm, or more precisely, the Iller estuary. It speaks volumes for the integrity of the indefatigable engineer that he expresses some doubt as to whether we might receive *any* result with the same delight, for the centre of gravity will always fall at *exactly* the place where it falls.

The fundamental question is whether we are to see the Danube – and with it, the truth – as some kind of discovery (aletheia), the discovery of a given order, that is to say, the apparently chaotic Danube is based on an order which we will (at some point) discern, because it is discernible, or, on the contrary, we are to admit that there is no such order, only eddies, spray and current, and the apparent order – for ultimately we are speaking of *something* here, after all, and *if* we board the hydrofoil in Vienna, *then* we can arrive in Budapest – is not something we have found, but something we have added ourselves, and then forgotten, and now, hearing the hydrofoil sound its horn, our smiles stretch all the way to our ears. In place of discovery, rediscovery. Flusser aptly remarks that Copernicus is not *truer* than Ptolemy, but simply more convenient! What order is, 'I' decide, who utter the letters o,r,d,e,r. The relationship between the law of Free Fall and geometrical progression (it gets better and better, just think of the man who fell from the tower of Ulm, or of 1, 4, and 9) is not some miracle, but a category of mind; the mind recognizing one of its own categories. But this, once again, can be called a miracle. The laws of nature are not the creation of God, or the angels, or even of nature herself, but of man! He is the only one who tampers with all thes things.

The following legendary story, with which Neweklowsky, as a genuine chaos-researcher, presents us, is actually quite typical, playing, as it does, on Goethe's Janus-faced *Mehr-Licht! / Mehr nicht!* After a life-long preoccupation with the Danube, the engineer is said to have cried out on his deathbed: Where, oh where, is the man who can distinguish between Danube, and not-Danube?! From the utterance of this sentence to the moment of his death (that is, some seventeen hours) he howled and hollered

---

Mehr-Licht!/Mehr nicht!: More light/There is no more [light]. Purportedly Goethe's last words

so loud that they had to close all the shutters in his house. But the people of Ulm could hear him all the same. Now the Danube is dying, they said, nodding their heads.

Ulm is the Danube's great (significant) graveyard. Here the Danube has died many a death. The town is frightfully quaint, the ins and outs of the Fischerviertel, with all its restaurants, taverns and medieval houses. A little Venice : *quaint*. So much so that even a (through–) traveller cannot resist the urge to sink to the level of the tourist, who, as we all know, is drawn to such quaintness like flies to an open wound. From here came the little Mozart, who never even saw the spire, which absolutely *everyone* has seen, even the still smaller Einstein, the great and moody Kepler, the Scholl brothers, who, as Golo Mann notes (page 79), fought with their bare hands against the might of the Third Reich. And it was here too that General Rommel deceitfully was laid out in state, before the town was reduced to a bombed-out debris of some 950,000 cubic metres.

In the highly detailed work, *The Dam's True Story, or The Water Won't Compromise* (Garzanti, Milan) it is suggested that the Undine Legend, or at least one of its earliest variants, originates from Ulm. According to a preliminary (and somewhat primitive) plan, von Stauffenberg was supposed to worm his way into Hitler's confidence on the U-boat *Undine*. As I am trying to get to the secret relationship between von Stauffenberg and Rommel, I have to mention the name of Lally Frenzel, the bravest of all fishermen, who walked the entire length of the frozen Danube, and also Achim von Arnim who, at another time and another place, cut a hole in the ice (cf. Ritter Peter von Stauffenberg und die Meerfeye), while, to put it somewhat picturesquely, living – forced to live – entirely on various types of fish (Fisch Arts?). The ancient traditions of the Ulm fishermen's guild still survive today. One need only mention the Fischerstechen, the spectacular Nabada-Festival which takes place every Schwörmmontag in August . . . But now let's listen in on a spoken variant of the Ulmer Blindtanz which dates from the seventeenth century. Listen with a heavy Ulmer heart:

DANUBE (*humanistically*): For twenty million years my waves have caressed this region which was formerly covered by sea. (Takes off mask, and sinks to her knees. Small and Great Blau gush inside her. The Danube prays haughtily.)

My Lord and Father,
make me an instrument of thy peace,
that I may bring love and hatred
to where till now the Empty Heart has reigned,
that I may prepare a bed for reconciliation and resentment
where the sands of Thoughtlessness run and Sympathy falls on its face,
help me to proclaim both truth and misunderstanding
where the mud of our Daily Round slips and slides,
to plant faith in place of doubt,
that the waterfall of hope may gush
where the backwaters of despair had formerly dwelled,
and to bring hopelessness
where light sits at the feast.
Dance! Amen.

(On the bank, where the spectators clap in unison, they begin singing *Ulm, Ulm, über alles.* Then suddenly there is silence, but for the splashing oars of the 'boxes'. Five minutes silence, then:)

EVA BRAUN: Adolf, I simply won't have it. I simply can't allow it, Adolf.

HITLER: You'll allow it all right, old girl ... You'll allow it because you've already allowed it to yourself. First one allows it to oneself, then one simply has no choice but to allow it ...:

GOEBBELS: Not so loud, for heaven's sake!

HITLER: Shut up, you stupid cow. We're going to do it ... You think I do everything from below, like you do? No, not me. I do everything from above. From above. With elegance. With dignity. But still so stupidly that no one ever suspects. Ha

75

ha (cf. Gounod). Murder simply has to be committed from above, Eva, not from below. But first go and get washed, you look like a madwoman. And then be a bit more attentive to the general staff ... And don't forget, I want carp served up for *hors d'oeuvre.*

I fancy a spot of carp. Yes, carp with sour cream. Good fish, that. Splendid.

EVA BRAUN: Carp? Carp? *(To Goebbels, gleefully :)* He's gone mad! Heaven be praised, he's out of his mind!

HITLER: Shut up! I haven't gone mad. Just have them serve carp.

GOEBBELS: My dear lady, my sweet pussy, carp in sour cream makes a first-rate *hors d'oeuvre.* I really can't see why they shouldn't serve carp.

EVA BRAUN: Well there won't be any carp! Adolf, don't drive me round the bend. I simply won't have them serve carp. Where are they going to get carp?

(Meanwhile, dressed as a master builder, a computer buff is climbing the steps of the cathedral spire, all 768 of them (as shown in the brochure!), ghosted by highly imaginative, multi-coloured searchlights. A paradigm of civic courage. The heads of the spectators turn to and fro, just like at Wimbledon. Legend comes to life: on top of Ulm cathedral one is closer to God. The legend tells of one ambitious youth, a certain Jacob, who, I quote, 'wanted above all else to be there when the spire was completed – close to God! – and then, in front of the whole town, he fell off, plunged like a meteor, which must have taken him, even leaving air-resistance out of the equation, at least five seconds! A town which thinks about life and death for a full five seconds ...: the Good Lord loved Ulm.' This is the legend that came to life, with the one difference that ... but more of that later!)

EVA BRAUN: I'm telling you, I won't have them serve carp. Why carp of all things? Why does it have to be carp?

HITLER: Look, if I say it's gotta be carp, then it's gotta be carp. Don't argue, or I'll beat the shit out of you. And I can if I want to, you know. I can beat you because I'm full of sin. I can do whatever I want, woman, I'm telling you, so you'd better start shaking in your boots. For I am full of sin! I am the Chancellor of Sin. (*Rapturous applause from the riverbank as a Neu-Ulm Table-Society, feigning a certain rowdiness, counts the steps out loud.*) Do you hear? The Chancellor of Stupidity, of Sin, of Violence, of Tears!

> DANUBE : And were I not myself the Rhine,
> I'd throw myself into the Rhine.

EVA BRAUN *(terror-stricken)* : Adolf!

HITLER *(somewhat more calmly)* : Well? Well? Give the order! Carp for supper! And invite all the top brass, all those wily old foxes who hide their hearts in their boots and hinder us like a thousand devils. (*More softly*) Eva, I'm sick and tired of all this cowardice, this shame, this fear – understand? I'm fed up with poetry, with flexibility, with wishy washyness. Now scram. Go on, get lost, my little cook. From above, that's right, from above. With dignity! (*Eva Braun hides her face in her hands, exit. From the riverbank random cries of: Uwe! Uwe! Üben, üben! etc.*) ... Goebbels?

GOEBBELS : At your command, Herr Shitler!

HITLER *(softly, gravely)* : Bow down before me ... I need you to bow down before me ...

So, the tragedy of Rommel in a nutshell (in Stroheim's sensitive rendition) : Goebbels babbled his way through a perfidious lecture about carp, about how it only appeared to be a rather humble fish, but was, in fact, in essence, an immortally, extraordinarily, aristocratic one. After all, one only needed to appeal to the fact that it was entirely boneless, except for fishbones, of course!

GOEBBELS : And that splendid sauce! We might mistakenly believe it to be nothing more than sour cream. But how much more magnificent it really is! The taste! Hot, piquant, para-doxical!

Then Hitler gets up and points, with a bloodcurdling thrust of the finger, at Rommel, screaming: 'He's choked to death! Choked to death on a fishbone! A fishbone in the throat! A fishbone I tell you! Well I never!' Rommel really is choking. Meanwhile it becomes crystal clear that the computer buff climbing up the spire had once worked for the Stasi, but he had only sold them his knowhow, and hadn't informed on anyone directly, apart from a few close friends, and these he warned in advance, even gave them the odd important tip. Then there is mild confusion. Goebbels sends, spectacularly, for Petersil, the undertaker (not by chance did we mention the death of the Danube). We'll never make it without Petersil, he repeats, half out of his mind. Then he falls to his knees, and that, yes, of course, that was the solution.

HITLER : We should have done that right at the beginning. (They all kneel down beside the Danube. All except Count von Stauffenberg.)

VON STAUFFENBERG : Excuse me, but what's going on?

GOEBBELS : What's the matter? (*He raises his eyebrows.*)

VON STAUFFENBERG : (*Remains silent.*)

DANUBE : Kneel!

HITLER : Quickly. You can't just stand there all alone. When everyone else is kneeling.

The rest is already common knowledge.

DANUBE : (Shares Witold Gombrowicz's opinion that men are bound together by Pain, Fear, Absurdity or Mystery, and their lives governed by unfathomable melodies and rhythms, bizarre connections and situations. That is to say, they are the product of their own creations.)

In the finale we return to the master builder, the embodiment of civic courage, who plunges from the cathedral spire, or *would have* plunged, had his rainbow-coloured parachute not opened in the nick of time, extending the original five seconds to several minutes, during which time the whole town : thinks of nothing ! Quaint. But not only quaint. This stretch of the Danube is also particularly well-stocked with fish. The deep, muddy, nutritious water provides an excellent environment. What is true is true, the Lower Danube can boast of many more, and larger, fish than the Upper Danube. One finds sturgeon of up to two hundred kilos. They are rather hard and gristly fish, whose black roe makes delicious caviar. Their younger brother is the sterlet. (Warning : no scales !) These fast, swirling waters demand special angling techniques, and the knowledge of dangerous depths, good fishing spots and varieties of fish is passed down from father to son. These are the kind of people who know that the upper arch of the sterlet's tail fin is longer than the lower arch, just as with sharks, and that it is advisable to wrap your hand in a rag before reaching down for one. On the deserted riverbank the dogs were howling.

In the same film they also said that New York is the kind of place where a person changes : *he becomes identical with his own self-image.*

14

The bar and eddy of Ulm,
continued

We had money again. Not even money, but 'better still' a cheque. It was the first time I had ever seen a cheque and I was suitably impressed. Like magic! And it didn't even cost any money.

We left Ulm. But then we seemed to go on treading water, until, with great difficulty, we reached Passau.

The two women came with us. Once I heard Breg say to Brigach: 'Yesterday I was so fat, forgive me.' I also saw one morning that they wore the same *rainbow-coloured* knickers.

It was a very beautiful morning, but not because of their knickers, which seemed like an added gift on this strange dawn. The evening before we had put in at perhaps the most beautiful spot on the German part of the Danube: the point at which the sublime and monumental pass between the Frankish Alps begins. This is the last point at which it is still possible to pet the Danube, Roberto explained as we pitched our tent. We camped beneath the shadow of the Weltenburg monastery, one of the oldest monasteries of Bavaria, which lies on a promontory that plummets sharply into the river. That afternoon we went to take a look, without – thank God – the women, who were, so to speak, taking the afternoon off.

Standing on the monastery pathway, we could see right into the steep breach of the Danube. The river disappeared among the precipices in boldly sweeping bends, accompanied on either side by huge, cranial rocks, spotted with random snatches of forest, like the tufts of a wig. A cumbrous opera set for Weber's *Der Freischütz*. Here and there one sees iron rings hammered into the rock, by means of which, in former times, the boats had pulled themselves upstream. These rocks, with their magnificent names – The Three Brothers, Napoleon, The Virgin, The Peter-Paul, etc – have seen several centuries of ships and barges pass ceremoniously beneath them. We visited the brewery, and I too was allowed to sample the monks' liqueur. 'Here the Catholics are in their element,' grumbled Roberto.

Our tents were already up – one for the two women, one for us – when the rain began to drizzle. We sat under the awning of our tent, Breg making sandwiches, Brigach boiling the milk she'd got in Eining, straight from the cow, as she put it. When they were busy working they were fine, and didn't get in the way. Roberto told us a story, the three of us crouching on the rubber mattress, gazing up at him. Now and then Breg stroked my back, then slipped her hand under my tracksuit and touched my bare skin. I didn't dare move, although I couldn't say why. What I felt was more a kind of goose-pimply hatred than gratitude. Her fingers spiralled down my spine.

Roberto was telling us about the Roman Empire, which came to an end somewhere right here in Eining. The border fortress had been called Abusina. He spoke about the lavish buildings of Louis I, and that it was not so much a Valhalla-temple that robbed him of his wealth as a dancing girl, Lola Montez. Then he spoke of Ödön Széchenyi, son of the great István Széchenyi, who went on conjuring until he had connected the Danube with the Seine – in so far as he travelled with the steamer *Mermaid* from Pest to Paris via the Ludwigskanal, along the Main and Rhine to the Rhine–Seine Canal. Then he told us about the bridge in Regensburg that had taken eleven years to build and was so detested by the people of Ulm. And then about Agnes of Straubing, the witch. Already half asleep, I heard Breg imploring

Roberto to let them spend the night with us, because of the rain. 'No, I'll look in on you,' he replied.

I am a very light sleeper. My mother would only have to whisper my name of a morning and I'd wake up at once. The screaming which woke me with a start the following dawn would have been enough for a thousand rude awakenings. Roberto slept beside me, as still as milk – not necessarily Eining cow's milk. The first thing I saw seemed utterly unbelievable. The women's tent stood some five or six metres away from ours and I wasn't in the least short-sighted. So what I saw I saw; even though I couldn't believe what I couldn't believe. A figure fell upon the tent like a raging hurricane and, like a giant uprooting a tree, tore it away from the two women and pulled down their bedclothes. The women woke up squinting and blinking. It was a sight I'd often seen and always loathed, those sleepy faces stretching and sighing, moaning and groaning and literally glowing with heat. The unknown attacker was already scattering their belongings in every imaginable direction, up into the oak tree, into the Danube, all over the place. And now and then, as if quite by chance, she gave the women the odd slap in the face.

The women went on screaming, and would have fled, had their attacker not brought them down with a single sweep of the foot that would have done credit to any bloodthirsty football fullback. I couldn't think of rushing to their defence, and even if I could have, I didn't. I simply nursed my own gloating pleasure at their misfortune. I began to shake Roberto. It was a struggle to wake him at the best of times, as if he were reluctant to leave something behind, or look something in the eye. When his heavy, blue-black eyelashes finally came untangled and he saw for himself what in me had aroused such a feeling of alarm, he simply grinned. It was then I noticed that the assailant was a woman. By now she was running after the other two, and, whenever she came within striking distance, she swung at them with her handbag, slinging it like a catapult.

Roberto sat up, his pyjamas open, and, scratching his belly as he sniggered, he encouraged the Amazons. The stranger brought the proceedings to a close by hounding Breg and Brigach into the Danube and forcing them to swim to the other side. Two hopelessly disappearing rainbows! Instead of turning back, the stranger continued along the bank, occasionally stamping her feet at the caterwauling women. Then she disappeared from view. Roberto shrugged merrily.

'We're on our own again,' he said, and I nodded approvingly, like a dog who has just been given a bone.

It was only after we had left Passau ('the lure of the finite') and were already in Austria, that I finally dared ask who the belligerent lady had been. Roberto gave the shortest of replies:

'Why, you know her. Effi Briest.' *

* heroine of the eponymous ("same name") novel.

15

Stairs

Since Ulm? I don't know since when. Yes, since Ulm, I have been heading continually and exclusively towards Mauthausen. I took every possible precaution: I lounged about in Regensburg, attended a lecture on the eight-centuries-old oak stake, and studied the dream-book they keep in the Kepler house, which tells of a voyage to the moon. 'A dazzling vision from the depths of a wretched room,' comments Aar. Kepler was a Danube scholar. Perhaps that is why he detested infinity?

I busied myself, in due form, with the great Passau flood which ravaged the town in 1954. Seen from the embankment promenade – Passau is almost nothing but promenade – the Danube seemed to hobble lamely a long way below. Then, however, the flood had even filled the riverside street lamps, which went on glowing under water. Meanwhile the water swirled and babbled overhead, rising all the way up to balcony level. Who could now speak of Inn, Ilz or Danube? Where now was the legendary Passau tricolor: the self-assured grey of the Danube, the ambitious, delicate blue and green of the Inn, or the weighty brown of the Ilz?

'Up there, way up there, that's where I rowed my boat,' said the woman with whom I had got talking, blithely pointing up to a two-storey building. She turned out to be a committed Inn-believer; for it is common knowledge that the Inn is wider and longer than the Danube at this point, and this encourages and entices many to go on calling the river the Inn, campaigning for it, which is rather an absurd idea, after all, what does it really mean to say that the Danube is the Inn (not to mention our Breg, whom we had just left behind) as if there were something worth striving for here, some clearly defined completeness, or emptiness, Nothingness or Eternity, to use the pseudo-witty language of the Baroque. It is here, at the latest, after the scandal and defeat of the Inn-believers, that one sees that the Danube is a 'Promenadenmischung'. In her younger days the woman had been, by her own account, a rather talented member of the Passau Rowing Club, and had won the East and South Bavarian championship for her age group. But by 1954 she had already outgrown the youth category. As the flood carried her canoe, she suddenly caught sight of a young man standing beside her on a second-floor balcony, shaving. She turned round and, by paddling against the current with all her might, managed to remain level with the youth. It was one almighty struggle. When the boy had finished shaving, he glanced at the girl in the canoe, and invited her inside. Grasping desperately at the balcony handrail, she made a jump for it, just as the Danube snatched the canoe (property of the Verein) from underneath her. She knocked the frail boy over as she landed, and at once, while they were both still in motion, locked him in the vice of her strong, sportive thighs.

Here I said farewell to my chance acquaintance.

When I left Linz, the Danube climbed into the so-called Linz Basin, and the river once again divided into several branches. Wooded hills on the left bank, a plain dotted with trees on the right.

On the left bank, 2112 kilometres downstream, lies the municipality of Mauthausen. As its name suggests, the town is the site of an ancient customs house, and, according to some accounts, sailors already had to pay customs duties here in the time of the Avars. And how they pestered Barbarossa on his way to the Holy Land! Frederick Barbarossa was a believer in simple solutions: when they tried to make him pay his dues, he simply burned the town to the ground. He waited for the red glow to die out in the mirror of the Danube, waited for the flying ashes whipped up by the light Linz wind to descend, then turned his glance to the *de facto* nonexistent town and shouted in a loud voice, so that all his soldiers and all the citizens of Mauthausen should hear him: What dues? What town? During the Middle Ages it was the salt trade that put the town back on the map. Its former rulers were the Pragers, from whom the old Pragstein Tower got its name. Stone quarries have been in operation for centuries on the town's perimeter, serving Vienna for generations with paving stones and the basic materials for barricades, as Heine notes in passing.

The innkeeper in Mauthausen was drunk. He looked a bit like Feri Steigerwald – if the name means anything to anyone. Steigerwald played centre-half for the small suburban football team with which I am (was) intimately associated. He was a first-class third-division player; that is, he dearly loved to win, and could persuade (force) others to share his passion. The second division would have been too much for him, but he was arguably a better player than many who came down to us from the league above.

When the innkeeper came over to my table, he neither greeted me nor spoke at all, just shut his eyes and waited. His freckles shone. I was still sober, even though, after extricating myself from Linz – a town I loathed, albeit superficially, from the bottom of my heart – I had stopped at the odd bar or two, by way of procrastination, and had drunk a large spritzer at each one. Here too I ordered the same. The innkeeper brought two glasses and sat down beside me. Behind the village, the Sun prepared to die. Romanticism, writes W. Kayzer in his famous open letter to Huisinga, that staggeringly beautiful and rugged document of male friendship which all but redefines the whole principle of masculinity, Romanticism is the kitsch of desire.

Below the terrace an American folk-dance group were warming up. One of the hulking great girls kept smiling at me with a full set of thirty-two teeth. I watched the swallows scour the last beams of sunlight. The dying Sun, the dancing Americans, the taciturn innkeeper, the diving swallows – suddenly fear deserted me, and there was nothing in my head, no memory, no desire, no imagination, only some charitable emptiness, emptiness as truth, Romanticism as the security of the moment. The American girl threw her legs high in the air, why weren't we already here yesterday . . .

Two more spritzers. Where did I come from? Budapest. And now? From Ulm. He had suspected as much; I looked like someone who had just come from Ulm. People came here, to Mauthausen, believing they had recovered their strength in Ulm. And no, he wouldn't deny it, he too had climbed to the top of the cathedral spire, believing he'd be closer to God the Father. But he was no fool, he hadn't drawn any conclusions from all this, neither about himself nor about God, none whatsoever, for he knew only too well that to see infinity as something finite was a risky business, just as it was risky – if not quite *so* risky – to see the nonexistent as something infinite. And that the woman next door had pulled a face and referred to Marx as the Jew who usurped God.

The American dancers packed up. No swallows. Two more spritzers. And as we happened to be talking about Ulm, did I understand Einstein's twin-paradox? He didn't understand it, but could explain it. (Spare me.) Take a couple of twins. One of them climbs the 768 steps in Ulm, while the other one over here – he pointed behind his back – that is, over *there* climbs the 168 steps of the quarry. Well, these 168 steps are the same as those 768. (Do go on.) Take the legend. The five seconds. Now then, if they push a Jew or a gypsy down the steps of the quarry, it takes him the same five seconds to reach the bottom as the master builder in Ulm, and it was the same with the eleven minutes of the parachute. For he was aware that these days the saints of Ulm all jumped with parachutes. Of course we could write a poem. Why ever not? Everyone writes poems, the twins, the parachutists, and that's just the point! That poems *can* be written! I was obviously an enlightened sort of bloke. The kind who knows what's what. That God lives! That God is dead! How charming, how anecdotal, the way the inmates of the camp are forced to stand in a line to watch the execution of a child. And someone whispers: So where's God now? At which the bloke standing next to him nods towards the child and says: Can't you see? Over there! Yes! Yes! But I'm not talking about God. I'm talking about stone. About the stone quarry. Not even about the quarry itself, but about any stone, any pebble or little brook, about the Danube, a clearing in the forest! You can get down on your knees and beg from God, but not from nature. If nature is hostile, there's nothing you can do to appease her. What can you do if you're frightened of the wind? I'll tell you: you can go on being frightened.

'Were you there too?'

He made no reply. Only that in the old days, before the war, it still mattered whether a person lived or died. If someone was taken from this world, his place would not immediately be occupied so that he should be forgotten. No, there was a hole, a gap, and the fellow was missed. Whatever grew took a long time growing, and whatever was destroyed was not forgotten for ages. In those days we survived through memory, whereas now we survive through our capacity to forget. Quickly and thoroughly. What Luther asked was: Show me a merciful God? What I ask is: Show me a merciful man?

Suddenly I could take no more. The Americans had disappeared, and so had the girl with all the teeth. I asked for the bill, *die Entlösung,* I said, and as I said it I knew that cause and effect had changed places in vain. This tall, freckled man was as frightened of every pebble as the prisoners he guarded.

As for me, I'm simply the one who trudges to and fro in the mud, between the buffet and the telephone box. More precisely,

dissolution; play on Endlösung (of debt)

I'm just the one they call 'I', and that is all you ever know about him.

––––––––––––

THE TRAVELLER AND THE WHY

(Five Wachau Bagatelles)
When he reached the Wachau – *why?* – perhaps because of the Willendorf Venus, the Traveller immediately fell in love.

★

Beside the High Gothic parish church of Melk, whose resurrection is probably the work of Raphael Donner, a woman entrusted her child to the Traveller for the afternoon. The little boy was like an angel – if that means anything to anyone. The Traveller wanders around with the child and grumbles. At the crossroads, he grabs the boy wherever he can. He himself can feel the boy's hostility to his clasp, but the child is so beautiful that the Traveller has no pangs of conscience. He remembers his father's fine, large hands. He thinks of his father's body in various situations, on top of a threshing machine, in the bath, in bed, beside the Danube. He strokes the boy's head for shame. But the boy immediately bursts into tears. They approach the Danube. Danyoo, Danyoo, twitters the boy. The Traveller glances at his watch. Once again there won't be a white Christmas. The bank is deserted. Suddenly the boy breaks into a run. His toddling turns into a helpless downward trundling, for he has failed to take into account the steep incline of the boat-slips. The Traveller sees the boy plop into the icy, fast-moving stream. He leaps after him like a goalkeeper with massive seven-mile steps. He lands on top of the boy and as good as pounds him into the gravel. They lie on top of each other, panting. At one and the same time, the Traveller sees the boy's radiant beauty and the lace-fine architecture of the cluster of Baroque buildings growing out of the abbey's rock, in perfect harmony with their natural surroundings. So as not to hurt the little boy, he quickly pulls himself up and brushes down his trousers. He does not, however, get to his feet, but crouches into his own body. The child stirs and begins to whimper like a kitten. The lapping of the waves. Then the Traveller asks his one and only question: *why?*

★

It was in the vicinity of Tulla, where the Danube once again flows peacefully. Approximately the spot where, in 1683, the armies of the Polish King Jan Sobieski joined forces with the German troops on their way to liberate Vienna. At dawn everything had been hidden by the fog, but by the time they reached the riverbank the sun was shining, the greyness had lifted and, although it was already autumn, the whole region shone a luscious green. Light is golden. The Traveller took his friend's arm and they sat in silence on a bench, ignoring the fact that everything was just *too* beautiful. They rowed out to a little island where they had carp *à la serbe* for lunch. His friend spoke about the struggle between good and evil. The Traveller began to perspire and gasp for breath. Misunderstanding this, his friend leaped to his feet and asked a question which the Traveller was unable to answer for gasping. His friend walked off and left him there. He listens to the plashing of oars; *why?*

★

The house must have been newly built, you could still smell the paint. One of the windows looked out onto the Danube, the other onto a rubbish tip. At this latter window stands the Traveller. The smell of paint merges with the smell of the woman. By the time an agricultural airplane comes spluttering down behind the rubbish tip, the woman's memory has entirely left his body. He breathes a habitual question onto the windowpane. The delicacy of this *why* stands in direct opposition to absolutely everything. For this reason, and from then on, throughout the Wachau dawn, he blames himself for absolutely everything. And this, somewhat insidiously, calms him.

★

Just as the Traveller fell in love, in the same way – *why*? – he waited impatiently each year for the arrival of March. Full of longing, anxiety and fear. Perhaps it was only the fear he really felt, the fear that somehow, this year, March would fail to arrive. Not out of malice or incompetence, but as a kind of oversight. For what did it matter, one month more or less? March was indeed an important month, a revolutionary month, but then, by the end of February, people have become so impatient, so weary of the stubborn cold. They live in a dark tunnel, devoid of memory and hope ('the future is eternal, and the past only comes thereafter'). February is that awful, rootless present. February is a moment of mercilessness, which is not to say it is a moment of truth, but if it just so happens that it is a moment of truth, then we are the bull in the arena. I dreamed of a bullfight, said the Traveller one morning in March. And? asked a distant, gentle voice. We lost, the Traveller confessed. So he went on searching for the tell-tale signs of March, encouraging, sparkling signs. He rummaged through ancient records, diaries, pocket notebooks, calendars. Thus he spent the second part of January and all of February. And then came March, then crazy April, and so on.

REPORT

As if we were alone, I waved to the captives of Stein (who, according to a malicious rumour, come equipped with Köchel numbers) and thought of the old and (und !) amusing wordgame *KREMS UND STEIN sind drei Städte*. With a deep sigh, I left Favianae (Frau Bacher) behind me and boarded a ship. When we reached shallow waters I took depth measurements. But before that I was genuinely offended that no one had come to see me off, and when our engines started – at first with a cough and splutter, then with an even murmur – I waved to the thousands of receding, diminishing women with their streaming hair, streaming handkerchiefs and screaming kids, as if each and every one were my own mother, lover or child.

At times the sounding line – which was a good four metres long and made to fit in a stronger palm than mine – played tricks on me. Even today one often hears the story of the boatswain Hubert Hegedűs. He was a jolly, even-tempered fellow in his sailing days. They used him to measure the water's depth. He would stab rhythmically at the riverbed and, according to specification, shouted the measurements up to the bridge, 24, 24, 33. Then, when the plummet no longer reached the bottom: no bottom, no bottom. Then suddenly, but still in the same impassive voice: no plummet! An unexpected mound on the riverbed had shot plummet and sounding line clean out of his hand.

The Danube is like my grandfather used to be: it too has its rules and regulations.

I was not settled, as they say.

For me, travelling is self-recognition. I do not seek the new and strange, but the old and familiar, so that I may finally recognize that which recognizes me. When I travel I am the guardian angel of that which exists. What I seek both in the world and in myself – and, according to my working hypothesis, there is no point distinguishing between the two – are the *models* according to which I can measure my experiences.

KREMS UND STEIN ...: Krems and Stein are three cities. (There is a city called 'Und'.)

The ship's captain was a 'cultivated, humorous Englishman', the very same Sir John Andrews to whom Kazinczy refers. He gave me a thorough once-over, then, seeing that I stood up to his inspection, clasped my right hand in his steely palm.

'I can see you are a genuine traveller. A traveller lives and dies for clichés.' Listening to this English gentleman, I was reminded of that rather arrogant period in my life when I toyed around with a certain travel-writerliness. But a Continental should never try to understand the English. They are *almost* definable according to their sober scrutiny of things, their respect for the object in hand. Yes, it is as if that's all there were to it : world domination as craftsmanship, greatness as mediocrity. Then suddenly you catch sight of that blazing blue sparkle in their eyes! For they are actually – let's be honest about this – quite dangerous madmen. And although their reliability is still reliability, we know from that moment on that it is based on something fundamentally uncertain, on peat and fen, on an unknown desire, fervour, sin.

The captain had just reached this point in his fiery *ars poetica*, that is to say he lived and died for clichés, emblems and, no, he wasn't one to mince matters, for myths too, simply loved 'em, the modern, inferior kind too, just as he loved kitsch and self-repetition and unoriginality, which should not be taken as a mark of resignation on his part, nor a lack of *niveau*, or if it was, then only in so far as defeat is the only credible form of victory, no, on the contrary, it was the thirst for knowledge that was at work here, ah yes, that was the most important thing of all, the passion, the passion for knowledge!

He finally let go of my hand. He was right. Who could fail to be uplifted by the idea that the history of travelling is as old as the history of man himself. For when the caveman, with his large head, short legs and bushy mane, set off on his first longer hunting adventure on the trail of reindeer, bison and bear, the *great* journey had begun, and it has been going on ever since.

93

Hurry up and get to the point about the Coral-Lady! Stop. Contractor (Hirer)

REPORT

Because I am the politest person in the world, who likes brown carp and believes, now and then, in the resurrection, I replied: 'We really are having jolly fine weather.'

This happened at the gentlemen's dinner the captain threw in honour of a capital carp. It should be mentioned that the carp of the Lower Danube are, on the whole, somewhat stubby, and their bodies (fig. 9) are covered with yellow-gold scales. It is also worth pointing out, however, that the lanky-carp has a higher profile index. Therefore the correct answer to the question, 'What is the greatest experience that our home waters have to offer?' is: playing a lanky-carp with a 30–35 line and spinning reel!

By the time dinner was over, we were already approaching the Iron Gate. The rabbit pâté with orange, the consommé with quails' eggs, the steak with green peas and the caramel soufflé had all, taken individually, been more than acceptable (although the vol-au-vents did seem a shade too dry). But something had gone wrong, something that represents the greatest adversary of all good dinners. The *whole* meal was ultimately a disappointment. For, all at once, it felt so *heavy* that we were forced to question not only every element it contained, but also ourselves. And all that remained, in place of the rapturous murmurings that signify the conclusion of a *good* meal, was a short and simple sentence: we had overeaten. Without having eaten all that much, we had eaten *over*.

That is the spirit of temptation which haunts old kitchens: not so much quantity as density. A solitary slice of fried meat – correction: Wienerschnitzel – dangling over the edge of the plate, is certainly a lot, but also enough. Old-fashioned cooking treats every supper as if it were the last, and does so with a certain social overtone (aftertaste), as if to say : now you can eat as much as you're not ashamed of eating. This is what French *nouvelle cuisine* finally brought to an end. Once it outgrew its initial ideological excesses, it really did change the world, and has every right to be mentioned in the same breath as the Great October Socialist Revolution – if this means anything to anyone. In vain did our ship employ genuine Viennese chefs, kitchen-wise, state-of-the-art specialists. Sailing downstream from Vienna, it is impossible to cook the same food, and in the same way, as in the Graben (or the Rasumofsky Gasse). Yes, Europe is broken in two, and there is no point in conscientiously trying to stick it together now, especially not with some kind of *Alleskleber* (Uhu). *Nota bene*, it is in the Razumovsky Quartet that Beethoven too finally breaks away from Papa Haydn. A young man of thirty-two suddenly yokes *Empfindsamkeit* to passion!

One by one, the captain bade us farewell. Harmless fathead. Meanwhile I got talking to the first officer. He had a high opinion of his boss. Unbelievably *talented*, he called him.

'How can a captain be talented ?' I asked.

'Let me give you just one example,' laughed the first officer. 'He is by far the fastest at solving crossword puzzles.'

'Are you joking ?'

'Naturally. But the water, my dear fellow, the water never jokes. As the old sailor's saying puts it: Never get fresh with the Danube !'

'I thought it was never get fresh with the ball, and that it was an old footballer's saying . . .'

'Such, my dear landlubber, is the nature of old sayings.'

I stared into his cheerful, manly face. And then the scales suddenly fell from my eyes –

Uhu : a brand of glue

Traveller! Why do I have to keep on reminding you? Do you think I have nothing better to do? I might inform you, off the record, that I too have my doubts about realism, but for fuck's sake it *was* a *gentlemen's* dinner, so it's hardly likely to *turn into* a Coral-Lady! And what do you mean by the Lower Danube?! We haven't even got to Vienna yet! Don't go telling me that the scales fell from your eyes! I believe you, but it simply isn't believable all the same. Try to render reality more real. After all, that's what I hired you for! I told you to live! Well? Didn't I? According to the supplementary contract, you are to live and die. You know how it is: either here or there, you have to live and die!

Or are you in some kind of trouble? Should I send money? I'm worried about you, my dear friend!

REPLY

Send money! Traveller

TELEGRAM

Wanna step outside? I'll thump you so hard you'll slide all the way to the Iron Gate on your own snot, you lousy scumbag. Yours sincerely, Contractor (Hirer)

REPLY

I don't consider reality to be banal. Nor do I live purely in order to travel. I kiss the hand of your good lady wife. Traveller

REPORT

As if I could see freckles on the woman's shoulder. A fleshy shoulder. The décolletage plunging all the way down to her bum. She was with a handsome hunk of a man and they were both in high spirits. 'I love that great big body of yours.' The man cleared his throat, and looked about him in embarrassment. This must have been all too much for the woman, because she leaped to her feet – at which we men also leaped to ours – and stormed out of the captain's mess. As she passed beside me she hissed angrily:

'What cabin?' And I told her. So women still went for me after all. And what is more, *parce qu'il est bien*! – as they say in the secret language of tenderness.

I cast a fleeting glance at the rock of Durnstein Castle, where, in the old days, the hero of so many adventure movies, Richard the Lionheart, had been imprisoned. We always called him Richard the Lionfart; why, I can't quite recall. Anyway, it was to this castle that he once fled in disguise, taking a menial job in the kitchens. But he was so steeped in the trappings of royalty and power, and so totally incapable of disregarding himself, that, silly thing, he didn't take off his splendid royal ring –

TELEGRAM

Do you think I don't know? Do you think I don't know that you're shamelessly plagiarizing and, what's more, from where? Well I do know. Meanwhile, the Coral-Lady is left unattended. Unchaperoned. Or is she too in flight? Too much of a good thing. Don't go believing you're all alone in the world. You're not alone in the world. The ruffe (*Acerine cernua*, fig. 19) is undoubtedly : superb. But by now you could have got round to the theme of the 'Devilish Strait of Grein'. It was here, according to my secret informant, that Franz Josef ran aground in the *Adler*. My secret informant informs me that the captain managed (*mit*

Muh' und Not !) to tow the boat ashore by the Haustein Rock, so that the Emperor of civil servants and the sad-fated Elisabeth von Wittelsbach could continue their journey in the *Hermine*. Last time he wrote that it was Franz Josef who founded the Danube. Well I never. Count Széchenyi fancies that he discovered the Danube, Metternich was wont to jest. (That's authentic !) Just one more thing : what has the Coral-Lady got to do with Elisabeth ?

REPLY

I never stated, nor even suggested, that I was prepared to carry out independent research. I am neither bound, nor even encouraged, to do so by any secret clause in the contract – and, without wishing to sound abusive, the contract is literally crawling with secret clauses, for tax purposes, I presume. I too know that my Contractor (Hirer) knows – from me, no less – that my main source is the Antos–Berényi–Vígh–Timár–Magris Danube Fishing Guide, which, according to the stamp, is the property of the Textile Workers Union library, Budapest (Third District). Do not vex me, do not deprive me of the illusion of independence, do not show up the shadows of my dignity, do not make pronouncements about my chances of clemency and salvation. In a word : lick my arse ! Traveller

SUPPLEMENTARY TELEGRAM

Previous telegram cancelled. Put everything down to printer's devil. Apologies to all concerned.

REPORT

So the refined and enigmatic English gentleman was turning the capon on the spit with the ring still on his finger, while a gossipy, snub-nosed kitchenhand sprinkled the beast with fat, and deftly caught the drips in a spoon. Whenever she missed one, the tall flames that leaped up from the fatty liquid (which was not entirely free of tarragon) literally punched her in the face, causing her to flush and recoil with a scream. The double-dealing lord and master of Buckingham Palace (?) went on turning the spit in silence. The girl meanwhile took a fancy to this Richard.

'Don't tell me you want to sleep alone tonight!?' she called over to him in some abominable dialect, for it goes without saying that, in addition to being a gossip, she was also something of a slut. To cut a long story short, the heir apparent to the English throne made a pass at the gossip from behind, while she, in her surprise, grabbed hold of the spit (I shan't go into the gastronomic side effects of this action just now), but then, partly because she recognized the ring, and partly because she didn't get the orgasm she desired – just couldn't make it stretch *quite* that far – she betrayed the 'diligent' kitchen-boy to the guards.

'A kitchen-boy in the bush ...!' Yes, that morning she had hoped as much (untranslatable, untravelable, wordplay), only international kitchen politics had intervened. And outside in the dark, dry Sherry Woody forest waited Robin Hood ... Well, let him wait!

16

Vienna :
the turning point

By Vienna a lot of water has come together in the Danube. By now there is no turning back, no humming and hawing, appealing to this and that. By now : the Danube simply has to go on flowing. It is in Vienna that the Danube first thinks of the Black Sea. But that is still a long way away. Vienna is the nadir of the Danube. Here there is no forwards or backwards. Here one cannot *want* anything. Vienna has always been definable in terms of a stormy absence of will. It is the city of resigned gestures.

Ach, Vienna ... waltzes ... cafés ... loose women ... fried chicken ... fiacres ... parliamentary scandals. Ach. Hungarians always arrive arrogantly in Vienna. There is no objective cause, nor even counter-cause, for this behaviour, not even the Hungarians' eternal belatedness, which only increases their self-importance. So, this behaviour is without cause, but not without basis, the basis being the mixture of dreams and illusions the Hungarians of Budapest nurse within themselves. Hungarians are like Woody Allen, who rediscovers New York for himself every day.

For a short time this arrogance was replaced by fawning and kowtowing. The barbed wire surrounding Hungary – which, at the end of '89, two hundred years after the French Revolution, we tried to sell in nice red-white-and-green packets – this iron curtain, was not impenetrable, but fluttered now and then, and all the peeping Hungarians were simply dumbfounded by what they saw. Wow, *hi-fi bananas*! Everything had become so formless that we longed disproportionately for form. We would never have dreamed of distinguishing between form and formality. And we knew nothing about the emptying of forms. We had forgotten, had lost, that European feeling (which is not simply a fashion, but history). And we were eternally grateful for the strait-laced, mechanical smiles of Viennese shopkeepers, their reserved politeness and soft, unmeaning phrases. In restaurants we disastrously overvalued the orderliness of the napkins, mistook the courtesy of waiters for genuine affection, and read the neatly-laid tables as a sign of moral strength.

In me the fawning and the arrogance intermingle. Coming from home, I feel I have arrived in a glittering western metropolis, and gratefully sink into my seat beside a nice clean tablecloth. Coming from the other direction, however, Vienna somehow seems all too familiar, and, seeing the streets deserted at evening, a doddering old man or woman with a dog, or a political report on television, I am seized by the *unheimlich* feeling of being at home. And I am obliged to remember that my country and this country were once one country.

I never really liked Vienna, mainly because I never knew it, or rather, I never knew the Vienna of Nothing (which is everything), only the Vienna of Abundance (which is relatively little in comparison with everything). I always mooched about in the same two or three polished downtown streets. Perhaps because I was, as a rule, merely passing *through*. (Passing through : that too is a kind of profession ; it would, however, be a frivolous simplification to identify it with pious, or religious, *travelling*.) I found everything excessively grand, convulsively grand, by which I probably mean : exclusively grand. In place of wise resignation, self-confident neckties. As for the legendary *Gemüt-lichkeit*, it was simply a kind of phosphorescent stupidity. And as for provincialism, Vienna is quite obviously provincial. It is above all the Viennese who'll tell you so, with proud, twinkling eyes. So it is as well to be cautious here. These days they say the whole world has grown provincial and the earth has reached its limits. There is no longer a Rome, where all roads lead, only an Ulm, indeed a thousand Ulms. One Ulm after the other. Enough Ulms to fill the Danube. World Province – this is clearly just as valid as Goethe's idea of World Literature. How can there be a *far away*, if there is no *from where*?

Actually, it was the way the Viennese looked at one that really put me off. That is, the way they never so much as glance at one. My problem here is less with the 'one', than with the 'never so much as'. To avoid any misunderstanding, let me put it in the third person. The Traveller was contemplating the glances of strange women. On the escalator, in bookshops, in the street. The way one simply forgets to remove one's gaze from another's face. It seemed to him that this was not the custom here. And this, he felt, cast the whole town in a rather bad light. In a friendly little town, men and women's gazes go scampering all over the place. It wasn't that he missed a kind of *bon vivant*-ish favouritism. He only wanted what he felt to be his due. In statistical, that is human, terms. He wasn't spoilt or anything like that, but what was due was due. After a day or two in Vienna, he felt as grey as a concrete bunker. A rather fragile concrete bunker. For example, the type built by a dejected Maria Theresa after a distasteful altercation with Fischer v. Erlach. (The object of the unfair dispute was the Palais Trautson, one of the finest Baroque palaces in Vienna. And it shouldn't be forgotten that the spirit of the Baroque was to weigh heavily over Vienna in later years. Vienna does not remember the Baroque with the greatest of affection, for the Baroque does not reveal its secrets to the town. The Baroque is Vienna's 'Before the Law'. The Palais Trautson, on the other hand, was once the seat of Maria Theresa's Hungarian Noble Bodyguard, which included the likes of György Bessenyei, Sándor Kisfaludy and György Klapka.)

Was this the liberal tolerance one read about, that sometimes turns into cynical indifference? From live and let live to die and let die (Polgar)? Ending up, according to the Traveller, as love and let love? Isn't there a line in Dylan Thomas about how the lovers collapse but their love lives on? (This was true of travelling too.) Anyway, if after a while, I looked into a shop window, say, in the Rotenturmstrasse, I was forced, on seeing the figure it reflected there, to believe that those jaded Viennese glances must have been right after all.

A busy Benedictine! The Gottweig anecdote came to mind about how, at the beginning of his reign, Joseph II visited the Abbey – in a frosty mood, it goes without saying – and standing there in the dizzy eighteenth century before all that 'impressive detail', saw a man hurrying between the hills, anticipating the fad for jogging by more than a hundred years (a scene the Protestant version equates unequivocally with the making of cider), at which the Emperor nodded appreciatively and said, not without a trace of malice: 'A busy Benedictine.'

So here I was, *busily* back in Vienna again: although I really didn't get much done. I booked into a room in the Josefstadt. My Roberto-research was getting nowhere. I can remember sentences, but never the whole thing. Roberto suddenly disappeared. I went over to Aunt Nelly's, rang the bell, and the chambermaid, as soon as she saw me, burst into tears.

'It's me,' I said to my aunt, who seemed unable to decide whether to embrace me or give me a good hiding.

'Fancy a game?' she said calmly in place of a greeting, and pointed to the chess table. 'You can be white.' As she set up the pieces I could see her hand was trembling.

By the time we got back to Vienna, Roberto had changed. If I'd had any sense, and not merely been a child – and a vain child to boot – I would surely have been frightened. Instead I was rather proud.

'Now your time has come,' said my uncle. I beamed with

satisfaction, failing to notice that he was using the same tone as the two rainbow-coloured women from Sigmaringen. Nor did I notice just how much responsibility was being heaped upon me, upon my shoulders, which were still small and weak shoulders at the time. Actually, looking back, I have to say that I was lucky. I could have come completely unstuck.

We seemed, at one and the same time, to be hiding and showing ourselves in public. Then our money ran out again, and we had apples and rolls for supper, although we still dressed in dinner jackets and laughed a great deal. Then we got to know a professional tap-dancer, and went to watch him perform every evening. Once Roberto went up on stage and danced too, but I don't remember where it was, for we went everywhere by taxi. Anyway, he danced the woman's part, which I found most amusing. I saw that he got money from the man. I had a very tight pair of pink corduroy jeans at the time (Roberto and I had bought them together). According to Roberto, it was these the tap-dancer was after. Another time he got the whole of a pub in Grinzing singing. He'd drunk a lot of beer and stood in the middle of the pub conducting. Everyone was happy. Outside he had to throw up. I held his head. 'Your hand was nice and cool,' he said later. Now and then he pointed people out to me. Waiters, shopkeepers, taxi drivers, even policemen. 'Take note.' He wound the town around me according to some plan, showing me downtown passageways and dark doorways.

'You'll be able to hide in here.'

'Why?'

'Grown men don't ask questions.'

I may have been a child, but I couldn't help chuckling at this. I wasn't that easily taken in and realized this 'grown man' stuff was nothing but a con. But I said nothing. And I also thought he was conning when one day he said he couldn't get up because of the pain in his leg. 'Periostitis,' he growled. 'Or arthritis.' And would I deliver a letter to the Riemergasse. In the meantime he would hold a tomato compress to his foot, which was supposed to be the best thing for it. Weren't tomatoes a bit expensive, and shouldn't I perhaps call for a doctor . . . ?

'No!' he shouted. 'Don't call anyone! No one!' And that enough was enough, I sounded like a pauper, and paupers never get rich. When I looked at him, he looked away, which was something he had never done before. And it was then that it occurred to me for the first time that even he didn't know everything, and that maybe he was the pauper who would never get rich, even though that was all he ever seemed to want. And then I thought of my father again, whom I felt I had just cheated or betrayed, without having done anything against him whatsoever. And I too looked away.

The Riemergasse was just the beginning. I never went to the same place twice. And wherever I went, I always had to wear different clothes. Usually I had to deliver letters to the people he had pointed out to me. Sometimes I had to bring back a reply. I always had to begin with the same sentence: *Ich bin in einem sehr komplizierten Sinn heimatlos geworden*, to which the correct reply was supposed to be: *Gelernter Österreicher?*

And that is how it always happened. Except for the first time, when I had to go and see the cashier at the Rondell cinema. I didn't notice that it was an 'adult' cinema. The cashier was an old biddy with grey hair, who tried to shoo me away. I smiled sagaciously, then, taking advantage of her pausing for breath, I triumphantly hissed the memorized sentence in her ear, explaining how, in a complicated sense, I had become homeless. Until then she had spoken to me sternly, as if I were her grandson. But now her mouth fell wide open, and I could see a string of saliva stretch between her teeth. She stared at me dumbfounded, as if I had just told her to stick her hands up. I looked over my shoulder to see who could have frightened her so. It must have

Ich bin . . . : I have become, in a very complicated sense, homeless
Gelernter Österreicher: a studied Austrian

been this that made her blow her top, the way I didn't seem to identify myself with myself, or rather, with whoever the secret sentence was meant to identify. Quite unexpectedly, she began to bawl in Hungarian : 'No ! No, that's just too much ! So they're sending child assassins(?) now ! That's just too much !' She flailed her arms as she screamed, scattering cinema tickets far and wide. Then a man in a suit appeared, with the same curly red hair my gym teacher used to have. 'Calm down,' he said, and here he uttered the woman's name which I shan't repeat in case she is still alive. Meanwhile I started edging away and ended up behind a thick, carpet-like curtain. A girl stood by the wall in a skirt and bra (black), smoking a cigarette. We looked at each other in silence. Outside the man was yelling at the top of his voice, looking for some 'kid'. The girl reached out towards me. I shrank back and started snarling like an animal.

'Be quiet,' said the girl in a melancholy voice. She led me to a rear exit. She exuded all kinds of strange smells. When I finally got back out in the open she gave me a friendly shove, and then, in the same sad voice, said : 'Motherfucker !'

I sat down in the appointed confessional in the Stephansdom. A cat ran among the pews. Pater Czakó, Montag, Dienstag, 11–12. When I whispered the sentence he leaned out of his box. 'Jesus Christ. Here. There you are, now go. Hurry. Gelernter Österreicher, hurry.' He pressed a bag of oranges into my hand and pushed me away. That day Roberto was as happy as a sand-boy. We went to see the tap-dancer, I fell asleep at the table and Roberto carried me out to the taxi in his arms. The following day I had to take the oranges to a bank. I remember that everywhere I went there were signs pointing to Prague. I even took a tram across the Danube. Roberto had told me what to do, step by step, and also what to expect at the bank. 'There won't be any surprises.' A safe had been registered in my name. When the bank clerk turned the key I waited for him to go outside as Roberto had said. Finally he shrugged and really did go outside. He hated me, and I was insolent in return. By way of revenge, I left him all my small change as a tip.

I got off the tram beside the Danube. There was a full moon. I walked along the embankment. Behind me, the Gelhaftskeller. In those days I still did not wear glasses, but even so I had to squint – 'Don't filter the light,' my old art master would say to me. He treated me with a certain favouritism because he abhorred the Russians so, although I can't quite remember the connection. I bent down to watch the light dancing on the water. The river was huge and grey. Once, when my face came very close to the water – his face was six inches from the Danube, they'd say in a novel – I suddenly caught sight of a tank at the bottom. A real tank, just lying there on the riverbed. I ran away. (The tank is still there today. Anyone can check this. Just ask for the head waiter at the Gelhaftskeller, Merrill Overturf, a charming, helpful fellow, almost as charming and helpful as Feri Oberfrank – if the name means anything to anyone. Six inches, don't forget.)

It was forbidden to wander off and eat an ice cream while on duty. Instead, by way of so-called technical detours, looking over my shoulder to see I wasn't being followed, I was to come *straight* home. From the Marienbrucke, an extension of the Rotenturmstrasse, I turned into the narrow Griechengasse. I hurried past the delightful little *Greek Orthodox Church*, decorated with icons, and then, on reaching the Fleischmarkt, past the *Greek Catholic Church* decorated with an octagonal tower. And there in front of the Griechenbeisel restaurant I spied a wildly gesticulating Roberto with the beautiful directrice whom I had already seen at the gentlemen's tailor's and who turned out to be none other than the Amazon who had given those two women of ill repute, Breg and Brigach, such a thorough hiding. She was still swinging the same handbag. I stopped in my tracks. They were arguing. Suddenly Roberto turned on his heel and, to my utter surprise, hobbled away grimacing with pain. And that was the last I saw of him. More or less. Or was it? No ... not quite the last. These days, according to authoritative sources, the Griechenbeisel is neither 'griechen' nor a 'Beisel', but rather a glass bead for tourists (Turistenglasperlenspiel). All the same, with its romantic ambience, ornamental balcony and cosy, vaulted rooms, it is still a forgotten little corner of the Middle Ages. The Griechenbeisel had shared Vienna's joys and sorrows for centuries, surviving two Turkish sieges (the building's steep, tower-like upper part dates from the beginning of the thirteenth century and was probably erected on the foundations of a Roman tower) and the odd earthquake, plague, flood and fire. It was here in the mid-seventeenth century that the hit song 'Oh Du Lieber Augustin' was born. In the restaurant's guest book, alongside the names of Beethoven, Wagner and Mozart, we find the great German surgeon, Billroth, and also Chaliapin. But Sven Hedin turned up here too, as did the inventor of the airship, Zeppelin, or, more precisely – Hungarian fate! – the inventor of the fixed-frame, navigable airship, the one time Hungarian timber merchant, David Schwarz. Count Zeppelin bought the rights from his widow, and that's the truth.

In the room we rented behind the Hohe Markt, in place of Roberto, a letter stood awaiting me. 'Noodle! I'm otherwise engaged. Tomorrow you're to go to Cafe Landtmann at one o'clock to meet "Effi Briest". You know who she is. Here's a thousand Schillings. You're to pay. That is, *invite her.* Insist on it. Take care. From tomorrow the world is ours! R.'

VIENNA: THE TRAVELLER LEADS A LIFE OF THE SPIRIT

Vienna is not a Danubian city. Vienna doesn't appreciate the Danube. As soon as it notices the river, it invites the canal to come in and show off, and splashes about a little in the Alte Donau. Perhaps this is why the Traveller, on reaching the Danube – and let's not forget he is a Danube traveller – begins to ruminate about his life. He sits down in a park, a Viennese park. These parks are Vienna's magic mirrors, in which the whole town can see itself reflected. And all at once everyone is there, Schnitzler and Trakl, 'the fire of rococo-hedonism' and 'the smoke of dry, brown, deathly, autumn brushwood'. (There's no smoke without fire.) The dead stroll along the well-kept paths. It is easier to join the ranks of the dead in Vienna. Young people exchanging grass and dope in the back alleyways of the Burggarten, old men in cravats, doddering old society dames, so many picture-postcards that will never be sent. Vienna has more than its fair share of dead. It has a fine bagatelle tradition in the living dead. The Traveller is seized by a passionate and somewhat ridiculous fit of self-pity.

In his younger days he had travelled widely and impetuously. His life had been a string of yesses, he had said yes to everything, taken on, tried out, desired everything. Actually he hardly travelled at all. He didn't find it *important*. He still had so much time, was full of time. And if he did travel, he felt it to be a kind of test that was not necessarily valid. Or rather, either it was valid or it wasn't, and it really wasn't worth trying to decide which: if I want it to count it counts, if not then not, but either way, it doesn't count. He clasped all the outstretched hands that were offered him, squeezing them, stroking them or kissing them. Or else he simply slapped them and laughed through his teeth. There was a time when he turned his nose up at 'globular' Passau and told the Danube to get lost, scram, beat it. Or not so much the Danube, as travelling itself, it was this he turned his back on. And he began studying maths, a bit haphazardly, like the puppy-dogs that yap on the riverbank. Then, after a short pause, he started going in for athletics somewhere between Mohács and Baja, and in the intervals, the intervals between the crippling one-minute 400-metre sessions, he translated Rilke and imagined he had a thousand lives, one in Eschingen, one in the obligatory Ulm, a gilt-edged one ('Catholic-Pagan') in Melk, one small life after Vienna in Petronell (alias Carnuntum), in the shadows of Marcus Aurelius, one in Komárom (where his friend had played the dandy in the fifties), one in Szentendre, one on the Mohács plain where, under the yoke of a wicked, but not altogether unattractive woman, he'd bring up his unruly kids on the banks of the Csele, one life in Újvidék on one of those boulevards that run down to the river, in a bedsit, embittered, alone, one in Orşova, one in Ruse, cherishing the memory of his former wives (whom, following in the footsteps of Nicola Bedő, he had loved to death), one pitiful life in Tulcea, and one at the end of the winding St George arm, originally dug by a dragon's tail and still preserving the memory of ancient battles, in silence, sinking ever deeper into the decaying mud of the riverbank . . . A thousand lives! And every day that floated lightly past only emphasized the thousand-ness. No, he didn't mourn the passing days, but flew and watched and laughed, devouring, inhaling all he saw, all the various breeds of fish, the instructions for treating white wines, the sauces and barges, the floods and steeples, the sandbanks, the ducks, the cormorants, the pelicans, the herons, the cranes, the egrets, the lines of poetry, the heroes of novels, the fords, the bridges, the fishermen, the sailors, the rolling hills, the trembling, the tiny bones, the nakedness, the things he saw, the things that are.

On one occasion, by the 'restless rocks' at Grein, he cricked his neck, or not so much cricked it as began to notice that it hurt. Or still less than that: he simply became aware of his neck's presence. That he had a neck. He reached round to his long trapezius muscle and clumsily pressed and pinched and massaged himself from behind. And as he caressed this *alien* cluster of muscles, he realized to his horror that he had fallen into a trap. Perhaps he had been too careless, too self-confident – but then he too had to be *one thing or another*. For until then he had always thought of himself as . . . No, it wasn't himself he thought of in this way, but the Danube, the thousand Danubes that he had been looking at – as the poet Attila József reminds us – for a thousand years. And it was only this looking that he considered real, or valid. It is true that there was something of the irresponsibility of procrastination in all this. In his sense of 'the way things were' as being far from finite. That things were 'like this' or 'like that' right now, but they could quite possibly be entirely different. But now, as he watched the ferry docking clumsily, he was forced to wake up to the fact that everything really was 'like this' or 'like that', and although they could quite possibly be different, this was the way they were *now.* It was Time itself that had touched him here and spoken to him so brutally. It was Time itself that had cricked and started retching.

Then two things happened. In his alarm, he grew ambitious. He rose with the dawn and travelled late into the night. He grew strict with himself – oh, you champagne bills from Cannes! And he reached Sulina in two days flat. At any other time he'd have spent years in a single godforsaken hole by the Danube (again: name not important). He devoted every moment of his life to travelling: by road, rail, sea or air. He would turn down the beer binges proposed by his friends in order to reach Regensburg that very day, where he would taste some fine Bavarian beer out of vocation. And all the while he missed his friends so much that he was utterly crushed by his rigorous solitude and radiated such childish defencelessness that two of the four women sitting at the neighbouring table in the tavern immediately came over to sit beside him and began at once to fondle his knees. And if, by mistake, they happened to fondle each other's knees as well they suddenly began snorting with laughter. The Traveller looked conscientiously over at the other two women, the two leftovers, who, however, sat quite contentedly chewing knuckles of pork – *à la maîtresse de la maison*, as far as the Traveller could see. But when one of the women beside him reached up towards his thigh, and the other gripped his free leg between hers, all three of them suddenly turned serious for a moment. Then, sniggering and laughing, they all stumbled up the wide, creaking wooden staircase to his room and, still in a fit of laughter, fell on top of one another on the bed. (On the dark stairway he had reached back into their crotches and, gripping them as tight as he could, had carried them up behind him, like a cat carrying her kittens by the scruff of the neck, miaow, miaow . . .) As they writhed and wrestled on the bed, on the floor, on the sour-smelling carpet, the women's hair kept flying into his mouth, and he chewed at it a little uncertainly. In the morning he stood in the window alone, watching the cargo ships. (The women had left him a little note : 'We don't know quite what to say. Ciao !!! PS. In your sleep you cried out something about the Free Port of Csepel. This doesn't mean much in German, but maybe it will help you. Anticipating your approval, we licked you like a couple of dogs while you slept. All the way from your Achilles tendon to the top of your head. We feel you should take care.') The unloading continued, the cranes like wading birds. The Danube–Main Canal is sometimes called the cock-up of the century. Others call it the century's great masterpiece. He looked in the mirror and found the person he saw there beautiful. He could smell strange smells on his own person. The girls had not been beautiful. They were young. And the Traveller remembered that he too had been young once.

And that was the other thing that happened. He began remembering things. He began collecting time, almost like a beggar, scratching in trash cans, rummaging in rubbish bins. He said things like : Now I am exactly the age my father was when we were deported. Now I am as old as a certain teacher of mine (indestructability personified) at the time of my matriculation. At this age my father had three children. Now I am as old as he was when he was beaten by the secret police. Mozart would already have been dead. There is a saying in the Lower Danube region concerning people who grow careless and foolish : *You're fishing for yourself!* (The saying is of Lipovenian origin. The Romanian version runs : *You're catching yourself in your own net!*

reflecting a somewhat harder, more critical view of the world. The Traveller first heard this in Constanţa, from the widow of a KuK officer, a tiny, debauched old woman, who went about without knickers and said : as for me, old boy, I'm a Roman lady, I draw my conclusions from the heart, I'm a lady of Rome ! And with a laugh and a dance she span round with her skirt about her neck, leaving the Traveller open-mouthed. He stood there in Constanţa allowing himself to be convinced of the truth of the old woman's words. Stood and was convinced.) And he really was fishing for himself, trying to piece himself together from the rubble of past years, which now seemed both important and unaccomplishable.

Again the years flew by. His ambition changed, but did not disappear. As if it had altered or lost its goal, and had turned into a kind of objectless desire, the kind which makes it necessary for one to feel something in order for the day to pass. He looked at the Danube : the water flows. The water flows every day. Now it is at Immendingen, now at Erkhartsau, now at Apatin, now at Chilia Veche, then once again at Immendingen. On a good day he could think of nothing but that the Danube was eternal. And that he was the Danube.

But the obligation of memory is also the obligation to face up to the idea of death. A lake is one thing, a river another, and an ocean another thing again. And all rivers are different. And all Danubes are different too.

Thus his life meandered

He no longer desired above all else to travel *better*, for although he knew, or thought he knew, that what *can* be known *must* be known, it was still possible to miss the Esztergom connection, or to sleep through that tender moment when the Száva comes towards us, which is only to say that travelling begins where knowledge leaves off, or, to put it more directly, is a form of both knowing and not knowing at the same time, both discarding and exploiting one's experience, which speaks to us of silent, stagnant waters where spotted or crested newts float peacefully, of rich backwaters and bands of current whose paths are redirected by protruding rocks, fallen trees, islands, dams, and of those secret, bankside currents, the cherished friend of the white-water canoeist, the experience that speaks of eddies and whirl-pools (in Hungary there are no whirlpools), of weirs and sand-banks, fords, islands, bridges, culverts, barrages, sluices, hydroelectric power stations, boat-slips and boat-lifts, pumping stations, harbour pontoons, buoys with their anchor tackle stretching into the distance, which can be so dangerous in the sparkling sunlight, and still more so when dusk falls, of parallel works and cross-dams, canals and banks (that, for example, a sand bank is good, but easily churned up by a dry wind, whereas a wet bank is stable, but you can easily take a bit of it with you on your boat, while a mud bank will, if allowed to dry out, crack and break apart, so you have to be careful when walking on it, and as for a reed bank, well, reed banks are as good as impossible, because of the stalks, of course).

The Traveller didn't really change that much. He hardly became more melancholy or disillusioned, nor even more romantic. But he did start getting up a little later in the mornings. He would sleep just that extra half hour longer. And as for *waking* up . . . he woke up very badly. Not so much in a bad mood, as exhausted. His ankles hurt, his neck hurt, everything felt that much heavier. He continued to desire – to need – solitude, but this didn't mean he hated the world any more than before. Indeed, in contrast to the hysterical isolation of his younger days, he could now stop and talk in the street for hours with the odd barge helmsman, ship's captain, or off-duty stoker, and while it's true he often wouldn't pay attention to a word they said, he liked to stand around and listen to the noise of human speech, whose music was not unlike the murmur of the Danube. He grew neither more wise, nor more thorough, nor more serious. He simply slept differently and awoke differently. He didn't even travel more frugally than before, or if he did, it was a decidedly Baroque frugality. The Traveller was not a Viennese.

Sitting in the Burggarten, there can be no doubt that the world is neither fragmented nor chaotic. It is, on the contrary, highly ordered, somewhat small, and thoroughly transparent.

17

Viennese secrets

Wherever I go, I always find little notes waiting for me. All kinds of notes delivered to all kinds of rooms.

> *Dear Sir, I have the distinct impression that you wish to meet me. You might have been a little more discreet. I'll expect you at one o'clock in the afternoon at the Eiles. If you are unable to attend ... Just be there! D. PS. Don't be alarmed. I was given your address by the Literaturgesellschaft.*

I had never seen such a tasteless envelope: blinding pink – peasant pink, as they would say in haughty Budapest – and dotted with darker and lighter hearts. And what is more, it seemed to be *scented*. At any rate, the girl at reception pulled a face as she handed it to me. By then I had been staying in the Josefstadt for almost a week. Gradually my days had taken on a kind of order or rhythm. Furthermore, I came to realize that if I pushed the door of the shower cabinet right back against the wall, I wouldn't bang my elbow every time I went to the bathroom. Thus I no longer had to think to myself each blessed time (word for word): 'What terrible conditions I'm forced to endure!'

The greatest catch of all, however, was the Cafe Eiles itself. At last I understood what a coffeehouse was. In the old days there were several good coffeehouses in Budapest, but none have survived, only coffee bars and the odd elegant tourist attraction. But not a single living coffeehouse. The unburied dead lie scattered around my home town and no one seems to take any notice. Instead they go on hypocritically talking about them, about the old days, the how-it-used-to-be and how-good-it-would-be-if ... In principle I understood what they were referring to, understood the common ground, the reveries from the forgotten Baroque *theatrum mundi*, the site of the slow and elegant passing of time, of the moment rather than the glance, of make-believe, of play, of deception, of misunderstanding as a moral act. Yes, that was the coffeehouse. The intentional misunderstanding as the exclusive basis for genuine understanding. The site of a history without qualities!

As I sat there in Vienna I suddenly became alone. That is, I lived alone, which is something I rarely do. I became particularly fussy and did all I could to calculate everything in advance, or at least to sound out the likely outcome of things. To this, the new-found structure of my days, belonged the lightest of lunches, taken in the early afternoon. A mixed salad from the nearby takeaway, perhaps the odd kebab, although this, because of the onions, would leave its stamp on the whole day, even putting my dinner at risk. I often simply skipped lunch altogether, which meant I would be ravenous by dinner time. A hair of the dog that bit you, I thought at such times, today I'll eat nothing! I'm good at fasting. For this too I see as a special case of eating, and I love eating. But by ten the situation would have grown intolerable. As I had discovered a friendly place in the nearby Lange-Gasse ('young, ambitious chef'), where the food was reliable and the prices only a little higher than they should have been, it seemed quite natural to look in, as they say, for a light *hors d'œuvre*. But often I changed my mind at the last minute, 'unable' to entertain even the thought of anyone speaking to me, or simply looking at me. And anyway, what would I do while eating? Where should I look? *At* someone again? Or into space? Into my plate, my empty plate? In my room, on the other hand, I was unbearably alone. I both longed for, and was repelled by, human company.

The Cafe Eiles solved my problem for me. 'The Cafe Central can be found on the latitude of Vienna and the longitude of loneliness. Its clientèle are driven as much by misanthropy as by the desire for company. They are the type of people who want to be alone, but cannot achieve this end without ~~society~~,' writes Alfred Polgar in his *Theorie des Cafe Central*, taking the words right out of my mouth. (It is possible that Umberto Eco also uses this quote in his *The Myth of the Absurd in Austrian Literature*, but I'm not a walking encyclopedia.)

I wandered round all the key locations of '63. I felt I hadn't found anything, but – as is often the case in such matters – I had, to a certain degree, been found myself. The letter I had just received suggested as much. Big Brother. I couldn't find any of the old waiters, shopkeepers or taxi drivers. The bank safe was no longer in my name. On my way back, I went down to the Danube and, holding my head six inches above the water, looked for the tank. Nothing. Although it's true there was no moon. In the Gelhaftskeller they had never heard of a waiter by the name of Overturf. In the Rondella I was propositioned by a homosexual, whom I turned down as politely as I could. But I did find Pater Czakó in the Stephansdom. *Montag, Dienstag 11–12.* I was as pleased as if I'd stumbled across an old friend. As I knelt down, instead of ~~Ladetur~~, I said: '*Ich bin in einem sehr komplizierten Sinn heimatlos geworden.*' As he reacted with utter puzzlement, I launched into a confession, starting out from the idea of homelessness. It was awful. At times I felt like a priest. The Danube's confessor, *Montag, Dienstag.* I cross-question the sources. It can't be easy, being a confessor. How can he who listens to all listen to one? Still, it is a pretty grandiose idea, that

Montag, Dienstag: Monday, Tuesday

the whole world is founded on love. What else is travelling meant to be?

EXCERPT FROM (ONE) SECRET CLAUSE OF THE TRAVELLER'S CONTRACT

In the ~~instance~~ *event* of the absence of a Contractor (Hirer), the latter is to be posited fictitiously. In all other regards the travelling is to be carried out as usual (discipline of documentation etc.) Reports are to be sent to Ulm *poste restante*. Settlement of accounts in June and December. (Signature missing.)

I walked down the Josefstadter Strasse and sat down in the Eiles. The elderly waiter stopped in his tracks, glanced at his watch and cried out:

'What is it, Herr Doktor, has someone died?' And then he hurried on. He had only known me for four days, but he behaved as if he had brought the Kleiner Brauner to my father and my *small brown [beer]* father's father. At this I too behaved differently, not so much self-confidently as sedately. (After all, I was *somebody*, not somebody frightfully important, but simply the kind of somebody whose father and whose father's father , etc.). I always arrived at four in the afternoon, and always sat down at the same table, a little divan-like alcove table for two, a *nook in a salon*, in the spirit of Polgar. On the fourth day a RESERVED sign sat on the marble tabletop. I hovered uncertainly, looking all about me, but it was only here that I could see such a sign. Peculiar. Then the old waiter came over, swept the table (hangedli!) and the reserved *?* sign disappeared. 'What can I get you, Herr Doktor? The usual, Herr Doktor?' So the table had been kept for me. The old fellow had observed that the man with the spectacles – whence the Herr Doktor – usually arrived at about this time, and had decided to keep my table free. I naturally found this, as I told

119

him, somewhat moving, coming, as I did, from the land of informality. The old man kept my sentimentality well in hand (as if he were familiar with Lehmann's frivolous work of scholarship, *From the Himmelpfortgasse to the Cafe Prückl*, Appendix: Guitar School, where we read that one must leave a coffeehouse at once if, during the course of any given conversation, the waiter oversteps the desired boundaries of intimacy; boundaries which the pragmatic Lehmann defines within the thematics of meteorology). The old man didn't even talk about the weather, in fact I don't know what he did talk about, only that he went on talking for some time.

I was surrounded by a pleasant murmuring; as if the inhabitants of the café were a benign menagerie of animals, panting, chirruping and grumbling. At times I followed new arrivals with a long, impertinent stare, or watched someone give their steamed-up glasses a flustered wipe. (At such times I always think of my father; steamed-up glasses always make me think of him.) Or I watched a series of irresolute movements towards a table, an alcove or a box, or simply stared at the newspaper, burying myself in the profound surface of the odd *feuilleton*, seeing, hearing nothing.

The elderly waiter never tired of hurrying to and fro, always late, always at a disadvantage, which would not prevent him from stopping at the odd table for several minutes, as if he had nothing else in the world to do. He toddled and danced and flew and somehow the 'system' never quite collapsed, everything just about managed to sustain its delicate order. He talked to himself too, and would wave furiously if someone interrupted him. 'Sshh, be quiet! Everyone's always wanting something! And all at the same time! Coffee, cakes, the bill, what an impossible crowd!' Then, as if under a spell, he suddenly became attentive again, sprinting backwards and forwards with his hands fluttering after him.

The old man was not so much faultless as unique. That is to say: faultless.

I was just reading about Handke, about how much he travelled these days (those days). He simply went to the airport, picked out a destination from the departure board, and off he flew, free as a bird. I like that story of his about the man who gives his shoes a *thorough* clean in Split, the Saint of Split, he thinks to himself for a moment, the Saint of Carefulness, the Saint of Tiny Weights, and then, months later, in Japan, his shoes still shine like mirrors, reflecting the promenade of Split in all its former, original light. 'We should make this man travel, our special correspondent István Handke . . .' – that was as far as I got in my thoughts when a shadow fell on my newspaper. I half looked up to find my head level with a woman's loins. (I can think of worse positions.)

When I stepped inside the Landtmann twenty-seven years earlier, I saw, sitting on a throne before me, a woman whose name I didn't know at the time. All I did know was that they called her Effi Briest (which I suspected to be a nickname or pseudonym), that she had a penchant for loud red blouses, and would occasionally beat the women away from my Uncle Roberto. She sat there enthroned, as if she'd come straight out of a fashion magazine. The light from her coral-red nails shone all the way to the door. When she saw me she leaped to her feet and almost knocked me flat with her gaze, she was so angry. She addressed me using the formal 'Sie'.

'So he sent you, did he?' She snarled with frustration. Suddenly her face smoothed and she gestured that I should sit down. Then, as if she had hit on some kind of solution, she said calmly: 'The cowardly shit.'

I found this quite incredible, and informed her that I should like to take her to lunch. She gave me a long, hard stare. Oh no, she couldn't have that. It was already far too late for that. She'd invite me. Impossible, Roberto had expressly stated that she was to be my guest.

'There is no Roberto. Only you and I.' I didn't then, but now

121

I blush at that sentence. For some reason I felt I had to stick to Roberto's (last) instructions. Heads or tails, I proposed, loser pays.

'Or the winner,' I added. She glared at me searchingly. Somehow I'd got the upper hand. She nodded and rummaged for small change. 'Oh no you don't!' And I insolently took the purse out of her hands. 'Only after the meal. Until then, no one's to know who's paying.' She nodded indifferently. At lunch I went crazy. I ordered two different starters, pâté and escargots provençale, cream of liver-sausage soup, trout (to give my stomach a rest), rabbit in mustard sauce, cheese, dessert and fruit. (It isn't only sentences I can remember, but meals too, whole menus.) Once during the meal I could have sworn I'd seen Gigi. I don't think I'd ever been more excited in my life than when, at the end of the meal, the woman came to toss the one-schilling piece. My mind went completely blank, except for one thought: either you win or you lose. And now somehow this seemed to apply to everything. Now or never. It was then I learned what people meant by a passion for gambling. I won and the woman paid.

'We had a good meal,' she smiled.

'No,' I replied. 'We played, and you lost.'

She went on smiling as if she attributed no importance to what I had just said.

'Roberto's had to go away. Now don't go home. Go straight to your Aunt Nelly.'

Once again I was nothing but a child. The following day Aunt Nelly put me on the Orient Express. On the border, the Hungarians bundled me off the train at once. A group of surly men led me to a room. They looked at my papers and asked questions about Roberto, but didn't seem terribly interested in my answers. For a while they left me on my own. It got dark. To my horror, I remembered that I still had Roberto's last letter in my pocket. At once I started to act as if I were in a novel (never do that, dear reader!). Pressing my back to the door, I started eating the letter, tearing it to pieces with my teeth and then swallowing them. I almost choked on the paper.

'Spit it out, you little shit!' shouted three men as they rushed into the room. Lying on the floor I *confessed*: 'I can't, my dear friends. Believe me. There's nothing I can do,' here I swallowed hard, 'not even with the best will in the world!' They didn't hurt me, after all. It was here, in the darkness of Hegyeshalom, that my Landtmann lunch finally came to an end.

TELEGRAM

It was a pleasant evening. Better than the Nuremberg trials.

Woody Allen

'You're interested in Roberto, of course.' I surfaced from my newspaper to find that the woman had already sat herself down, made herself comfortable, and had both ordered and finished her tea. It was as if she were still wearing that same tight grey skirt. Once again, she looked like a fashion photograph. She allowed me to look at her. In a nice, leisurely manner, I lifted my gaze to her face. She had grown old, but that wasn't the real difference. I didn't even notice at first. And later I could see that she didn't try to hide it at all, was neither ashamed of it, nor proud. From the corner of her right eye all the way to her cheekbone ran a long, ugly scar. 'Looking at my worm?' she asked. 'Well just you go ahead and look at it. Maybe by tomorrow it'll have crawled a little lower.' And then, in an unexpectedly gentle voice, she added: 'Because I will see you tomorrow, won't I?' I didn't reply, and she, like some adolescent, simply shrugged. The scar was at once horrifying, like a crack or cavity in her face, the mark of some *ancient* affair, some archaic scandal, about which the less said the better, and at the same time seemed to dismiss all such thoughts as trifles, and actually made the woman look younger, projecting onto her face the image of a somewhat wicked child. And the reason for all this was, I think, her eyes, which were so mysterious, enigmatic jewels, tiger's eyes (can inspiration repeat itself?), but also the eyes of a terrified child, a chattery teenager, a radiant young woman, an attractive, wild, middle-aged woman, an embittered woman, a grand, generous woman, a cruel woman, a petty woman, a happy woman, a jolly woman, a melancholy woman, a superficial woman, a terrified old woman who believes in nothing but her body, the very body which is about to betray her, to leave her in the lurch, to wither away. Enough. I agree with Count Waldstein, who was Széchenyi's travelling companion on his famous Danube tour of 1830, and who wrote in his diary: 'Never describe a single landscape, a single painting, never, never anything painterly, picturesque: only hint at it, just enough to drop a fuse into the powder keg of the imagination.' A face, too, is a landscape.

'No, no, don't you go counting on Roberto, my boy ... Got a light? Of course not, why should you have ... Herr Ober ...!'

That I couldn't keep up with her was the least of my worries. From then on, from that table at the Eiles, I did nothing but try to keep up with her. Even in the street she walked half a pace in front of me, and I trudged after her like a faithful horse, if not quite a dog. We walked a great deal, she forced me to, all over the city. As a rule we set out from the Eiles, sometimes in *conversation*, sometimes silent for hours. I would never have thought her capable of silence. But she could be very silent indeed. Once we sat out on the bank of the Alt-Donau, autumn had suddenly become summer, and we didn't say a word all morning. We were as silent as the night. There was a swan too. The Zur Alten Kaisermühle was already shut, so we walked over to the Danubio where, since the Zur Alten Donau degenerated into a pizzeria, the clientèle feel just like they're in Italy.

But Italy didn't help either. There was no place for us, and that is what we were really looking for. What were we, how were we, and where? Who was she, and who was I? What was there between us? Roberto was between us, that was clear. But not like a wall, not dividing us, yet equally powerless to link us together. And ultimately we were looking for some place in the city where we could talk about him. Where we could begin. So that Dalma could make up her mind. For she could see on my face, on my person, or my surroundings, that it was not only possible for her to speak, but necessary too.

'I've asked two young friends of mine to join us,' she announced one day in the Eiles. 'So that we shouldn't be alone ... I think it's for the best.' She didn't look at me.

The 'two young friends' were a phenomenal couple, about twenty years old. The girl was probably Italian, at least she often spoke Italian, and laughed the whole time ('you all think I'm just a silly little happy-go-lucky Italian girl'). They radiated talent and strength. One could see that the world belonged to them and they were just stepping out into it, bright, intelligent, hungry for everything. When Dalma wasn't there, they spoke of her with the utmost respect. They could remember whole passages of her music-historical writings by heart, and spoke with the complex voice of tenderness and admiration.

Vienna began to spin as they dragged us to and fro, or more precisely, only me, because Dalma at once (and annoyingly) became as young as they were, adopting their rhythm, their opinions, even their words. (Traitor, I hissed at her one morning. She said nothing, but knew exactly what I meant.) Thus I became the eldest, a sullen, grumbling, grey old man. But I enjoyed this sense of drifting, I didn't have to make decisions, and Vienna span. They chattered and nattered in several languages, laughing, taking my arm, letting it go again, taking one another's arms, moving me, openly and secretly, and then once more by making the secret open. At times a single glance could last an inexplicably long time. ('You know that feeling when everything's fine and cheerful, only deep down inside something's not quite right.') We went to the theatre (offendedly, but not without pleasure, the Burgtheater audience swallowed everything that was thrown at them from the stage), to concerts and to restaurants (after midnight, Dalma would only drink apricot brandy and eat oysters and chocolate mousse), wandering all over town, from the Salzamt to the Oswald und Kalb, from there to the Santo Spirito, where Beethoven sounds like Pink Floyd, and then by taxi to the Europa, where Dalma unexpectedly asked me to scratch her back, and when I timidly began to oblige, I could feel that the girl was scratching mine, at which Dalma began scratching the boy's back, and he the girl's, so that there in the Europa we were all scratching one another's backs in a circle, then off we went once more to some place in the vicinity of the Bauernmarkt, some bar (Bela live), where, sighed Dalma, 'I always have such good conversations,' but it didn't work there either ('in that hall you had to play at a different rhythm'), then once again, stylishly and systematically, in the Bermuda Triangle, or stuck in the Mapitom, or drinking all kinds of beer in the Krah Krah. And I forgot to mention the Miljöö where we ate pork sausages and chitterings. This extravagant familiarity with an unfamiliar city became increasingly agreeable. By contrast, Budapest represented a lack of familiarity with a place familiar to the last nook and cranny – increasingly disagreeable.

Vienna came (in dribs and drabs) to an end and I had to leave. I told Dalma. She nodded. 'Now the poor man's Danube begins.'

Early one morning the following message awaited me (on a piece of square, yellow paper with almost printed letters):

> Zimmer 411 Clara aus San Fransisco
> hat angerufen. Sie versucht es vielleicht
> morgen nochmal. Danilo ist gestorben.
> Anruf 13.25 16.10.89

Zimmer 411: Room 411. Clara from San Francisco called. She may try again tomorrow. Danilo is dead. 13.25, 16.10.89

I tried telephoning here and there, but to no avail. Then I set off into town alone to get well and properly plastered. But I soon grew weary of this, and returned to my hotel room to sleep.

On the last day, quite contrary to custom, Dalma asked me to accompany her home. But only as far as the Schwarzenberg, as it turned out. It was a dark, warm evening. By the Russian war memorial the fountain suddenly started up, with its coloured lights, then immediately stopped again. It was like a single breath. We had sat the whole afternoon in the Kleines Cafe on Franziskanerplatz (*'wer viel hingeht, wird leicht alt da'*). When we reached a darker part of the street, she suddenly and impetuously showed me her breasts. (The pullover she lifted up was the one the girl had worn the day before.) They gleamed white in the dark. 'Look for as long as you think they're worth. It's time you stopped putting me off.' If I travel, I read in a book somewhere, love will grow inside me. The way she waved after me; it was as if she belonged to me.

If I were 'I', I'd say farewell to Vienna with an anecdote. It would be about my grandfather who, whenever he travelled by train, always went second-class, saying: 'You arrive at the same place.' Even when – and this would be the 'punch-line' – as Prime Minister of Hungary, he had to go and see King Charles, 'up in Vienna'.

The twentieth-century novelist has fared with the 'I' rather like the boy who cried wolf in the fable, and laughed when his companions came to his aid. One day, of course, the wolf really did appear, and however much the little shepherd boy shouted, no one budged. Instead of over-scrupulously trying to project this metaphor onto so-called reality – explaining what and who

'*wer viel hingeht . . .*' : 'who goes there often, may easily grow old there'

corresponds to the wolf, the shepherd boy, the prank, the fable, the no-one-budged, the however-much, etc. – allow me to go on. I could say: let's pour fresh water into the glass – but the glass leaks (I don't call it a pipe for the simple reason that we don't want to *completely* lose heart). Or I could say: I am Madame Bovary. Or I could say, pleading for attention: P.E. – *c'est moi*. And then again, I could simply say: I, but this 'I' is not some fabricated figure, but the novelist, who knows his business, a bitter, disappointed man. But no 'I' will make my heart pound with excitement, nor do I keep my fingers crossed for 'it', wishing it all the very best of luck. *Necessity is not in itself virtue.* Help. Wolf.

But enough of sorrow. All aboard!

18

Ship's log

For the Traveller the relationship between voyage and adventure
was not self-evident. Concerning such matters, the contracts
were . . . not so much ambiguous, as unhelpful. There were those
Contractors (Hirers) – although the Traveller was increasingly
less able, or less inclined to make such distinctions: there were
Contractors (Hirers) and that was that, he travelled and that was
that, and as for contracts, let them flutter in the autumn wind –
who insisted that travelling was adventure first and foremost.
There were those who simply wanted plenty of action. They
were not interested in the story, or rather, in the problem of
whether or not there was a story ('You are not a Wanderer, your
path does not lead to where one story begins and another ends,
nor does it dwell on the frontier between sleep and wakefulness,
nor in the grip of dreams and nightmares, nor in the chasm
between fact and fantasy!'), or, more precisely, in whether or
not we have a history (for a long time half of Europe lived in a
great collective lack of history, while the other half lived in the
thousands of unnarratable histories of individuals), for only the
collective history is history. The action-oriented Contractor
(Hirer) was left cold by the condition of Europe (which has now
anyway changed, although precisely how, it would be difficult
to say). He saw history as either expressly or inexpressly glorious
and triumphant, like the regulation of rivers or hydroelectric
power stations.

No, the Traveller was beyond appraising his Contractors (Hirers). Isn't history anyway just a question of who is broken and how? And who, in all this, remains unbroken? He did not claim that no one was. The Traveller was an asker of questions. – He simply met a demand, offering a service, code-named 'The Danube Pilot', on the principle of pay for one, get two. Exclusive details! Adventures! Spies! Women! Men! Love! – He was, however, prepared to recognize that travelling was a form of searching, and thus something romantic. The Traveller escapes, while knowing all along that there is no escape.

Die grellsten Geschichte sind Zitate, the wildest stories are quotations – this is what we bring with us from Vienna.

In his novel about the Danube – which anticipates the works of H.C. Artman and Italo Calvino – the seventeenth-century oddball Martin Fiegl ('the Sterne of the Salzkammergut') writes that there may well be those who have longer, wider and merrier Danubes (note the paradigmatic Renaissance *joie de vivre* exuded by every attribute, like the explosive, new, disturbing, frightening and unfamiliar strength, flood, ice-drift, eddy and whirlpool that erupt in the sulphurous night of an adolescent), but there is no other Danube that flows across more histories, ages, political and social alternatives and general ways of life. The incidental music of the 'Wirtschaftswunder' dies away in Vienna, and we leave the 'Weisswurstäquator' behind. Liver sausage, *n'est-ce pas*. 1929 kilometres still to go. Even a river doesn't remain humble. Something greater, coarser, wilder is still to come. Once I read an article about Israel in which an elderly Hungarian Jewess said: 'You can say all you like about Hungarian culture and poetry; for as long as I live the Danube will always be red to me. I don't give *nowt* for your Hungarian culture.' Wiener Blut, as it streams into the Donauwalzer at Novi Sad. Die Donau so ... *Wie ist sie?* The drunken Danube, Danube of the rabble. Danube of Pain: Don Au. Now there will only be secrets and turning points. But can the Danube really be, if everything is the Danube? A Central

site of a massacre in 1941. Hungarian army killing thousands of Jews.

European question. How can I unveil the veil itself? But perhaps one shouldn't talk so much.

Dalma took command of things, saying that I should follow my instincts. That was the best thing to do. She called me her dear boy. And she was already discussing the details with the director of the Erste Donau-Dampschiffahrts-Gesellschaft, a certain Herr Z, who was utterly *charming, amenable* and *generous*, just like his sweet little shipping company itself, which had been founded on 13 March 1829.

'My dear boy, you must write that down.'

'What?'

'Charming, amenable and generous.'

'Why?'

'It might come in handy some day. For you, a word can always come in handy. You want to put the Danube into words, if I've understood correctly.' She began roaring with laughter, then suddenly stopped again, just like that fountain. She looked at me quizzically, like a little girl. 'Or was it the other way round? That you want to build the Danube with words?' Silence. 'Doesn't that amount to the same thing? Can it amount to anything *but* the same thing?' Anyway, she went on, we now had two cabins on the *Theodor Körner* all the way to the Black Sea. The cabin came with shower and WC, and – it went without saying – was air-conditioned. Although it didn't have adjustable air-conditioning, like on the MS *Mozart* or the MS *Volga*. As for Körner, he was cruelly snatched from this world at the age of twenty-two, by a Napoleonic death. His highly successful tragedy about Zrínyi was damningly criticized by Ferenc Kölcsey.

Fiegl puts the words in Metternich's mouth, so to speak, when he describes the hustle and bustle of Mexico Platz. One is struck by a certain Balkan odour, what with all the bartering, exchanging and black-marketeering. A gold tooth sparkles in the grainy sunlight, an old man embraces a satchel-breasted old woman, then looks about him proudly, raising his balls in the palm of his hand. A pack of Kent will lighten the burden of their lives. This is the magic and menace of Central Europe: that a pack of Kent can lighten the burden of our lives. West of the river Leitha a pack of Kent has never lightened any burden whatsoever, except perhaps for nicotine addicts. That Austria too belongs to Central Europe only becomes clear when one leaves Austria behind.

If Prague is the heart of Central Europe, says György Konrád, Budapest is its crotch. Okay, that's fine, heart, crotch, there's not a lot to lose here. But the way the breasts and buttocks sing or caterwaul, dance or shrivel, is not a matter of indifference. Show me the town that would accept such an idea with its head (breasts, etc.) held high? Central Europe's ankle? Zagreb as Central Europe's nipple? Vienna as its earlobe? And how about the whole woman? What is she like? Well? Well she's fond of her homeland and has lovely earlobes.

To me, Central Europe is nothing but a beautiful crystal ball that Kundera invented for himself in his sorry Parisian solitude. (He was melancholy in distant Paris, and knew it would be futile to return to Prague: that would be just as *distant* . . .) Once they played a parlour game where they passed this crystal ball round in a circle. Each of them pawed it for a moment or two, then rolled it on. But all their fine words were uttered in vain: poor Mr Kundera went on grieving, sometimes thinking of Prague and sometimes not.

TELEGRAM

It's all the same to me! You can go ahead and be envious if you want to, but it's pretty childish . . . Did you say glass ball, or bell-glass? (Joke, forgive me.) But now it has come true . . . Okay, so it appears to be made of plastic, or wood, or *aluminium*. Aluminium crystal ball. Not to mention the Germans. Bonn voyage!

One more thing. You write that 'Dernschwam, as an agent of the Fuggers, travelled the length of the Danube in 1553 to visit the Turks, making the fatal mistake of not recognizing the importance of America. Thus they were ruined.' I presume you mean the Fuggers. I notice that you're fond of scattering *objective trifles* between two *hors d'oeuvres*. My dear friend, in choosing between the roles of fool and prophet, don't hesitate: the former.

Tell me, aren't you growing old? That's a stupid question, of course. If you are not growing old, you will say no, and if you are growing old, you won't be aware of the fact – which is a symptom of growing old – so what else could you say but: no. Okay, point taken: no, you're not growing old.

Is it really true that Dernschwam, together with Veranić, discovered the political testament of Augustus near Ankara? And did you really think that this was as big a sensation as the discovery of a new drama by Sophocles?

One more thing. You're having too much fun again! I want you to enjoy yourself all right, that animates me too. But this 'the Lady measured me with her icy gaze' stuff is a bit much. The icy, I mean. My father always told us that if we were late for school we should say either that the tram cable snapped at Calvin Square, or that we'd been attacked by a man-eating tiger. But to say we'd been held in check by a man-eating tiger with a broken tram cable was pushing things too far and the teacher was bound to get suspicious. Think about it, sweetheart.

You're often in my thoughts, you know. You're not angry, are you? Or has something happened without my noticing? Some of your reports I read over and over again. I try to picture your days: how you get up, shower, brush your teeth and then just travel, travel ... I read somewhere that the Hungarians are a simple and friendly people. Not that you're particularly friendly. And that Hungary makes people happy. Are you happy? Flaubert writes of the 'aesthetic of unfulfilled delights'. Bullshit. I took twenty-four red roses to my father's grave, for five dollars ninety-nine cents. Stop. Contractor (Hirer)

The Danube is perpetually changing, its affairs eternally clouded in obscurity. Traveller

———————

I enclose (sic!) some observations by Timothy Garton Ash, who, we may confidently say, carries the dream of Central Europe on his tender, slender English shoulders. In his brilliant *New Yorker* essay. 'The Spawning of Danube Fish on the Ruins of Communism', he makes the following claim: 'He who holds the fish holds the power.' This is indeed the fundamental drama of our region. Garton Ash, of course, poses his questions, one rainy Wednesday afternoon, so to speak, as if they were two or three hundred years old. (Garton Ash is, of course, an Englishman.) That he finds this *so* reassuring ... well that's his problem. Of Michnik's essential strength and intractability he comments appreciatively: *Pisces vivunt in aqua.* I agree whole-heartedly with these lines of praise for the great Pole. About Kundera he is less inclined to offer an opinion (he only allows us to suspect that, in the Dostoevsky debate, he sides with Brodsky). A fish both does and doesn't offend another fish. The ambiguity of the saying that 'you can tell a fish is a fish from its head' (smells fishy!!!) does not allude to Havel, nor even to the Slovaks, but to the 'whole thing' – that is, to the question of whether the whole is the whole, or a fish is a fish, even if it is one according to its head. Only an Englishman could ask the question: 'When is a fish a fish?', without his national bias crying out: 'Trianon!' Regarding Konrád, he rather dis-

Trianon: According to the Treaty of Trianon, the post-First World War settlement between Hungary and the victorious Allied powers (4 June 1920), Hungary lost approximately two-thirds of her former territory and one-third of her former population to the new successor states.

ingenuously allows us to believe, initially at least, that he is referring to Joseph Conrad, and when he finally lets the cat out of the bag – 'A fish in the hand is worth two fishermen in the bush' – we can't help feeling that he has taken the easy way out. The closing passage masterfully summarizes the confusion of the new Europe: 'The fish has four legs, but still it stumbles' – modestly rejecting the pessimism of 'the big fish eat the little fish'. Stop, as it were. Ach, Mitteleuropa ...

At half-past twelve in the afternoon we pushed off from the Vienna embankment, right in front of the Hugelman Cafe. Here all classes and genders are lumped together. Powdered hairdressers in overcoats and old gossips come here for coffee, just as barons and counts come here for their liqueurs. The current carries us downstream, but wherever possible we also open our sails. If the wind dies down, or we reach a stretch where the Danube is wider and the current slower, those travellers who win free passage thus, take up their oars.

'The Bucintoro!' cries out Gyula Antallfy beside me. And there indeed stands Tivadar Batthyány's curious construction. This round wooden structure, equipped with its massive paddles, has been attracting attention since 1797. It emits neither steam nor smoke, but remains fixed to the embankment, standing fast and silent against the current. The great paddle appears to have been rotated by a wheel pulled by horses in the hull. Or by oxen. Or, according to one rumour, by women. Young, naked women going round and round in circles. And not slaves, either, but apparently working of their own free will. At the top of the steps that recede into the bottomless depths of his vessel, Tivadar sits and watches his 'horde of women', stamping their feet, flexing their muscles, and casting the odd fleeting smile at the man overhead. The cradle of the Age of Reform, as the disagreeable old Grillparzer might have said.

At Orth we visited the Danube exhibition housed in the castle. I found it rather boring. Rudolf used to go hunting in these parts : still boring. We went by coach out to the Uferhaus, where we had a jolly good meal, fishlights soup and Serbian carp with garlic. We drank more wine than we should have, and sat out on the Danube bank panting. The sun shining, the water flowing, the taste of garlic in my mouth.

At that time – when we arrived in Orth ? – Europe was just in the process of changing. It turned out that the finite was not infinite after all, and that history was not the frozen milk-bottle we had once thought it to be. The travellers no longer mentioned names in their reports, and jailbirds became ministers, presidents and so forth. Just as in a novel by Balzac, the rising tide threw up new destinies, carriers were born from one minute to the next, and we could see – sometimes the television even showed us – how this or that person's star had fallen, then and there, in a matter of moments.

What was one to think ? All kinds of things. That the vacuum left behind by the Austro-Hungarian Empire could finally be removed. Europe had caved in on itself, like a mouldy rubber ball. Europe had been living in deceitful calm, wedged between the jaws of two great powers. As the band Bikini sing : What a girl America, and Russia what a man. And the song goes on about how both of them grip the Danube between their thighs and squeeze, squeeze, squeeze.

This region was just like a work of genius : it instilled uncertainty and uneasiness into the world. ('Do you know, sir, when Central Europe was created ? When they didn't let the Czechs join in the fun and games of the Empire !')

Near Bruck an der Leitha (Királyhida), Vodička, the old sapper, announced that he resented the Hungarians, to which Schweik replied :

'Not all Hungarians can help being Hungarian.'

'What do you mean they can't help it ?' erupted Vodička. 'Of course they can help it ! They can all help it ! Nonsense.'

En route to the Holy Land, the Bishop of Friesing, Otto von

Babenburg (brother of the Austrian Prince Henry II, who was at war with our King Géza II), glared with a similar mixture of fear and hatred at the Hungarians on the riverbank, with their grim faces, sunken eyes, stocky bodies, wild attire and barbarian language – which is why one either had to curse fate, or wonder at the patience of the Lord, who gave such a monstrous people such a beautiful land.

In his highly entertaining 'Danube Diary', Grillparzer maintains that it would be hard to disparage the ambition of the Hungarians if there were at least thirty million of them. But the way things were made it all pretty laughable. This he jots down in Pozsony, just as parliament is convening in 1843! At the height of the Age of Reform! Sailing farther downstream, he is inclined to moderate his position. For beholding this enchanting region, he feels that he can better understand the Hungarians' ambitious ideas. '*Ich habe mich ein wenig mit ihren Superlativen ausgesöhnt.*'

I can hardly escape him as he goes on and on about how his belly aches. He has no other conversation. Except for something about one beautiful Mrs Horváth. And how frightful my pronunciation is.

The three of us stood on deck, Grillparzer, Lady Mary Wortley Montagu (the wife of the Turkish Ambassador, Wortley Montagu) and my good self. Grillparzer spoke to himself, which was, in one way, embarrassing, but in another, enabled me to establish a certain contact with the woman.

Here, *bittschön*, everything is falling apart. A new emptiness is forming in place of the old, and enormous rats, about one metre long, are about to break into our houses. Europe has collapsed, and it is this collapse itself which we refer to as the New Europe. But no one has any new ideas, the old legal framework no longer functions and there is no new one with which to replace it. And

'*Ich habe mich . . .*' : 'I have become a little reconciled to their superlatives.'

there is absolutely no hope of ending the nastiest and most total of all wars – he was thinking of the war against nature.

'Indeed nothing can be more melancholic than travelling through Hungary,' writes the Lady to Pope in a letter of January 1716, sent from Győr. (N.B. it was from the same Pope that our Csokonai stole his *Dorothy.*)

I'd had enough of Europe. As usual. We hadn't yet reached Komárom. The little island at the mouth of the Concó is connected to the bank by a stone dam. In the lower corner of the island the bream go plundering! A little farther down, by Almásfüzitő, the water is so dirty, especially in the shallows, that the fish are often inedible. What consolation is it to know that there are plenty of rose carp around Neszmély? What consolation?

In Neszmély we visited Fritzi Hegedüs and his wines. We got utterly drunk. He read us the lewder bits from Martin Opitz's *Buch von der deutschen Poetery.* He'd had both his legs amputated, but he still swam, did gymnastics and was stronger than ever. The heart grows no wrinkles.

We awoke to a splendid dawn. It was grey, grey, grey – as if absolutely nothing had happened the day before. As they say in Ulm: Travelling isn't born of good intentions.

Meanwhile some kind of infection had raised its ugly head on board ship and we returned to utter chaos. The captain palely offered his excuses. At first I didn't understand. Soon, however, I was to understand only too well. It was if I were losing my bowels, as if my insides were falling out of me and slithering away like an unfaithful snake, away, away from me. First my bowels, my colon, my small intestine, my appendix (Fig. IV: appendix, delatur), then my inner organs fell away too, until 'I' became less and less. Withdrawing into a corner of my cabin I immediately understood the disintegrational tendencies of the postmodern condition, which recognizes only contingent, decentred and deconstructing 'systems'.

I was deconstructing.

I could not avoid the consequences of this radical indeterminacy. The question of ontological uncertainty became absolutely crucial, and as I looked out of the tiny, round portholes between moans and groans and genuine suffering, seeing the grey and powerful current (in that Husserlian sense according to which the fundamental existence-theoretical property of the logos is that it is not owned by anyone, does not belong to anyone, simply *is*) and with everything that was liver and spleen falling away from me (or so I felt), and the beautiful shrubs of my leafy lungs swirling out of me and into the Danube – it was as if I were giving birth : to myself. And that is why the Danube can be interpreted as a self-creating work of art.

There is no direct route from poetry to life, or from life to poetry, I moaned out loud, and, continuing to cower in the dubious intimacy of my cabin toilet, wasting away, I created for myself, perforce, the necessary conditions for the demolition of the subject. Meanwhile the lace-like features of Visegrád were covered by an ugly fog, and restless, swirling rain wound itself around the ship. Everything seemed to wriggle out of me, even my tongue – an advantageously ambivalent word here in Pannonia – a dry, white, crustaceous extremity, while I substituted myself for precisely the material that was departing from me.

As mentioned earlier, I had already erased the 'I' in the recognition that man had to be reassembled anew : from modes of discourse, proverbs, senseless relations, delicate, nameless nuances. *Ecce homo*, a man, in quotation marks.

The repetition of words and motifs : we hammer ideas into the wall like nails and then hang jokes on them.

Descent, course of life – nonsense ! Most stem fom Juterbog or Königsberg, and all end up in the Black Forest !

Today we classify trains of thought ; we take geography, insert a few pipe dreams, then throw it aside again. We no longer link things together motifically or psychologically. We only ever begin things, but never complete them. Everything remains open, anti-synthetical.

On this we insist, in opposition to the irreconcilable. How do my aesthetic representations take place? My aesthetic representations only take place in accordance with the inorganic structure of decentred reality. That is the theory.

I got to know two stokers, twins from Dunaszerdahely. Their mother was a cook in the fish restaurant at Gönyü, their father a Yugoslav guest-worker, an eternally cheerful Croat who told his children jokes. He explained, for example, the difference between theory and practice and the little rascals' faces sparkled like black diamonds. 'Go into the kitchen and tell your mother she has to sleep with a stranger for fifty thousand forints.' After a lot of persuading the boys return to announce that Mummy is ready and willing. 'Fine, now go over to your sister with the same proposition.' In no time the boys report that she too has given her consent. 'You see,' says their father, 'in theory we now have one hundred thousand forints. In practice we have a couple of whores.' There was a knock at the door. 'Who is it?' I whispered. 'Lady Mary Wortley Montagu,' whispered Lady Mary Wortley Montagu. 'Go away,' I whispered. 'Believe me, I know how you feel,' whispered the lady. 'I'm not interested. Forgive me, but please get lost,' I whispered. 'All right, I'm going,' whispered Lady Mary. 'I know you are the perfect conversationalist, but please leave me alone,' I whispered, 'only promise me you'll never be thirty-five years old.' 'I promise. I promise,' whispered Lady Mary, and I could hear her footsteps receding down the corridor. With all the remaining strength of my desire and disenchantment I reached for the heroic element . . . I opened the window and the thin, cold strands of pirate rain began to prick my face and hands. The air had grown heavy, like in a steaming sauna. Everyone on board was waiting for the bend, the famous, perilous Danube Bend (which every sailor we asked described differently). WHAT WILL BE WILL BE, the lamb within, the wolf without, the world is thought into confusion, the myth had been lying, *woher, wohin, nicht Nacht, nicht Morgen*, with one last spasm everything was set to pour out of me, every 'lost I' prepared to perish, on the warm cabin toilet-seat I felt like a spatial Möbius strip, a nut within a nut. Over there, already, the lights of Budapest.

woher, wohin . . . : from where, to where, not night, not morning

19

Le città invisibile
(Invisible Cities)

I

TELEGRAM

I don't believe you. Contractor (Hirer).

REPLY

No comment. Traveller.

And he thought to himself: *in the life of every* Contractor (Hirer) *there is a moment which follows pride in the boundless extension of the territories he has conquered, and the melancholy and relief of knowing he shall soon give up any thought of knowing and understanding them* – and if at such a moment the Contractor (Hirer) looks out of the window of his lonely room he will be overcome by a sense of emptiness, impossible exclusiveness, motionlessness, as if the Danube had frozen over, and he will be plagued by doubts and uncertainties, which he will anxiously try to distinguish from despair.

This moment is identical to that in which he, the Traveller, arrives in the city of his birth ...

Cities and Memory. 1.

Leaving there and proceeding for three days towards the east, you reach Budapest, *a city* which delights in allowing the snake of the Danube to crawl between its breasts. Here the river is very wide. Seeing this, the foreigner immediately feels at home.

Cities and Memory. 2.

When a man rides a long time through wild regions, he feels the desire for a city. Finally he comes to Budapest, the city which swirls around his own memory like some cheap funfair merry-go-round, the city *where the foreigner hesitating between two women always encounters a third,* where on the banks of the Danube (mainly on the Pest side) pensioners wickedly trip each other up, then, laughing hoarsely, shriek : penalty ! penalty ! Witnessing this, the foreigner feels so utterly foreign that he begins to itch all over, is seized by a scratching fit, and this sensation is already quite close to the feeling of being at home.

Cities and Desire. 1.

There are two ways of describing the city of Budapest : you can speak about 'the form of the city', that is about its topology, the relationship between centre and periphery, kernel and outskirts, working-class and upper-class districts, about culture and nature (in the city), and all this would be no different from those images we see with half-shut eyes after long and aimless days of roving, and which we might call geometric fantasies ; *bearing in mind that the nubile girls of each quarter marry youths of other quarters, you can make calculations telling you all you need to know about the city's past present and future, or else you can say, like the traveller who took me there, 'I arrived here in my first youth, one morning,* and I had hardly been in Budapest two days when I met a little woman with dark hair and fell deeply in love. The woman rarely spoke, she simply smiled. Every day she'd call on me at my hotel, arriving on the dot of ten and leaving at exactly 12.15. It was very good to be with her, at once calm and stormy, sometimes we wrestled like children, cuffing each other lightly, rolling up and down on the bed. Gay Science! At times we simply lay in a motionless embrace. She died years ago, but I never left the city. On the dot of ten I shut my eyes, and at exactly 12.15 I open them again. I hate this city.'

Cities and Memory. 3.
In vain, great-hearted Contractor (Hirer), *shall I attempt to describe* how Budapest is a *city of high bastions* built of words, in vain shall I suggest the foreignness of this language, the foreignness of the words, which for precisely this reason impress the visitor with such overwhelming power, as on the corner of Nagymező Street and Andrássy Avenue (the Broadway of Pest and the Hungarian Champs-Elysées, the latter leading to Heroes Square, in contrast to its French counterpart which, in a manner of speaking, stretches out into eternity) he stands in the turmoil and (like the dreamer of Ruse) 'dreams of a man who has forgotten all the languages of the world, until at last he cannot understand a single word spoken in a single country. What lurks in language? What does language conceal? What does it steal from us? The visitor did not attempt to learn a single word during the weeks he spent in Hungary. He didn't want to lose anything of the power of the alien-sounding cries. He wanted the sounds to strike him in all their inner truth, with no remnants of imperfect or artificial knowledge diluting their effect. The snippets of information everyone picks up during his life about various countries and peoples, he shed in the first few hours.'

My lord, noble Contractor (Hirer), it would be superfluous to describe the foreignness of this language, the unexpected ingenuity it sometimes manifests (the Hungarians proudly claim their language is like a whore, it does anything you ask – allow me not to qualify this from the point of view of sexual culture), that strange sloppiness which appears at once liberating and boorish, light-footed and imprecise, poetical and poeticizing, boldly visionary and obscurely pottering. At times this language is concise, primordial and melodious, at times unctuous, crowing, lisping.

In vain! For this city is silent, reticent, has been struck dumb, has lost its tongue. *A description of* Budapest *as it is today should contain all* Budapest's *past. The city, however, does not tell its past, but contains it like the lines of a hand, written in the corners of the streets, the gratings of the windows, the banisters of the steps, the antennae of the lightning rods, the poles of the flags, every segment marked in turn with scratches, indentations, scrolls.*

Cities and Desire. 2.

The inhabitants of this city define happiness as follows: On Szentendre Island, bathing in pre-sunset radiance, the very same radiance – we might say, were this a tiny Greek island – from which classical philosophy was born, from that and that alone, just sitting there on a rickety, worn-out chair which almost keels over, collapses, watching the easy, inveterate movements of fishermen returning from the Danube, and for one short moment unable to tell if you are the sand of the riverbank, the water, a fisherman, a shell, a fish, the light, or the sinking wreck of your chair. Such is the power of Budapest, *the city of deceit.*

Cities and Signs. 1.

All cities have their secrets. Budapest's secret is its deceitfulness. A cheap veil descends upon this city, like on a third-rate dancing girl, you see her flabby belly, the fulsome pleats of fat, the caved-in thighs, the swollen ankles – and then the veil is lifted by the lightest of breezes, perhaps only because you meet a savage glance outside the synagogue, or the bus driver starts whistling a Donizetti melody (Don Pasquale Overture!) as you rumble down Andrássy Avenue, or, almost in spite of yourself, you notice two youths on the lake of the City Park taking each other by the hand and, in a fit of laughter, capsizing with their punt into the water crying 'Shark! Shark!', and in this nakedness you see into a crazy city which makes you think not of Vienna

('Budapest is just like Vienna, only Vienna actually works'), but of the eccentricity of Berlin in the 1920s.

You let them watch you, you join in with the Donizetti melody, you gaze longingly after the disappearing boys, and you realize that the city is beautiful. Provocative, dangerous, vulgar, grandiose, selfish and vain: beautiful. You are overcome by sadness, you wait for the veil to settle again and for the artiste to shake her 'despondent derrière'. You really have no business with this woman so you can return to your wandering in peace.

Cities and Memory. 4.
Of secrets one cannot speak. All cities have their secrets. Blood-bathville, says Örkény.

Cities and Desire. 3.
From an old Serbian reader: If you wish to savour a combination of inimitable Hungarian temperament and high culinary art, and should you prefer Bohemian atmosphere to impeccable cleanliness, be sure to lunch *chez* the three old maids at The Buffalo out by the Roman Baths.
From the same work: Travelling is sickness.

Cities and Signs. 2.
In the days when the Lenin Ring became the Teréz Ring and some resourceful students made money selling tin cans with the label: 'Socialism's Last Breath', there lived in Gozsdu Court – one of the 'largest and most mysterious arcade buildings' in Budapest – at 13 Mayakovsky Street (by then, once again, Király Street), a woman who, in spite of being as fat and pink as a piglet, was well loved by everyone in the district, indeed she even had admirers in Ráckeve and Újpest, perhaps because of her smell, she did have such a good smell. This woman, who lived alone, collected the water of the Danube in tiny phials. She had Evening Danube, Dawn Danube, Spring Danube, Angry Danube, Drift-Ice Danube (which she kept in the fridge), Green

Danube, Fair, Grey and Blue Danube, and God only knows how many others; she lined them up on a hand-carved shelf above her bed, and whoever came to see her, her each and every admirer, would have to inspect the collection from beginning to end.

Her and her Danube, the men would grumble.

Thin Cities. 1.
No one can say for sure where the gods of the city (Budapest) dwell. There are various theories.

II

TELEGRAM

I cannot believe you. Contractor (Hirer).

REPLY

Literally! *The cool breeze brings the fragrance of the muddy estuary.* Traveller

To himself, meanwhile, he thought: You ask, do you travel *to relive your past? That is to recover your future?* My answer would be: *Elsewhere is a negative mirror. The traveller recognizes the little that is his, discovering the much he has not had and never will have.*

Cities and Memory. 5.
Budapest is the kind of town where on 14 August 1980 an unheard-of whirlwind snatched a pleasure steamer from the Danube, lifted it right out of the water and threw it over the most celebrated bridge on the river, the Chain Bridge. The granite for the foundation stone (and all the others too!) was brought from Mauthausen in 1842. When the bridge was opened in 1849, the keen-eyed people of Budapest soon began to jibe

that the grandiose lions which lay at each end had no tongues; their sculptor, one János Marschalkó, threw himself, as legend has it, into the Danube in his despair. Who was the first to cross the bridge? Haynau to be sure, the hangman! And who never crossed it at all? That's right, Széchenyi. All the passengers of the vaporetto drowned to a man, apart from a certain Szörényi. He was held to be a child of fortune, even though he really came off worst, for all the other passengers, all the victims – at least according to the Good Lord's own account – went straight to heaven.

Cities and Desire. 4.

When Cortazar arrived in Budapest (in secret, wearing dark glasses) he at once – here followed a gesture of the hand, as might illustrate a wave or a downhill run, a dive or a big-dipper at the fun-fair, an avalanche or a diving header – in other words, *just like that*, at once, with, for, or even in, a beautiful gypsy girl, depending on how you interpret the gesture. Oh, Julio.

Cities and Signs. 3.

The city of Budapest, which we had just walked from top to bottom, does not appear densely populated. We instructed the coachman to drive at once to the best inn in town. The coachman swung onto the bridge which is about four hundred *sazheny* in length (1 *sazheny* = 2.134m) From the bridge a magnificent spectacle unfolded before us; the Danube rolling from Donau-wörth to Kilia, witness to so many battles, graveyard to so many thousand luckless warriors, winding its way between the wide banks.

We saw the theatre on one of the parades. A rather cumbrous building. In the vestibule of the Thalia church an Italian clown was putting up his tent. A meagre audience watched the Neo-politan hunchback's immortal, if already somewhat faded, drama. '*Povero signor Pulcinella!*' But whose attention did he seek, on what deaf ears did he squander the gems of his sarcasm, his scornful laughter, his Lazzaroni dialect? The earnest Hungarians who stopped to look thought him a fool and most of them went on at once, leaving smoke rings from their pipes behind as signs of their disdain.

Thin Cities. 2.

Towards the end of the year, when it is already turning cold and getting dark earlier, and fog descends upon the city like a stray and hungry pack of wolves, one receives a letter from Donaueschingen, a love letter, a wonderfully extravagant, beautiful, vulgar, impetuous letter. According to some theories it is in these wolves that the gods of the city dwell.

Trading Cities. 1.

Proceeding eighty miles into the northwest wind, you reach the city of Budapest, *where the* hatred *of seven nations gathers at every solstice and equinox.* Swop for swop, tick for tack, now I'll never give it back.

III

Meanwhile he thought to himself . . .

Each time I arrive in Budapest, the city of my birth, I am plagued by doubts and uncertainties, and however anxiously I try to distinguish them from despair, I cannot change my almost ritual sense of helplessness.

I tried not to desert the well beaten track for one as yet untrodden, I leafed through foreign publications which sang the praises of the city (*Geo Spezial, Stern*, etc.), in those days Central Europe was decidely 'in'; for a while the West was not simply killing time with its own glorification, or rather had chosen a more complex, and thus at once more sympathetic, way of doing it.

In essence, I followed the example of Adam Zagajewski, who, in a piece entitled 'Wysoki mur' ('The High Wall'; in *Zeszyty*

Literackie, 7 (1984), 16–14), asks what it would be like if he, the writer, came to Poland as a Dane, what would he see, understand, believe, comprehend of the unexpected moods and passions he encountered, and would he be able to crawl inside the invisible underground tunnels of national intimacy and complexity with, for the most part, velvety darkness as his sole companion?

Pretending to be a Dane, a German, a Dutchman, I too trod the tourist trail. I remember in the early seventies Western tourists were obliged to buy restaurant vouchers, and we would use up my aunt's leftover vouchers (for naturally she lived and ate with us), which meant we had to pretend we were foreigners. I remember how courteously we were treated, we ate at the Rózsadomb restaurant and even at the Carpathian. My father was chief clown, I've never seen him more positively cheerful than then, even though in those days he probably still worked as an unskilled labourer somewhere . . .

Cities and Desire. 5.

After six days and seven nights you arrive at Budapest, *the white city, well exposed to the moon, with streets wound about themselves as in a skein. They tell this tale of its foundation :* after the Paleolithic age, traces of which can still be found in many places, for example in objects excavated from the Hermit's Cave, the Celto-Eraviscusians founded settlements on the site of present-day Budapest. It so happened that one night these Celto-Eraviscusians all *had an identical dream. They saw a woman running at night through an unknown city ; she was seen from behind, with long hair, and she was naked. They dreamed of pursuing her. As they twisted and turned, each of them lost her. After the dream they set out in search of that city ; they never found it, but they found one another; they decided to build a city like the one in the dream. In laying down the streets, each followed the course of his pursuit ; at the spot where they had lost the fugitive's trail, they arranged spaces and walls differently from the dream, so she would be unable to escape again.*

And this became the city of Budapest.

Thin Cities. 3.

New men arrived from other lands, having had the same dream as those before them. The Romans reached this part of the Danube in the first century AD. On account of the same woman they built Aquincum (network of roads, public utilities).

Trading Cities. 2.

With the Romans retreating from the waves of the great migrations, the site was occupied by the Huns. Then came Charles the Great. Then the Slavs. That was the time when *the people who moved through the streets were all strangers. At each encounter they imagined a thousand things about one another; meetings which might take place between them, conversations, surprises, caresses, bites.*

That was the time in the city's past when *no one greeted anyone.*

Cities and Eyes. 1.

The medieval monuments in Pest and Buda (Romanesque style) where the dream woman had appeared were swept away in the Mongol invasion of 1241. Later, in the Gothic period, her streaming fair hair reappeared in the chancel of the Inner City Parish Church and in the severe courtyard of the Dominican Convent on Margaret Island, later in King Zsigmond's palace, which drew the attention of all Europe ; later, during the Turkish occupation, she was seen in various baths, the Király Baths, the Rudas Baths, the Imre Baths and also in the Gül Baba sepulchral chapel on the Rózsadomb, later in the Baroque era she was seen mainly in the House of Christ (today the Százéves restaurant), in the early spring flood of 1838 she was seen in the barge of the hero Wesselényi, and in the age of eclecticism she was seen all over most of the public and apartment buildings of Budapest.

Still more recent times (the period of the emergence of the labour movement, the Horthy era, the liberation etc.) *all recognized something of the streets of the dream and they changed the positions of the arcades and stairways to resemble more closely the path of the pursued woman and so, at the spot where she had vanished, there would remain no avenue of escape.*

Those who had arrived earlier could not understand what drew those who arrived later to Budapest, *this ugly city, this trap.*

IV

TELEGRAM

I don't believe you. Your Budapest does not exist. Perhaps it has never existed. Certainly it will never exist again. Why do you delude yourself *with consolatory fables? I know well that my empire is rotting like a corpse in a swamp, whose contagion affects the crows that peck at it as well as the bamboo that grows, fertilized by its humours. Why do you not speak to me of this? Why do you lie to your* Contractor (Hirer), *foreigner?* Contractor (Hirer)

REPLY

No comment. *This is the aim of my exploration : examining the traces of happiness still to be glimpsed, I gauge its short supply. If you want to know how much darkness there is around you, you must sharpen your eyes, peering at the faint lights in the distance.* Traveller

Cities and Signs. 4.
No one, wise Contractor (Hirer), *knows better than you that the city must never be confused with the words that describe it. And yet between the one and the other there is a connection.* If I describe the swinging hips of the women of Budapest which set the Octagon alight and make the Danube overflow, leaving little barges to roam the waterlogged streets of the inner city, 'in the Venice of Central Europe', then *from these words you will realize at once how* Budapest *is shrouded in a cloud of soot and grease that sticks to the houses, that in the brawling streets the shifting trailers crush pedestrians against the walls.* And if I describe the elegant hats and parting coral-red-

painted lips, it is only to remind you of the scandalous 'state' of restaurant bills these days.

You must therefore understand the following, Oh wanderer: if, let's say in the Hungaria coffeehouse, you see flawless old ladies with heavy ancient jewellery, or, leaving the famous McDonalds and arriving at Gerbeaud on Vörösmarty Square, you feel, surveying the elderly gentlemen sitting at their tables in bow ties, that you are back in the days of the Austro-Hungarian Empire (or at least a shabbier version of the same) – no, no, it's not aristocrats you see, nor heralds, but simply *old people* doing their best to preserve the time that once was theirs, but is no more. No more.

Falsehood is never in words; it is in things.

Thin Cities. 4.

Whether Budapest *is like this because it is unfinished or because it has been demolished, whether the cause is some enchantment or only a whim, I do not know.* But it is a fact that years ago the city was infested by rats. The smaller ones were the size of piglets, the larger ones as big as lorries (Csepel). But very few of them were wild, or even malevolent. The only conflicts with the natives – if there were any at all – were most probably the result of a lack of understanding, or simple misunderstanding. Some of the rats now act as tourist guides, offering insider-sightseeing, cultural tours, etc., or they simply trudge up to the Vienna Gate, a site of markets in the Middle Ages, take a look at the statue of the bronze girl, said to be the muse of Ferenc Kazinczy (1759–1831), then pop into the Lutheran church where in summer they hold organ concerts and the service is in German. (Tickets from Vörösmarty Square, Tel: 1 176 222). I should add, however, that their English pronunciation is not too good, indeed their English pronunciation is appalling.

Noble Contractor, illustrious Hirer! This is the one thing – this dark shadow, this playful sunspot – about which, if you treasure your life, you should never question the people of

Budapest! Not even if a rat nibbles off the corner of your most expensive snakeskin handbag, and another brings you breakfast in bed. (*In any case, they seem content now, those creatures: in the morning you can hear them singing.*)

Trading Cities. 3.

Italo Calvino needs little introduction to Hungarian readers, but it would surely surprise them to hear that some see him as the most eminent representative of 'ennobled' Sci-Fi. This book of his is a dialogue between Marco Polo and Kubla Khan. The great globetrotter reveals before his despotic Contractor (Hirer) – and the reader – a multicoloured world of improbable diversity and thrilling marvels, and it is only at the end of the dialogue that the Traveller's joke becomes clear: he has been speaking of one and the same city all along, the city of his birth.

Cities and Eyes. 2.

It is the mood of the beholder which gives the city of Budapest *its form.* Come on, come on, whoever you are, let's go and make ourselves a Budapest!

Cities and Names. 1.

'You're an intelligent person. Do I have to explain the interests of the Party to you? We want names. You know, I know ... I understand ... You honestly believe, rat, that pain is some inferior *physical* affair. Well you're mistaken. If we rinse your urethra through with broken glass you'll soon feel your prick's meta-physical dimensions. Then you'll understand all about *sein* and *sollen* ... And take my advice: tremble, this time really tremble.

The four symmetrical buildings on what used to be November 7 Square (now Octagon) glorify the name of Antal Szkalnitzky (1873). The first house on the right-hand side of the Ring is the Registry Office, an imitation of the Palazzo Strozzi in Florence. The inner courtyard of the Pallavicini Palace (98 Andrássy

Avenue) is among the finest in the city (atrium thick with ivy, etc.). Between the two, at 60 Andrássy Avenue, was the whatsitsname of the State Security Authorities . . . *the Hauptquartier.*

V

. . . he went to the nearby post office to send his reply-paid telegram.

REPLY

Bills attached. *If existence in all of its moments is all of itself,* Budapest *is the place of indivisible existence. But why, then, does the city exist? What line separates the inside from the outside, the rumble of wheels from the howl of wolves?* Traveller.

He got chatting to the young post-office clerk who was thin and pale and blushed whenever she had to utter a number; fifty-seven forints, she whispered, for example, bathing the whole booth in a russet twilight. He arranged a rendezvous on the banks of the Danube and immediately forgot all about it.

Somehow they still managed to meet. They walked hand in hand, the wind blowing, leaves floating like paper airplanes. The river is very wide just here. Now and again the man would ask wicked questions which the girl would have to answer with numbers. The Danube glowed like a red sunset. Then the girl said:

'You know your telephone's bugged, don't you?' The man shook his head with a smile, no, the thought had never crossed his mind. 'There was this man who came over from the centre. He told us.' The girl's hand was cold and sticky. The man squeezed it tight, then, in an indifferent tone of voice, like one who means the opposite of what he says, he replied:

155

'I'm really not such an important person.' The girl cut in enthusiastically:

'Of course not! Not you, silly! It's some ancient affair. Some Roberto, or whatever his name is . . .'

'I don't know any Roberto,' replied the man, his heart pounding, and he clasped the little post-office clerk in his arms. The afternoon boat to Vienna cut its way through the water, its pot belly floundering with all the dignified majesty of a plump priest. The funnels billowed haughty puffs of smoke, the paddle wheels scooped water faithfully and earnestly, and out on deck fat foreigners sat at tables laid with fine white linen eating ham and drinking ice-cold beer; beside the railings girls in bright print dresses and large straw hats stood waving their little handkerchiefs at the men.

'Repeat after me: one two three . . .' (At such times our hero – whom, in all modesty, we might call Sinbad – wished he were the ship's captain in white trousers and a gold-braid cap. He'd pace the deck dreamily in his snow-white shoes and cast conquering glances at the Romanian women with their big, round eyes and raw silk dresses.)

Thin Cities. 5.
If you believe me, fine.

Trading Cities. 4.
Today even the oldest inhabitants can hardly remember the times when the Antichrist ruled this city (cf. trade union stamps and pathfinder – alias Pioneer – scarves). Just to give you an idea of the absurdity of the situation, in those days Budapest was Szolnok, Szolnok was Lovasberény, Lovasberény was Szeged (consequently the Tisza was the Danube, the Danube was the Yenisei, and the Yenisei the Tisza), Szeged was Kőszeg, and Kőszeg was Budapest. You had to be very careful. If you got the Yenisei mixed up with the Yesinin, for example, you were gambling with your life.

Cities and Eyes. 3.

There is another Budapest. In the mirror of the Danube. *At times the Danube* increases a thing's value, at times denies it. *Not everything that seems valuable above the mirror maintains its force when mirrored. The twin cities are not equal, because nothing that exists or happens in* Budapest *is symmetrical: every face and gesture is answered, from the mirror, by a face and gesture inverted, point by point. The two* Budapests *live for each other, their eyes interlocked; but there is no love between them.*

Cities and Names. 2.

'I've spent all morning spying on you through the peephole. You're in a bad way ... the bruises ... the swellings ... I can even see how you open your jaws with your hands to let them stuff wet bread inside. You cannot see yourself, but I can see you. You're very beautiful. I know you know this. I can see it in your eyes. Funny how deceptive it is. What's in a name after all? A row of letters. No?'

At 39 Andrássy Avenue stands a proud Renaissance building, the former Grand Paris department store (1909). It used to house the Teréz-Town Casino. On the ceiling of the main hall is an allegory of the city of Budapest, surrounded by figures representing the arts and crafts. Now they sell camping equipment and bed-linen here. 88–9 Andrássy Avenue was built in Tuscan style. On the façade are coats of arms from all the regions served by the Hungarian Railway. Between the two is 60 Andrássy Avenue where the *Hauptquartier* of the State Security Authorities used to be.

Cities and the Dead. 1.

Budapest is a big village. Everyone knows everyone else. They know me too. We know you, fair mask, smile my fellow villagers. One of them is making jam. 'Marmalade,' she says. My God, I sigh, a marmalade-lady, and like a blithe assassin I shut the kitchen door behind me. When I am about to leave, she declares I am the spitting image of my Uncle Roberto. And she runs her fingers through my hair.

<h1 style="text-align:center">VI</h1>

... this fiction, that I walk around the city as a Western tourist, was a rather simple idea, but it created a certain amount of freedom to manoeuvre. The reason why it didn't really work, why I couldn't carry it out consistently, was that I got bored. And the reason I got bored was that the fiction inevitably did turn me into a tourist, rather than a traveller, which is what I wanted to be. I could say, with a certain Central European arrogance, that I sank to the feeble-mindedness of a Westerner. This in itself I enjoyed – let us be greatful for every new stupidity – only, I had done it all before and, to tell the truth, it didn't add any new dimensions to the game.

I stayed at the Forum Hotel and raved about the beautiful view of the Danube. I could stand for hours in front of the enormous panoramic window in my room looking at the water, the floating restaurant (Chinese cuisine), the throbbing of the Chain Bridge, and, on the other side, the Buda Hills, the Castle, the funicular. I hired a car, went to the casino and even found my way into private card-playing clubs. I attended the parties of the nouveau riche and downtown intelligentsia, and I visited every restaurant of note. I changed my Deutschmarks at the black-market rate, which was neither particularly risky, nor particularly exciting. Then I went to stay at the campsite on the edge of town. I dodged paying the fare on the underground – 'Nix daytsch, pardon, ungarisch!' – and ate standing up. I knew where you could get good 'langosh', although I didn't sink as low as hotdogs. And I discovered good little eating houses, the Kádár, for example on Klauzal Square, or the 'Little Secret' on Nagymező Street. I was the last East German, pursuing the trail of *le temps perdu* ...

Trading Cities. 5.

Most honoured Contractor (Hirer), in this city's books one reads the following (The Traveller *knew it was best to fall in with the* Contractor's (Hirer's) *dark mood*): Again and again I am surprised, because unprepared, to hear people – mostly foreigners – referring to the place where I live as a *city*. So Budapest really is a city? Like Paris, Amsterdam or Stockholm? So it really does lie picturesquely on the two banks of the Danube? Our bridges arch like a fabulously beautiful thought? And do we really have secret tips to offer about restaurants, about a little inn, or better still a woman, a lady, who does a whole roasted goose in a surprising garlic sauce, better even than in Lyon, not to mention, of course, our lively cafés, oozing with the sentimental decadence of the *fin-de-siècle* ... And the atmosphere! That special murmuring and hidden dance which makes one city different from another. And the faces in the street, in which our own reflections bathe, simply because we know something about ourselves that you won't find *anywhere* else. Our cultural life effervesces like our famous spas? Budapest is a famous spa! The irrepressible will to live seethes everywhere, those East European survival jokes, polished with talent and cunning, a little southeast of Schweik? Yet again, we are a great power at some poetry symposium? Let's not mince matters: a little double-bottomed jewellery box in the lap of the Carpathians, that's what we are! Or as the hit song has it: 'I always dream of Budapest, that's the Paris I like best? Do we really have it *that* good?'

Cities and Eyes. 4.

'For Budapest I didn't need to make any plans. I simply possessed and used the city as a matter of course. My basic geographical knowledge of the city of my birth was centred around football pitches and their surrounding public houses. I was for some time, after all, a suburban footballer with a promising future. Then that time passed. The promising future became a promising present, then a promising past, *et nos mutamur in illis*. Hidden paths invisibly intersect the city, from one little dirt track to another – paths known to no one but washed up third-division footballers and the secret society of football-club hangers-on. Fantastic characters come together in such places, an exclusive species well on the road to extinction. Thus my knowledge of the city depended entirely on the *whims* of the draw – presided over by the Budapest Football Association. A team like the Csillaghegy Workers' Gymnastics Club (where I played, enjoying the confidence of the expert directorate) would only very occasionally get as far as, say, Saroksár, and for a Cup tie at best. And we were soon knocked out of the Cup ... I never lifted a finger on behalf of Budapest itself; the thought never entered my head.'

Cities and Names. 3.
'Give me a name.'
Topography.

Cities and the Dead. 2.
Imagine, good Contractor (Hirer), that it is night. Not just dark, but a darkness that weighs several tons. You are standing at the top of a mountain, or a hill rather – it is only here they call it a mountain – and the whole city lies before you, minute, like a doll's house, hundreds of tiny, flickering points of light ... (Later I'll send a simile too. For example : like phosphorescent crabs in the Bay of Balaclava ... which is where, by the way, the Russian fleet lies underneath a cliff ... The person who told me this had been a prisoner of war there. 'Just imagine, we were given women's underwear, the whole camp went around in bright lace panties. Half of Yalta laughed at us.') Behind you stands a woman, closer than is physically possible. You can hear the air swirling in her lungs. Maybe she wants to stab you in the back. I have some good advice for you : tremble. She speaks in a whisper of some man she had dearly loved, who was by *then* already a nobody,

not even a nobody, but an emptiness, a pile of nothing, they had beaten everything out of him, his body, his soul, his past, his memories, a name, the women, the women, even the women they had beaten out of him. (Dalma had been speaking of Roberto.) The river is so wide here.

Cities and the Sky. 1.
This road is the boulevard of the suburb. It is lined with poplars and runs, straight as an arrow, down to the Danube. Every Saturday, every Saturday for twenty-five years, come rain or shine, between half past seven and half past nine, a woman stands on the third corner of the street — counting from the railway line — wearing a nightdress and a blanket. Twenty-five years ago she was already old; now she is even tinier, more wizened, whiter, and now and then her head begins to shake. When anyone passes, she asks them the time, then thanks them by raising her stick. Whenever she sees me she seems pleased. I have always been frightened of her, and never dared ask her why she stands there. Today I finally made up my mind to do so. A repulsive caterpillar grin crawled across her face and she shook with laughter. 'My daughter-in-law ... and my son ... we only have one room ...' It was revolting, that superior, choking laughter. But then, as was her custom, she raised her stick, high into the air, and everything blew over.

VII

In his Report, the Traveller *describes a bridge, stone by stone.*

TELEGRAM

But which is the stone that supports the bridge? Contractor (Hirer)

The bridge is not supported by one stone or another, but by the line of the arch that they form. Traveller

Why do you speak of the stones? It is only the arch that matters to me. Contractor (Hirer)

Without stones there is no arch. Traveller
Or as a woman acquaintance of mine put it : no tail.

Cities and Eyes. 5.
Goethe's eyes are the only sight worth seeing in Weimar.

Cities and Names. 4.
'Believe me, it is not just you who is tired. I'm tired too. I could say, look out of the window, but in a basement, that's a rotten joke. Or do you think I'm having you on ? I'm as disappointed as you are. And as dejected ... I think you've finally understood, even if it has taken you longer than expected, that down here in the basement neither outstanding moral strength nor outstanding physical strength have any real significance. We do not differ in those respects where you would like us to differ. By the way, I live alone. You'll have to think up something else. I don't say it can't be done. Only that I've never seen it done. No one has ever left this place in such a way that ... Whoever did get away with it died in the process ... It's a shame about the window story ... The roof garden is just like in Paris ... Europe ... I know, you're exhausted. Look, I'll say the names, you just nod. Don't be frightened.'

Cities and the Dead. 3.

I showed Dalma the place on the Danube embankment where once, a long time ago, I'd slept with a girl.

'My dear boy, your standards of taste are not very high.' But she took me warmly by the arm. She was sucking on a long, ivory cigarette-holder. 'You know, that uncle of yours ... Yes I know, distant and not even a relative, stop being so defensive! ... that uncle of yours became a puppet! They could do whatever they wanted with him. You only have to take one brick from the wall and then, one brick after another, the whole wall comes crashing down and there's nothing left! That nothing was Roberto. And it was on that nothing that those fine tweed suits hung ... perhaps that's why they suited him so well ... there was nothing of him to spoil them.' I clasped her arm tightly. Now and then the spring flood carried whole, leafy trees with it down the Danube. 'After the revolution they sent him to the West. First he did fairly minor jobs, reports about émigrés, about the general atmosphere, then various bits of recruitment work, lists of agents and double-agents, agents who had gone over to the other side and come back again. He was good at his job. He lacked a certain natural fear and was as reckless as the devil, right up until ...' She stopped talking and chewed her lip.

'Right up until?'

'You know, so why ask?'

'Until he fell in love with you.'

'Oh, he never loved anyone. I loved him.'

'Didn't he even love me?' The woman shrugged. 'He did, you know. He did love me.'

'He didn't love anyone. Forget it. Then in '63 came the Danube mission! This time there could be no fooling around ... The Russians were in charge ... Well, they always were ... Roberto became impossible. He was, as he put it, going to double the Danube ... He drank a lot in those days ... And he really did double the Danube! Working for both the Russians and the Americans at the same time. It wasn't for the money. At that time his interest in money was totally *en passant*. No ... He did it simply to lead the whole world by the nose. To be a somebody after all. When we all knew he was a nobody.'

Suddenly she stopped.

'Why don't you ever kiss me? Have you noticed? You've never once kissed me ... Don't think I can't see that you haven't changed your shirt since yesterday.' She never missed a thing. Sometimes this annoyed me, at other times it filled me with a pleasing sense of self-importance. 'I already knew him from Hungary. I'd been to visit him on the plains. I was one of his lovers ... but it was only later, in Vienna, that he really noticed me. I'd travel down to the plain by bus, every third Friday in the month ... I'd arrive late in the afternoon, the dogs always barking ... I had to ring the bell ... There was this bell on the garden gate ... I love the Great Hungarian Plain ... And when I went in to see him, in the wattle house, I hurried straight to the window. If he had been unfaithful he'd leave a sweetie there for me, by way of consolation ... It was in the Landtmann that the Danube came to an end.'

'I don't understand.'

'What don't you understand? Someone gave him away.'

'Who?'

'Me.'

I started to run.

'Stop! Stop! You fool. Not out of jealousy, simply because I could see how they were destroying him! I saved him! Stop, for heaven's sake! Halt! Halt!'

Cities and the Sky. 2.

If you believe me, fine. Budapest is the kind of city where it rains cats and dogs. A man is carrying a large painting. You can see that it is heavy. The painting shows the inside of a studio. Right at the bottom, almost slipping out of the frame, is a chair, a profane cross. The painting is sacred. Exactly what is lacking in Vermeer, one might argue. All this takes place in Mártírok Street, where the carbon monoxide concentration is the highest in town. Somehow the air gets caught between the buildings. Europe's smelliest street: as such, a curiosity.

Continuous Cities. 1.
There was a day in the history of Budapest when everyone and everything lost a mother – every worm, every beetle, every poplar. Even those who no longer existed lost their mothers. In short, every mother who had ever lived or ever would live died that day in Budapest. On that day Budapest was itself that death. But this didn't change anything at all. When I, understandably, burst out crying, a woman's voice said to me softly: 'Don't cry, darling.' But when I went on blubbering all the same, it said: 'Go on then, darling, cry.' And when I finally stopped crying it anxiously and repeatedly called me by my name, saying: 'Everything is all right, isn't it? You are okay, aren't you?'

VIII

... in the beginning I thought I'd give each chapter a culinary title, like Tripe or Brisket Of Veal Stuffed With Truffles. And at the end of every longer section I'd supply a festive menu. A Danube menu. Exactly what a Danube menu was, I didn't know and would have to find out. I wrote letters to famous chefs asking them to give the matter some thought and then to rattle or bluff on about it at length, sparing neither pains nor money. I looked up great Danubian chefs like Herr Aspacher from Illereichen, or Frau Bacher from Wachau. I dined with the renowned Pál Kövi, and ate my way through the living legend of good old Imre Gundel.

But I was somehow unable to lend my gluttony a truly Central European dimension, and all I seemed to do was highlight the contours of snobbery. In all this, even one-course pub lunches didn't help. Still, the description of food really does constitute a kind of topography, and it is quite possible to turn chefs into mythical figures, servants, specialists, artists, entertainers, creators, mothers, all of whom : feed us.

The idea was that the Danube would somehow come together from all these conversations, menus, recipes and meals. Or rather, through their traditions, dreams and everyday practice, the Danubian differences and similarities would somehow manifest themselves. But the idea was too luxurious, even if it did prove extremely fruitful. Always make sure, Oh Contractor (Hirer), never to order soup in an Italian restaurant! (Reiseführerprosa)

Cities and Names. 5.

'This too is Budapest. Here in the basement there is no difference between man and woman, persecutor and persecuted. Here only the moment exists. Don't blame yourself, all that has happened is what could happen. And don't blame me either, this is not a battle where there are victors and vanquished; it is more like when it either rains or the sun shines. It is true that there is both flood and drought. I don't say this as a warning. No one is going to hurt you now. You will be going home tomorrow. The day after tomorrow you will be deported to the plains. It's not dangerous. Can I visit you? My name is Dalma.'

Cities and the Dead. 4.

Or did I secretly imagine that things would be better on the banks of the Danube? Dalma showed me the various movements of the water, the whirlpools, hidden currents, and smaller spillways. She had done a lot of rowing in these parts, she told me. She'd been part of a proper gang, the only girl. And they had discovered mines too, which they exploded on the islands. And when she

Reiseführerprosa : guidebook prose

went to the Soviet Union they showed her the Great Yenisei Barrage. There is none other like it in all the world; the water almost does somersaults. There isn't a single ship that can pass it. This, of course, is a great blow to the Soviet economy. Dalma talked a lot. She was right, we were afraid of silence. Her lipstick smudged, the bags beneath her eyes pulsated and her face became not only ugly, but alarming. As if it were somehow trying to allude to itself: I was once this way or that, *that* beautiful – it was this that was so ugly.

'My dear boy is getting fed up with me,' she said suddenly. 'But don't go tearing off again.'

'And why did Roberto take me with him?'

'You were the only person in all the world he trusted. From Tokyo to New York, you were the only one.'

'What about you?'

'Come off it!'

'And my father?'

'You're joking.'

'And my mother?'

To this she made no reply. I asked again. No reply. I asked once more.

'And my mother?'

'If you ask me that once more I'll box your ears.' I couldn't help laughing, although it was clear she had really meant she'd kill me, chop me up into little pieces and throw me into the Danube. They had locked Roberto up in '63 and only let him out in '83 which meant he had served his full sentence, which was rare. But for some reason they hadn't wanted to exchange him.

'You mean Roberto is alive?'

She continued in the same vein. That she, Dalma, had the feeling they were afraid of him, and that it was better for everyone that he remained locked up. She, at any rate, had never loved him more than during those twenty years. By the time he got out on 2 September 1983 and rang the bell of her little flat on

Mariahilfer Strasse, she no longer loved him. By then she too was only afraid. Roberto gave her one hell of a beating. She thought he'd never stop, and was going to kill her. Then he moved into the little room at the back of her flat, and only ever came out to use the bathroom. Like the hero of a novel, I thought sneeringly.

'And what does he do?'

Dalma shrugged.

'He studies maps, hatches plans, makes notes. It makes no difference. Just now ... the other day, he said let's do the Danube mission together ... What if this time I don't betray him. It makes no difference.'

'I don't understand.'

'You don't have to understand. You just have to sail down to Tulcea.'

'But I thought ... that I ... that you and I ...'

Again she merely shrugged.

'You don't have to think, either. Hold me.'

I held her in my arms as if she were a piece of wood. I felt ashamed of how old she was. I could smell her cigarette-holder and could see that she was losing her hair. But I kissed her all the same. From above. The top of her head.

'And does Roberto know that I ... that we ...?'

'He knows everything.'

'And didn't he send me any message?'

'No.'

'Doesn't he even want to see me?'

'No. He doesn't want to see anyone. He's like an old man. Like a lonely widower, grudgingly waiting for death. And he finds everything such a trial, every step, every breath, every blow of his nose. He whimpers the whole night long and drinks as much as he can during the day. He doesn't want anything ... Or rather, there is one thing he still wants ...'

'But I want to see him!'

'Don't you go wanting anything just now! He didn't even

send you a message. But he sent me one. That I was to stay out of his way!'

'Where is he now?'

'Don't even ask.'

'Tell me, for God's sake, I'm not a child.'

She screwed up her mouth. I still held her in my arms.

'Now let me go!' and she brushed me aside. The ship from Vienna stood motionless before us. Our ship. It lay in the water with all the dignity of a portly priest. In the softest of voices, Dalma said:

'He's there. With us.'

Evening had arrived. A single rowing boat could be seen, riding on the old unpolished silver back of the Danube. In the boat sat a group of women in white dresses, fluttering a long white veil above the water. Then, out of the darkness of the far bank, the lanterns of the harbour appeared. At that moment silence descended over the great river Danube. The waves glided invisibly on their sleepy way, carrying word of our fears and helplessness to distant shores . . .

Cities and the Sky. 3.

If you believe me, fine. Budapest is the kind of town where a stranger has been brushing his teeth in my bathroom every morning for several years. I have never seen him. He weighs a ton, not counting his flannel pyjamas. He is his own corpse, or so they say.

Continuous Cities. 2.

There was one day in the history of Budapest when everyone succeeded at everything. May that day never recur in my dreams! The city had never seen such suffering.

Hidden Cities. 1.

Budapest is no more. It has fled.

IX

. . . Perhaps the terraces of this garden overlook only the lake of our mind . . . Contractor (Hirer)

And here, in fact, we are. Traveller

Cities and the Dead. 5.

What makes Budapest *different from other cities is that it has earth instead of air. The streets are completely filled with dirt, clay packs the rooms to the ceiling, on every stair another stairway is set in negative, over the roofs of the houses hang layers of rocky terrain like skies with clouds . . . At night, putting your ear to the ground, you can sometimes hear a door slam.*

Cities and the Sky. 4.

At one time, maybe even still today, the best veal casserole was served at the Góbé on the József Ring. Once, in the second half of the sixties, after a Latin class – *sic itur ad astra* – I was sitting by a wide picture window that looked out onto Berkovics Street, when I saw, some inches away, on the other side of the window, a woman in an imitation-leather slit skirt. She was screaming at someone, but I couldn't see whom. I asked the waiter for a cherry brandy. By this time the woman was being violently beaten by a man. After one almighty blow her face began pouring with blood. When she reached for her wound the man struck her again and she fell onto the window pane. Her face and lips pressed hard against the glass, she started sliding slowly downwards, leaving a smear of blood and saliva behind. It was as if we are in an aquarium, where it is impossible to say who is inside and who is outside. Meanwhile I go on eating, trembling with fear. The casserole is superb. The woman's blouse is torn and you can see her white breasts. They are just like leavened dough. That was the first time in my life I had seen a woman's breasts in the flesh.

The smudged bloodstain on the windowpane – that was exactly how high the water had risen that terrible Lent when the ice broke and the Danube overflowed its banks. The ice had become congested by the sandbanks above Csepel Island, and the water, whose path had been blocked by the ice, first broke the banks at the Klopfinger house ('the fissure was stopped up at once'). At its height the water reached the point indicated by the bloodstain – on the evening of 15 March at exactly eleven o'clock. Twenty-nine feet and nine inches.

Continuous Cities. 3.
There was one day in the history of Budapest when everyone suffered from an attack of wind. Hence the many windmills on Csepel Island. But the whole thing didn't last too long, perhaps because of the carbon tablets. *A city, which, only when it shits, is not miserly, calculating, greedy.*

Hidden Cities. 2.
There is a wicked Budapest, a hedonistic Budapest, a power-hungry Budapest, a happy-go-lucky, a melancholy, a profound, a witty, a shitty Budapest, a deceitful, a rascally, a formless Budapest (plastic), a city of poetasters and economists, of exaggerated arrogance and exaggerated humility. One could also describe it like this: *In Budapest, life is not happy. People wring their hands as they walk in the streets, curse the crying children, lean on the railings over the river and press their fists to their temples. In the morning you wake from one bad dream and another begins ... And yet –* etc., one could also say that *at every second the unhappy city contains a happy city unaware of its own existence.*

Cities and the Sky. 5.
As part of the three-year plan initiated on 1 April 1947, the working people of the city of Budapest have begun rebuilding their capital. The city's manufacturing industry has developed in unprecedented leaps and bounds, while entire, new, modern districts and housing estates have been created. Budapest is the kind of city in which, in an apartment belonging to one such housing estate, an old woman proudly cries out each night before going to bed: 'I can hardly hear! Hey! What! I can hardly see! I wet the bed! Every part of me hurts! Nobody loves me! My bowels are bubbling!' Victory sounding from the concrete walls. As if she were shouting: 'I'm getting closer to God!'

Continuous Cities. 4.
There was one day in the history of the city when it was filled to the brim, completo, completo, there wasn't a single empty bed. Increasingly impatient strangers wandered through the city, up to the Castle district, back into the centre, out to the Hotel Volga, then once more to the 'Bottomless Lake', and in the mad rush you kept meeting the same faces, a pair of twins, a group of Danes, an elegant Coral Lady, growing ever wearier, completo, completo, and if the city hadn't been Budapest, but, say, Venice, you might already have been in Mestre swarming like a horde of bees from one hotel to the next, then all the way along the Brenta to Bologna, while in the dark evening the elegant patrician villas merge with their shadows, the moon too being completo, and what is more the new motels are all booked up too, just like the cars and motorboats, which is when it suddenly dawns on you that you have lost, that you belong to the losing side, and all the hotels and motels in the world are completo, and Budapest is no more, has simply ceased to be, and you can't just leave, for there isn't anywhere to go in all the world, and although by this time you would accept anything, from a bed of fleas to a luxury hotel, nothing matters any more, not even finding someone to let you in, when suddenly an old witch appears and winks at you, she

has a room, and gives you an enormous key which opens the door to an almost empty hall with one gigantic bed, as big as a ship, bang in the middle, and this bed is full of people, guests, lying in rows, and you turn round in despair, but the old woman pushes you back in, and by this time you're really beyond caring, so you put your suitcase by the bed (it's just like a child), undress to your underpants and climb in with everyone else, throwing your clothes on the suitcase, beside you lie two large, elderly women, their long grey hair spread over the pillow, and if you touch them in the night while half asleep you can feel how hot their bodies are.

On such days Budapest is like John Lennon and Yoko Ono's chess set: all the pieces are white, all thirty-two.

Hidden Cities. 3.

Budapest is no more, it has been stolen, has disappeared leaving no trace, has come unstuck, has been sucked out like an appendectomy, has wandered off like an unfaithful mutt. The poundmasters have already won the contract. Now, where little streets once stood, stand little streets; in place of the dynamic semicircular Ring, the Ring; where the Castle once stood steeped in history, now stands the Castle steeped in history, and all this is true of people too, including the present writer, and of the Danube too, and, of course, of Joliot-Curie Square.

Continuous Cities. 5.

There was one day when the pricks of all the men of Budapest stood to attention. They had hardly enough room to pass one another in the narrow alleyways (medieval city centre). For this reason the city was *delicately* rebuilt. If you can't see this, stranger, you can see nothing of this city.

Hidden Cities. 4.
—

Hidden Cities. 5.

A city is what it imagines itself to be. Its own fantasies. Its own lies, fibs, fables. Its own distortions, forgeries, fabrications. A city is the very star whose place in the sky it denies!

From my stories *you will have reached the conclusion that the real* Budapest *is a temporal succession of different cities, alternately just and unjust. But what I wanted to warn you about is something else : all the future* Budapests *are already present in this instant, wrapped one within the other, confined, crammed, inextricable.*

20

The truth

When I arrived back from Vienna, a message concerning shipping matters awaited me. Up until Budapest I had been 'doing'
the Danube in stretches, and right at the beginning, after having
seen one of their advertisements, I had planned to have the
Danube Steam Shipping Company take me from Budapest to
Sulina and back, strictly on business. We had even agreed on a
date in the spring. But in the meantime, as the journalists say,
freedom had broken out, and every Tom, Dick and Harry wanted
to come and look at this freedom. (They had grown too used to
their own and found it a little boring; but these brand new
freedoms seemed rather interesting.) This meant that I slipped
ever lower down the waiting list, until finally I missed out
altogether, which offended me somewhat.

   In Vienna I had been asked to give a 'musical' reading. Jürg
Laederach played saxophone (in his own wonderfully, relentlessly
free style) and I filled in the gaps. The reading began at eight in the
evening, exactly when the Mödling Film Theatre (Babenberger
Gasse 5) was showing Ferry Radex's utopian, experimental short
film, *Sonne, halt!* (as Thomas Bernhard Praschl puts it: *ein
verspieltes Traktat über Liebe und Einsamkeit*). The film's leading
actor was Konrad Bayer who took his own life in 1964 (Wiener

---

ein verspieltes Traktat . . . : a playful treatise on love and loneliness

Gruppe). Back in those days, Radax is said to have been given a 35-millimetre movie camera by Disney's son-in-law, and with this he and his crew went down to that miserable, distant Danubian village, Monterosso al Mareba. The scandal that broke out when the film was first shown on television is part and parcel of the film's whole legend. Supposedly, this was the first time a naked breast had been seen on Austrian television, so one can imagine the excitement of a small nation with a great history.

According to the message, my steamship voyage had come up(?) after all, did I want it or not, decide.

This was unexpected news, as I had already given up the idea, and anyway I hate making decisions – I'd rather simply wait for what has to happen to go ahead and happen. It was no simple matter. Throughout my voyage I had been continually (and uncharacteristically) tortured by pangs of conscience. Basically, I was enchanted by the spell of completeness, Engineer Neweklowsky's 'Danubian absolutism', and my own sense of the impossibility of all this. I continually felt that I had overlooked something, or missed something out, some *crucial centimetre* of the Danube, and however ridiculous I knew this feeling to be, I could somehow never really seem to settle. I seriously thought that if I were travelling *decently*, I'd be bound to get caught up somewhere along the way and spend several years on some muddy or picturesque stretch of the river. And yet I knew that I wouldn't get caught up anywhere. I increasingly came to identify writing (or, more presumptuously, being a writer) with travelling (while writing about travelling interested me less and less), until I was finally, and self-critically, forced to establish that I wasn't really a traveller at all! And the most deceptive and misleading thing in all this is the Danube itself! It simply offers such a bad example – by eternally advancing forwards! As if that were a kind of victory. Behold, in spite of so much conflict we none the less ... yes, come hell or high water we shall ... flow ever onwards into the sea!

Not that I seriously thought of changing my life. The pangs of conscience stemmed rather from the fact that I never limited myself in my writing (which naturally reached its own limitations), whereas I most certainly did in my travelling, in so far as I simply *pretended* to be travelling, while in reality I was merely writing. Saying so may cast me in a bad light, but I had just experienced writing as a self-limitation for the first time. It was not a good feeling.

Meanwhile I was making good progress with the book. I had reached Budapest, which meant that I had completed the Rich Danube and could now begin the Poor Danube, which was no longer suitable for travelling by ship. I had anyway given up gathering experiences and I already knew the region between here and Belgrade (twenty years earlier I had also travelled the 'lower waters' with friends). By now I'd had enough of libraries and had read *quantum statis* every existing book on the Danube – never again! I was now working at full steam (doing *nothing* but writing) and for a while I kidded myself that my cabin was nothing less than a floating study. Actually, however, the words, the written words were holding me captive, fencing me in, and I knew myself well enough to realize that at such times I could be influenced by *anything*, so I avoided taking risks. (One could object that, if I could be influenced by anything, then not-travelling-by-ship must also count as an influence. True.) I dropped the idea of a further voyage by ship.

REPORT

Welcome aboard, *bienvenu à bord*. I like being spoiled, but I know that at times like this nothing is ever enough, money leads to more money, generosity to more generosity, one whim to another whim, if there is a sauna, then where is the fitness centre, if they give us fresh towels every day, then what about the customary dressing gown, in other words, why isn't *that* part of the service? For the greater the luxury in which one travels, the more penny-pinching one becomes.

'Can't you talk about anything but money?' asked Lady Mary Wortley Montagu disparagingly.

One grows accustomed to the bright and breezy Swedish stewards like a dog to its fleas. For if one knows that food arrives from the left, and drink from the right, and that the drinks steward wears red, and the food steward wears blue, then, seeing a flash of blue in the corner of one's eye, one immediately leans a little to the left, whereas if one sees a flash of red, one leans a little to the right. And that's all there is to it.

According to the Lady's conjecture, the stain on my jacket – whose shape was not unlike that of Csepel Island – derived from a bottle of Château Latour, 1976. Should I attend the bridge course or a lecture on George Lukács? A thousand worries. And it's high time I did something about my tennis serve.

'Can you waltz anti-clockwise?' I asked Lady Mary, taking her completely by surprise.

'Can you talk of nothing but idle pleasures? Never a word about anything else?'

I should also mention a fine-boned, blonde-haired women with translucent white skin and hands that flitted like birds. On every inch of her you could see (feel) the bone, fingerbone, cheekbone, collarbone, anklebone, neckbone, I had never seen such *sensual* bones. She read Joseph Conrad day and night and confessed to the Captain that she too would dearly love to captain a ship. The Captain hung his head and blushed.

'My life has grown hard,' he said quietly, 'like the shit in my bowels.'

THE TRAVELLER ON BOARD PAYS FOR ONE, GETS TWO

On board ship the Traveller begs for/buys stories.

'If only something would happen,' whispered a woman below the bridge.

'Excuse me,' said he, withdrawing sheepishly to his inner chambers. Another time, however: 'Okay baby, let's get it on!' he cried out, in a no less cowardly fashion. But there were some men and women he simply couldn't fool like that. These he cherished, storing them away inside himself, here and there, in his heart, in his lungs, in his liver, etc., etc.

21

The truth, continued

From so much Danube and so much talk of Central Europe I didn't so much get sick – which is anyway the wrong word – as get angry. (In matters of patriotism, Thomas Bernhard remains the crucial authority, although as far as Hungary is concerned, you have to change *Hochgebirgstrottl* to *Tiefebenetrottl* . . .) All that stuff about Danubian thought, Danubian ethos, Danubian past, Danubian history, Danubian suffering, Danubian tragedy, Danubian dignity, Danubian present, Danubian future! What does it all mean? All that flowing became suspicious. Danubian nothingness, Danubian hatred, Danubian stench, Danubian anarchy, Danubian provincialism, Danubian Danube. Poor Gertrude Stein, were she alive to hear this! The Danube is the Danube is the Danube . . .

According to a rather weak joke, the answer to the question of what holds a football team together is partly alcohol and partly a shared hatred of the coach. And that's all. That's all Central Europe ever was. At least, it was only the Soviet Union that kept Kundera's definition alive. How it appealed to me in those days! And how obtuse and immature I found Handke when he called Central Europe a purely meteorological concept. Yet how right

---

Hochgebirgstrottl: high-mountain idiot
Tiefebenetrottl: low-plain idiot

he was! And in no way was this a condescending treatment of the subject. Nature, as a court of appeal, is no trifle. Just try talking to someone from Murmansk about the cold. Or to an Indian about heat or rain. It's cold, it's raining, there's a storm raging and the Inn bursts its banks : here I know what I'm talking about. Clouds, stars, winds and storms, water-level, rainfall, common wisdom, folklore (Mátyás the ice-breaker, April showers, St Swithin's Day).

To sum up : we are neighbours. The same horse looks through the window, we look out onto the same garden, can appeal to the shared knowledge of hailstorms and floods, forks of lightning, the August horizon, snatches of fog, slippery roads at dawn, a spellbinding woman, an angelic little boy, an unmovable man, great, public, orgiastic misunderstandings.

The neighbour is : he who is. We are never, nor ever could be, without him. The neighbour is eternal. And he sees all. And we are neighbours too, our neighbours' neighbours. So we know one another a little better than necessary. Nothing ever remains hidden. Face to face : 'love, hate, good and evil, victor and vanquished, life and death.' We have to face up to everything. Our neighbour forces us to be free ... We know everything there is to know – about the other. Less about ourselves, which is why the neighbour is the stranger. Who restricts us. Obstructs us. The neighbour is captivity, the personification of the fence. And if that fat hen of his crosses over to our side again I'll wring its rotten neck. Or I'll make soup out of it and offer him some. We'll remember this colossal feast for years. Plus cucumber salad. Later he'll accuse me of cooking his hen. *Was für eine hen ?* Next thing he'll be saying the cucumber salad also crawled through the fence ! Then he invites me for a cosy little supper.

After plucking and chopping up the suspiciously familiar hen, boil in three and a half litres of water. Add a one-pound bone of beef, salt, pepper and a pinch of paprika. Next stir in a table-spoonful of tomato purée, onions, garlic and four or five mush-rooms. Simmer until soft. When ready, sprinkle surface of soup with a tablespoonful of cold water and leave to stand without lid for five minutes. (My grandmother's method.) Strain, take out hen, and strip meat from bone. Replace soup on stove and cook liver dumplings therein. Add vegetables and one egg per person. Boil for three minutes, making sure that the whites are hard, but the yolks remain soft. Serve in a soup dish and garnish with chives and parsley. In summer, green peas may also be added if desired.

There is always a certain inexplicable and arrogant loftiness in the way one speaks about Central Europe – the soft, accommodating, falsetto voice of a guide, a pleasant, engaging, if somewhat offended voice, discussing fragments from Roman times, the achievements of the Baroque, the absence of the (likewise Baroque) handkerchief of Grillparzer's secret mistress, which, in that it anticipates Wittgenstein, serves as a memento for the region. That is to say, cultural history as a kind of sedative tablet. Cultivation as a form of museum, the museum as a form of assignment and a so-called solution – here even suffering and humiliation sparkle like triumphant decorations, medals for valiant service and distinction. As if suffering elevated us *in advance.* As if 'the long, hard years' had produced some kind of reserve or knowledge, the fruit of that *other* way of thinking which the world somehow needs. There is probably a grain of truth in this (there is always a need for any kind of *other*), but not in that 'enlightened', didactic way, only privately. Within the *individual,* not within the community. The individual, who is part of the community. And this knowledge is not *something,* something namable, but a voice, a register, and – to be a little lofty myself – a colour on the palette of the European chorus, a squeak in the Gregorian howling of wolves.

In the film I mentioned earlier, a Hungarian man stands beside a woman in the empty fifth-floor office of a New York skyscraper. The man tries to draw the map of Hungary on the woman's face. He sketches a fine line across her forehead with his finger (Győr, Komárom), sweeping into the socket of her eye (Visegrád), down along her bumpy nose to the coral-red lips (Baja).

'The Danube,' he whispers intimately to the woman.

THE TRAVELLER AND RÁCKEVE

Now and then he took on private jobs too, illicitly, for they were generally forbidden in the contract (income tax, etc.). But the Traveller was only moderately interested in contracts. He did study them meticulously, arguing over percentages, upping advances, but essentially only out of respect for the Contractor (Hirer) whose self-esteem was based entirely on his sense of his own generosity.

For the people of Ráckeve he travelled free. It was Laci Szőke's idea, who hired the traveller for a couple of days each year. Laci Szőke was simply crazy about Ráckeve, which had been founded on Csepel Island by forty thousand Serbs fleeing, under the leadership of the patriarch Arsenije Čvarnojević, from the Turks, and whose main tourist attraction was the almost stagnant Saroksár Danube arm. It is locked between sluices, above and below, and consists of boats, boathouses, reeds, anglers' camps, summer houses, parks, footpaths, woodlands, beaches and a healthy population of fish. One of Ráckeve's more interesting curiosities is the fifteenth-century Gothic Greek Orthodox Church, with its unique, separately-built tower and sixteenth-century Byzantine-style frescoes and icons. Not far away in the Kiskunság region is Apaj (riding school) and the dredged lake of Lacháza, Délegyháza ! – five crystal-clear lakes, beach and nudist colony. (Boy, what tits !)

Laci Szőke would tell you that Ráckeve was the centre of the world : here the Danube was utterly enchanting, the old men wise, the young as fresh as daisies, the middle-aged hardworking, and as for the Serbian carp they served at Jóska Pataki's place – it was simply beyond words.

'Ráckeve has forgotten Ráckeve,' said Laci Szőke sombrely. The Traveller nodded. To discover a region for oneself (i.e. for one's Contractor (Hirer), or rather, to have it discovered for one by the locals, was in Europe a pretty routine affair. It wasn't the most promising of prospects, but then the Traveller was not contracted to win great glory, but . . . but for a certain ephemerality, like a kind of Sisyphus, so he was the last person to have to go explaining himself all the time. If they wanted idle chatter, there was always the Danube.

Now he was particularly glad to travel. The ocean in a drop, the Danube in a bowl of fish soup – that too is a kind of *recognition*. An idea both serious and true to style. Wherever he stayed in Ráckeve, he was treated at once as a member of the family. He could have, they'd say, the attic room, which belonged to their adolescent son, who, almost miraculously, bore not the slightest of grudges and even vacuumed the heavy carpet for him. Naturally enough, the men of the house refused to take him seriously and saw him as a kind of muddled, distant aunt. At any event, he was always in the way. The strict rule of the matriarch was occasionally interrupted by the great and wicked outbursts of the men. Hungary is a pre-emancipated country. Strong women *and* male domination, intimidated men *and* exploited women.

The Traveller's situation and status was not altered by the fact that he liked hot peppers and could take his drink. 'Eh by gum,' they'd say, "'e's a raight old sissy!" (In such matters it was only good old Bandi Kasza who could really embarrass the Traveller. At Bandi's place, whenever Aunt Lizi left the room, he'd have to gulp down masses of the hidden apple schnapps which, God only knows why, they called Calvados. Whenever there was any mishap in the town, the people of Ráckeve would raise their austere forefingers and say: 'It were the Calvados what done it.')

The men weren't jealous of him – of course they weren't! –

although they were a little bit mistaken not to be. But only a little bit. He was always surrounded by women – women of all ages, girls, housewives, grannies. But it was above all the old dears who spoiled him, offering him liqueurs and telling him with their shrill whinnying voices of their pregnancies of long, long ago. 'My womb fell off to sleep, that's what that blockhead of a doctor said, my womb fell off to sleep, and I was already in my fourth month.' The teenage girls told him of their latest lovers, and even introduced them to him. They stood there before him, shifting from one foot to the other, while he nodded in approval. Now and then the woman from next door called in and invited him to taste her apple fritters. Or her pig-trotter stew. 'What a nice big appetite you have,' she sighed.

Laci Szőke followed him about like a shadow, eager to see how his beloved town opened itself up to the Traveller's friendly but penetrating gaze. The truth was that Ráckeve had not forgotten Ráckeve, but that Laci Szőke had forgotten Ráckeve. That is to say, a town like Ráckeve only ever forgets itself in so far as a man like Laci Szőke forgets it (and perhaps himself as well).

First, as was only proper, they paid their respects to Misi Pesta and his household. He was the greatest of all Danube fishermen. He knew all there was to know about the Danube. Everybody said these same two sentences about Misi Pesta. His family had run a bus service in the old days. There is now a pub where the old garage used to stand.

'You see, that's where the buses used to pass.' He always showed the Traveller this spot. His mother, old Tante Pesta, had been the driver. 'Once we sued the local newspaper because they claimed she smoked cigars, which wasn't true.' They went bankrupt in the First World War, started up anew, but went under again in the Second. They managed to get started once again, only to end up on the kulak list. The Hireling (this being how the Traveller saw himself when he was in a bad mood) would let out a deep sigh: the same stories over and over again.

The authorities came out to nationalize them. 'Well, Tante Pesta, you know why we've come.' 'Why, my dear boy?' They had someone with them from Budapest; he knew exactly what to say. 'We're going to give the people back what's rightfully theirs.' Tante Pesta, née Rákhel Vida, nodded cheerfully: 'Oh that's good, that is. Oh yes, I'd like it to belong to the people again.' She went inside, as if to get wine, her every movement smooth and self-assured. 'Well, cheerio, let's drink to the people. I'm the people, so are you, just as one and one make two.'

But instead of wine she brought a rope. She walked out among the men – who scattered like chickens – and tossed the rope over one of the thick, lower branches of the little pear tree. She went on talking as she fastened and fiddled with the rope: 'Everything you see before you is the work of my own two hands. I can tell you the times of all the buses since 1928. I can account for every kilometre, every rotten metre. I remember every wheel-change, in snow, sandstorm or spring flood. And I can tell you exactly how much of me there is in every brick of this house, how much of my sweat and toil. I know the names of all the passengers too,' and here she turned to the men, 'your father, and yours, and your father's father, and yours ...' She pointed at them one by one. When she reached the man from Budapest, no member of whose family she'd ever driven on her bus, she glared into his face. Everything flashed through her mind at once, all the suffering, the three attempts to start again, the fire, the flood, the Russians. And it wasn't rage or dread that seized her then, but tiredness. She no longer saw the men standing about her, nor even the house. All she saw was the little pear tree and the rope.

'Have I ever told you this before?' asked Misi Pesta.

'Aye, once or twice,' nodded the Hireling.

'You know they didn't even nationalize the house after all that ... or rather, they didn't take it from us. My mother's tempestuous grief simply blew them away.'

'Tempestuous grief,' mumbled the Hireling every year. They

went fishing. He only watched. Misi Pesta became perceptibly excited beside the Danube, or rather, more attentive. He knew exactly where the fish were hiding. The Hireling always tried to learn the secret, to understand this special power, but to no avail. Misi Pesta and Pista Mike. Here in Ráckeve they knew best.

'See ? See how big it is ?!' But the Hireling never saw. At most he noticed the reeds swaying as the carp nibbled at their stalks.

'I see it. Looks like a good 'un,' he lied politely.

They sat together like this for hours without so much as uttering a word. Misi Pesta did not flaunt his talents.

'There !' he pointed from time to time. More often than not they didn't catch any fish. The Hireling caught the odd wellington boot or anorak. Seen from a distance he was just like any of the others. The quiet did him good. But he wasn't moved by the people of Ráckeve. He simply did his job as a Traveller – he arrived, found somewhere to stay, checked shipping and train timetables. He learned what spoon-bait was, that the priest-louse was a kind of fish, that coots taste of fish, that Pista Mike was the best pike fisherman, that stamping one's feet allegedly affects the sexual urge of catfish, that freshwater carp are so stupid, you only have to imitate the sound of an iron barge and they swallow the hook, because they've grown used to their food arriving in iron barges back at the fish farms ; he knew at precisely which spot beneath the bridge the giant catfish had thrashed about among the geese, the water bubbling up around him, he must have been all of fifty kilos, they had even given him a name, but they never uttered it out loud, out of respect, and it was only somewhat reluctantly that they betrayed it to the Hireling, it was Vili Csukás (Djugashvili, that is, after Stalin) so it wasn't really out of respect that they kept the name quiet, but out of fear, at most they'd say 'Vili's been here again,' or 'They saw Vili down by Rózsa Island,' and thus they drew closer to the spectre, the horror, which in those days weighed upon their every moment, their every breath, they anthropomorphized Stalin and entertained the *realistic* hope of one day catching him, and there were denunciations too, and interrogations, but then, as they said *high up*, how could a catfish be called *csukás* when a 'csuka', in Hungarian, is a pike, and as the policemen were themselves seasoned, practising fishermen, the whole affair soon blew over.

'We never could catch him. Never.'

They paid a formal visit to Jani Szále's 'champignon stable'. 'It grows like Jani Szále's champignons,' people had been saying mischievously on the island for centuries, which meant quite simply that the object in question both did and didn't grow, was both Roundhead and Cavalier, something that was one thing, but as soon as you called it one thing, was another, and so on. The saying illustrated the deeply lived quality of Hungarian history, which was like a winding backwater. The Száles were a famous family in these parts, boasting of poachers and heroes from the Turkish wars, every second one of whom was called János. They tried to maintain that their name derived from the word *szála*, on the basis that their ancestors danced with the girls of Ráckeve in great *salons*. Another explanation started out from the word *csálé* ('gee ho!') and claimed that the family descended from a line of village idiots, an equally honourable lineage. The Hireling was fond of this giant of a man, who was himself not unlike the champignon-saying, belonged in his own sur-roundings and knew exactly where he lived; not cultivated, but intelligent. According to the Hireling's rather wicked interpret-ation, he had sacrificed his life to his champignons, herding his family – all the many little Száles – into a single room, while keeping all the others for his champignons.

'This here is the leading champignon,' he was wont to say to the Hireling. 'The strongest of the lot. All the others rally together behind him and then: charge! They start to grow like mushrooms. It's a bit like the queen among bees.'

Then they did a Calvados-lap-of-honour down towards Bandi Kasza's place. Bandi Kasza had done time in prison after 1956 for illegally crossing the border. This 'damned hard kid' was already on free soil when he went back for his friend's shoe, and that was when he got caught. (According to a second version of the story, he went back for a necktie. That's the dandy version. But there was a whore-catcher version too, according to which his downfall was brought about by a pair of women's panties.) For this reason he would get ceremoniously drunk on 23 October each year, planning the whole thing in advance, starting with beer, then moving onto spritzers of light sand wines, before graduating to heavier red wines. He interrupted this carefully structured process with the odd arbitrary and hysterical Calvados and the odd 'constitutional' stroll down to the 'Little Cormorant Inn', followed by a good twenty-four hours' sleep. 'I keep the memory of the revolution alive.' In the beginning Aunty Ilcsi had tried to lock him inside the house, but good old Uncle Bandi simply climbed out of the window, taking frame, mosquito net and everything else with him. 'They'll never lock up another Kasza!'

Every year Laci Szőke showed the Hireling the 'beach' – a small clearing between the trees where the legendary, and often bloody, heading matches were played. He pointed out the spot where Szepi Garai spat blood, which turned out to be red wine, after nodding in four goals for his team, and they visited the little nook, now overgrown with reeds, where, in '64, all the forwards fell out of their barge and Marci Zsák drowned. 'Just like Manchester United.' They did a bit of rowing, avoiding No-Man's Island, and they failed to find the ford where you can walk back to Round Sandbank Island . . .

He listened to the familiar stories with growing indifference, watching these people go on about the good old days when television had not destroyed the art of conversation (during which time the television was constantly on, and the Hireling saw for the first time how his countrymen watched it: that is, they always had it on without anyone actually watching, or at most for a couple of minutes now and then, just like America!). So much self-delusion and nostalgia, Laci Szőke searching for his lost youth, knee-deep in sentimentality, oohs and aahs. It has to be said, my dear old friend, whether you believe it or not, Ráckeve is not the centre of the world. At which Laci Szőke starts blithely shaking his head, aah, for him, for him that's exactly what it is! The Hireling can't help giving his shoulders a definitive shrug: so what?

He always made time for an aimless stroll in the general direction of the horizon. To go as far as the eye could see. (At one Danube-bend of the book, I decided to walk all the way along the Danube's path through Hungary. Everyone I told voiced their doubts – to put it mildly – they laughed at me. K. was the only one to give me any practical advice, although even she seemed to grin as she drew my attention to the importance of the appropriate footwear. Basics, tools, she said with her characteristic reticence. K. has two boys, two girls and a rather unfortunate marriage. She once tried to break herself free after falling in love with one of her students, but in the end she couldn't bring herself to cause so much pain for so much pleasure (assuming that pain and pleasure stood as equals). Once I met her lover in the lift of a downtown hotel. There was music playing as we floated upwards. For some time we avoided each other's eyes. Then the boy suddenly said, in place of a greeting:

'I wish her all the best.'

'You want me to tell her that?'

'Yes, that's all.'

'I think that's quite a lot,' I said, a little pompously. He nodded a farewell, brushing my shoulder as he got out of the lift. I bet he's going to somebody's room, I thought indignantly. Now, all of a sudden, I can't remember if I ever did deliver his message.) To walk along the narrow embankment early in the spring when, thank God, everything is still empty, the little huts and weekend refuges all wide open, at most the odd pensioner pottering in his shed. How awful it must be when all this is packed with people, all rubbing up against one another, everything tiny, low and narrow. Mediocre. Botchery. Botched houses, botched weekends, botched couples, botched marriages, botched lives.

Botchery: the keyword of the Kádár regime. There are freedoms but no freedom. Botchery means something like the phrase 'the gayest barrack' once meant in an external, *feuilleton* sense. Botchery is the same, only in an internal, practical sense.

From the inside, the 'gayest barrack' was neither gay, nor cheerless, just grey. And from the inside, you couldn't even see the barrack itself, only the linoleum, the insulating tape, the rows of Bonanza cupboards and so on. From the inside, you could see only the endless signs of strain, the plastic, the glue, the foam, the patches, the quick repairs, the doors and windows made in Hong Kong, and all the stamping of feet, all the built-in furniture, the pranks, the dullness, the aptitude, amnesia and attention, all the things the barrack was made of, things you can't identify, but which had been things once, all the same, for people lived here (unrealistically, as it were, without existing), in something thrown together, concocted, scrounged: botchery.

Botchery is at once a knack, a certain adroitness, and a know-ledge of the terrain, of how to get by, whom to call, how much to pay; a kind of perpetual wrangling. But it isn't simply – or rather exclusively – a matter of cheating, or of cunningly adapting oneself to the circumstances. Botchery is above all a form of victory. Everything may well be worthless around here, and I don't deny that I'm no exception, but all this is still *my* botchery. And it isn't just a form of victory, but also a form of defeat. Botchers have no dreams, nor will they ever dream again. Botchery is a statement – a statement that is tantamount to defeat, but we still win a point for it, which could come in handy at the end of the championships. Botchery is survival – only it is impossible to say at what cost.

The Hireling went on walking in Villains' Valley and out to the lakes, to the anglers' camps, and then inland, away from the riverbank, along the backwater of Becse. Fallen trees, dry reeds, 'at the sound of his step' the frogs leaped so high you'd think he had kicked them, the would-be footballer. And then, when he reached the fields of Kisház, he suddenly saw in his mind's eye the image that represents the goal of all travelling : *he comprehended Ráckeve*. The simple fact that, while there may be hundreds of other similar settlements along the Danube, this one was : this one. The inventory of stories is finite, monotonous, and everywhere one goes one finds a Misi Pesta, but only this one, after five hours of silence, wheezes in asthmatic excitement the word : There ! One finds heading matches on every beach, but it was only here that one could see father and son standing face to face with entirely *identical* bodies (later the grandfather joins them, it's almost too much : three generations of muscles). The Hireling stopped in his tracks. A dusty ZIL lorry trundled past him like an (unjustifiably) enthusiastic elephant. Once again he was pondering the question of uniqueness. Ráckeve too was given meaning by death. That was why he was there. In Becse, he quickly popped into the pub (whenever a pub just happened to fall on his way, he always popped in, quickly, slowly) for a 'medicinal' spritzer. Was that all there was ? An asthmatic wheeze, a bundle of muscle, a sloping riverbank, a broken branch ? Is that all it required for a place to be the centre of the world ? Maybe. As always, he looked in at the André Kertész museum to see the 'Village Madonna' – a young peasant woman suckling her baby, surrounded by poverty, her breasts the only signs of richness. The photo was taken at Szigetbecse, 26 September 1920.

They took him for a foreigner. The ticket collector urged him along amicably : 'Off you go, off you go ... stop looking at me like that ... nix Geld ... hurry along now, sweetheart, I've got to have my lunch sometime too, you know.' The Hireling looked at the woman for some time.

It turned hot. The asphalt steamed as he passed back along the highway. At every bus stop he studied the timetable and checked the departure times. They were about five minutes out. Again he thought of the film where the swimming-pool attendant says that the world has no heart. He won't say this to Laci Szőke. Or maybe he will. Again he had seen himself, *Fata*

Morgana – the simple Nietzschean *nicht ich denke, es denkt* – melting down his 'I', scattering it far and wide, stuffing it between the molecules of the water, in the rotting sedge, into the mouths of the carp and, of course, into the Danube-smelling crotches of women.

Ráckeve comes to a ceremonious end with Jóska Pataki's Serbian carp. Under the oak tree in his Uncle Jani's courtyard, Laci Szőke lays the pushed-together tables. It is as if the whole of Ráckeve were there, bustling women offering and pouring wine, Marika shouting orders from the kitchen. The conversation turns to serious matters. Captain Cousteau will be coming to inspect the Danube. After visiting the Nile and the Amazon, he is going to assess the state of the Danube, purity of water and effects of the Bős-Nagymaros dam. The Captain is of the opinion that all life stems from water. The Hireling sits in silence, listening, eating. The Serbian carp is indeed flawless.

'Sauces and spices,' nods Pataki humbly. 'Believe me, old chap, it all depends on the fat.' He repeats this several times, as if the Hireling doubts his word.

'On the fat. And on the weather.' At this they all laugh. They laugh at everything. Someone was a *horse painter* in America. For a wine glass to sound beautiful you have to grab it down below, just like a woman.

'Do I sound beautiful?' The Hireling looks round to see who spoke. In the distance a pair of sparkling woman's eyes. Or is it a cat? Miaow, miaow. A cat. The lamps that hang from the oak tree sway in the light breeze. The table rocks, the courtyard. A botched courtyard to be sure, but the sky, the mighty oak, the long table, the clatter of cutlery – these things are genuine, as if we were sitting in a Chekhovian garden, although it is true that the women with white dresses and wide-brimmed hats are missing, the three sisters, and we are not exactly thinking to

nicht ich denke, es denkt: not I think, it thinks

193

ourselves Moscow, Moscow, if only we could get to Moscow, then everything would be all right.

'One can only travel *from below*,' mumbled the Hireling, not really wanting to talk to anyone any more. He knew that getting talking with someone, speaking to someone, could be a dangerous business.

ONE ROTTEN, FISH-SMELLING MORNING IN BAJA THE HIRELING LOOKS INTO THE MIRROR

'Judging by my carefully shaven face and my thick, raven-black hair, I can hardly be more than thirty years old.' (Hungarian men are highly reminiscent of the sack-racers in the opera *The Nymph of the Dnieper*.) Fish soup for breakfast – he would have never believed himself capable of such a thing.

22

The continuation of the continuation of the truth (travel diary)

The voice on the telephone was a distant voice, faint, unavoid-able, refined and brutal, as if it came straight from heaven. Actually it was Andras Tüske calling from Nagyvárad, which did indeed sound like the end of the world, but that still isn't the same thing as heaven (in my opinion). Was it still on, what we had agreed, of course it was, it always is, I said, without the faintest idea of what he was referring to. Okay then, maestro, said he, not quite in jest, I'll be waiting for you in Kocsárd at midnight. And here we were cut off.

I got to know Andris Tüske in Kolozsvár at the beginning of the summer. There were a thousand and one reasons for getting to know him (in short: he is a most likeable man), but at that time I was a bit like old Pavlov's dog – all I had to do was hear the word 'Danube' and I was off. I had heard that Andris Tüske's family had in the old days been deported to the Danube Delta. So I pounced on him, tenderly. We sat in a barn-like restaurant drinking beer that tasted – let's not mince words – like horse-piss, and that, if accused, I'd never own up to having drunk. But we undoubtedly drank it all the same. And in the end it wasn't his Danube Delta stories I ended up listening to. His father, a clergyman, had been sent to prison, while his mother and her seven children had been packed off to the Delta, to Feteşti on the banks of the Small Danube by the Borcea backwater. The mother didn't speak Romanian, and there was this *slave boat* the Romanians had brought from the French, the *Gironde*, which used to take convicts out to the colonies, and the children had to find out whether their father was on board, and there was a ten-to-fifteen-metre-high sand wall on the riverbank and they sat one behind the other holding hands, with Miklós at the front, who was as brave as a lion, digging out the odd chunk from the wall, which was more or less directly underneath him and which finally collapsed with an enormous crash into the Danube. But Miklós wasn't only brave, he was also unbelievably talented with all things technical, and after he had constructed a washing machine for his mother at the age of twelve, all the people in the neighbourhood started bringing their junk to the boy, and the ice, and the flood, and the fish, and the way a whole life can be determined by the water, the river ... There was something so balanced about Tüske's tone of voice, cheerful, but neither humorous nor ironical, rather an expression of the composure that comes from understanding what has happened, is happening, to one. He spoke exclusively of suffering, of evil, of vilification, later on too, when the Securitate were watching him, the interrogations, the fear; but there was not a hint of self-pity in his voice, only that wonderful uncertainty which is a mark of the most certain truth, the fear of saying something and then the rapture of having finally said it. I studied the way he spoke, the way he strung words together, seemed about to remove them, then left them there after all. We sat drinking our dishwater beer and a bizarre band started playing, violin, keyboard and drum-machine, two shop-stewards from the early seventies, and farther away, at the long table by the wall, men in suits were drinking toasts (lunching or dining at four o'clock in the afternoon), there was one woman among them, looking very flushed, and more and more people kept joining them, the whole town flocking towards the music, old and young alike, African students, or Arabs, Palestinians, and I sat listening to this sensitive young man, looking at his slender wrists and thanking my lucky stars that I'd stumbled across him. It wasn't a sensation of love or friendship that seized me, but something both more and less than that, less because it had nothing to do with me, and more because it made me realize that there must be something fundamentally *friendly* in the world, the world in which I lived, if it were possible, so easily, without any special effort, to stumble across a character like that.

We were cut off, and with that the matter was settled. In Eastern Europe (I know, I know: Central! Central Europe!) fate often takes the form of a telephone. Romania is practically unreachable by phone. A feeling of helplessness and defence-lessness flooded through my body like a kind of tingling warmth. I became calm and cheerful – I didn't have to think, to ponder over whether or not I'd be met in Kocsárd the following day at midnight. At that very moment – to exaggerate a little – the radio announced that there was a cholera epidemic in the Delta. There were already a number of casualties and the border with Romania had been closed. Fine. What do I do now? Go on writing my book, or start writing my will? Or should I take all this seriously? Just how dangerous was it? Better find out.

*

Today I finally found Kocsárd on the map. It is actually Szék-elykocsárd. 'O Székelykocsárd! Dark secret of my life!'

Somehow, I want to get out of booking my ticket. I'll try to get my sister-in-law to do it, she works near the station. Or my brother, who is good at getting things done. But first I'll try my son. – Not so very long ago, a charming lady came to visit us from the West, an enthusiastic champion of all things Hungarian, who was spending her first longer stay in the country, travelling alone for the first time and feeling a little lonely in the city. With much gloating and satisfaction, I heard that she, after having successfully come through all the thousand little trials and tribulations that we hardly even notice any more, had finally gone to a travel agent to buy a train ticket. When, however, the girl behind the counter didn't offer the slightest response to her greeting, she burst into tears. Just stood there and sobbed. (I should add that she would not have got a train ticket there anyway, greeting or no greeting ...)

My son has just phoned to say that the queue is three hundred metres long, what should he do.

'Join it,' I said with my father's indignant voice, before slamming down the receiver.

I sit in my study while others change my life. *Du musst sein (ihr) Leben ändern*. Twaddle.

My sister-in-law is here with the ticket. The plot thickens. I shouldn't even try the Orient Express, I won't get a seat, and anyway it doesn't stop at Kocsárd, only at Războieni. But there is a relief train in the afternoon. One way or another I'll have to change at Kolozsvár. Two weeks later my sister-in-law gives birth; now every part of her is nice and round.

I'm worried. I'm one of the significant worriers of our time. I imagine sitting in the dark, deserted station at Kolozsvár, dogs howling in the distance, and sorry old nags drawing their carts beneath the veil of night. A blue-faced corpse in the straw. It will be dark, it will be quiet and I shall be freezing cold. And frightened. I haven't been frightened for ages. Not since my childhood. Midnight awakening to the sound of loud adult voices: 'If you say another word I'll kill you.' (A woman's voice, mezzo-soprano.) Or when I got lost in a Second World War bunker. That was the worst, because it was just like being in a film, which means that anything could happen, but all the time I knew it was real.

Du musst sein (ihr) Leben ändern: You must change his (her) life.

Since then I always confuse that bunker and that fear with Clara's. Her too I asked about the Danube – 'Say whatever comes to mind.' Instead of a letter, she sent me a pile of notes. She didn't even write the sender's name on the envelope, but I recognized her handwriting. The notes were numbered. (Why?)

1. Der Tod ist ein Meister aus Deutschland. (Celan) Know it?

2. Ceausescu = King Von

legends – Attila, Suleiman, Charles the Great; the six names of the Danube; the Rhine, Main, Danube = rivers of Attila

Passau = Bavarian Venice

The Piazza Navona; in Bernini's group of sculptures the Danube as symbol of Europe

Linz = Ruhrgebiet; its rhythm found its way into Bruckner's Seventh Symphony

Ady = looking West – oppressed from the East

ideas flow down the Danube

3. Unfortunately the Danube brings to mind the fact that my boyfriend (he was eleven and a half years old) and his parents were executed into the river in '44. Márti Taub, who was fifteen years old, survived, in spite of being shot three times. She grabbed hold of the corner of a towboat and spent an hour or two in the icy water before swimming back to the – by then deserted – bank. (She has turned into a beautiful, cocky Jewish woman who knows absolutely everyone and pretends to have four children. And everyone believes her, she has such enormous breasts. She suffers constantly from inflammation of the joints. The joints of her fingers, for example, have grown as big as ping-pong balls. But now she's receiving treatment from a Russian 'energeticist' who puts something on her hands. Some Jura. Thirty years old! Thirty years old, she shouts at me down the telephone. She always shouts these days.)

As I've already told you, I left the line because I couldn't bear to go through the tunnel, which stank of pee – even when I'd played there earlier on. They didn't come after me. I didn't know where they had wanted to take us, so I went back to the

Jewish house at 41 Sziget Street, just in case my mother had come back – she had been taken away. (I look back over what I've written and see I was so worked up that I've committed – or rather, made – all kinds of spelling mistakes.)

It is raining. Are there no leak-proof shoes in this world? – I'll take half a salami and a bottle of schnapps; that's for us. But no coffee. Last time I was hardly able to *hand it over*. How does it go? Pearls to the swine? Or simply: help! How I adored my Western relatives for their Suchard chocolate ... Coffee as a nation-preserving force. If the world is God's cap, Hungary is the feather therein. If. If you need me, Jagger-Richards, if.

★

Station (Western). An old woman arguing with her son, stamping, fretting, panicking. 'Hurry up now. Quickly,' she urges the boy. A difficult boyhood, one can see.

By a string of coincidences it became clear that Războieni and Székelykocsárd were one and the same place. Good thing I speak Hungarian and know this city like the back of my hand. This way I can just about get by. Five years ago, experienced man of the world that I was, I put my sister-in-law (another sister-in-law, who isn't a sister-in-law any longer), who was going back to Vienna, on a train coming *from* Vienna and heading for Bucharest. ('Is this the Vienna train?' I asked. 'Yes,' they replied.) We jumped off at the last minute – it was just like jumping off a tram – and wandered across the track as if across the fields. I had to carry six (6!) suitcases all at once. I brimmed with pride, my brother's wife brimmed with hatred. Both feelings have faded since then, but have not altogether disappeared.

I have a seat reservation, that much is certain. 'My brother has gone to buy trousers. *After all* there's still ten minutes,' I hear from the corridor – or am I over-stylizing the anxiety of 'going East'? Nothing more than a bit of Reisefieber? Maybe. But then we really are entering another world. A different 'yes', a different 'no', a different never, a different forever, a different eternity – that is, a different geometry; a different sense of honour, of giving one's word, of revenge, a different understanding of right and obligation. Or, to cut a long story short: I'm travelling a few hundred kilometres and I'm going to meet a completely different interpretation of – Aristotle. (Here syntax has been sacrificed to enhance the humble punchline.) (I shall soon see that the difference is not quite like that. It is more simple. More wordless, without words. – Note added later.) 'Wicked trousers! Won't crease a bit! You get on the train at Torda and get off at Arad like a proper gent.'

How many oily faces! – We set off with a groan.

HIRELING HEADS SOUTH,
ARM IN ARM WITH DANUBE LEAVES
HUNGARY

Pah! (That is to say. Splendid, free land, enchanting country – I must take my leave of you, your memory will burn forever in my heart and soul, snap, crackle, pop. All this happened 1433 kilometres downstream, round about the river's half-way mark, taking into consideration the initial beating about the bush.)

TELEGRAM ABOUT 'IF ONE DAY ...'

Our ship was approaching Novi Sad where once, in days of old, the water had carried bloated corpses on their way to Belgrade. The Danube, just like a human being, can endure anything.

Reisefieber: travel-fever

201

Here the river doesn't seem to know what it wants, like a seasoned actor playing the part of a drunk. It is not a matter of staggering, or stuttering, or vomiting all over the stage, but of the pure exertion of concealing the state one is in, a matter of pure and – if the actor is really good – *futile* exertion. Fruška Gora watches our labours from afar. The mountain is calm, say the locals, addressing the mountain itself so that the Danube too should understand what is meant. The mountain is calm, the Danube forgives.

I imagined everything to be Serbian, the women, the Danube, the air, the sun, the night. Every movement and every word was Serbian, and so were the Serbs themselves. I can love anyone. I remembered one of your telegrams; you were very angry with me. 'If one day you are able to hate someone, you will at last have found peace and reached your journey's end.' That was the first time you addressed me in the '*du*' form.

REPORT ON CORPSES
DENTISTRY AND MATHEMATICS

I draw on the contemporary records of Georges Tim Aar, who from his prodigal childhood onwards crawled at the feet of Prince Eugene of Savoy. I shall demonstrate his credibility with a short anecdote. Towards evening on 12 September 1683, they asked their superior, Karl von Lothringen, whether they should deal a decisive blow to the over-confident, dallying, Kara Mustafa that night, or wait until the following morning. The experienced Karl replied with an argument unique in military history: 'I am an old man, and I wish to die at night, in comfort.'

Thirty-three years later the Prince's advisers stood scratching their troubled heads. But Eugene was, in the language of today, a 'brilliant' man, as brilliant as the sun. On a hazy August morning in 1716, the great Turkish leader Damad Ali was casually pottering about in the forest of Pétervárad, when the Prince of Savoy, with one flank of his army concealed by the forest, the other by that great protector of European values, the Danube, charged at the right flank of the unsuspecting Turks. Like all great ideas Eugene's was a simple one ('He thinks that I think that ... therefore I shan't think that at all.'). It was simple, but not trivial: that is to say, a great number of people died. The riverside swamps swallowed up six thousand Turks alone.

The Danube is a hearty eater in these parts. (January 1942, November 1944, etc., holes in the ice, Jews, Serbs executed into the water, babies thrown against the wall, the tying together, shooting and burning of Hungarian executees, prisoners made to walk barefoot over hot coals, skinned alive, testicles torn off with pincers, mines fastened to the legs of children, blazing away until the target falls, people sawn in two at the waist, impalings and etcetera, etcetera. Etcetera: history's other name. Etcetera: the weight of time, sullied impersonality. Etcetera: the law; my lord and master, I place my life and death in your hands.)

Even Damad Ali's personal courage could not help him. Concerning the dimensions of his magnificent tent, one need only mention that it took the combined labour of five hundred men to set it up.

Aar cannot fail to report the horrible death of Count von Breuner. The latter was the uncle of the Schwarzenberg children, a man of many talents, poet, physician, fanatical mathematician, and favourite of Prince Eugene's general staff.

I came across his activities in the field of dentistry in the manuscript archive of Zagreb library, among the notes of Klaudia Mágris. This was – forgive me for saying so myself – in its own way something of a find, even if not a particularly interesting one. Von Breuner, the father of dentistry!

Klaudia Mágris was an interesting and colourful figure in the Hungary of her day, a famous, enlightened and emancipated woman of the late eighteenth and early nineteenth centuries, who corresponded with George Sand. According to all the evidence, she was a beautiful moon-eyed woman, who, however, was in the habit of bringing calamity crashing down on her pretty little head. She had literary aspirations too, but her book about the Habsburgs won the approval only of Joseph II (who was hardly a Habsburg at all). Rumour has it that, already as a child, Mágris fell for the highly respected Empress, and later fell equally madly in love with Lajos Kossuth. A typical Central European phenomenon by all means, but not in those days (there was no need for it then). The age could sense the contradiction here. Even such a passionate woman of defeat could not be tolerated by the century of triumph, and the fair Klaudia was forced to flee, at breakneck speed, what is more, and in men's clothing (the latter – especially the fine, lightweight Italian jacket – being something for which she had always yearned). She settled in Trieste, becoming a kind of *grande dame* of that city. It was on her that Italo Svevo based his *As a Man Grows Older*. And from Flaubert, who, outside of his books, was a terrible gossip, we know that Turgenev was never at a loss for words when this hugely talented, eclectically-fated and curvy-hipped lady of Trieste was being discussed. Allegedly she planned to write a book about the Danube, but no written trace of this is anywhere to be found, unless – he said with a bow of the head – right *here*!

Von Breuner laid the foundations of the modern dental filling, by mixing ground Danube gravel with copper and lead-silver melted in mercury. (Cavity-Buster was his nickname in the camp.) But it was above all in his delicate, empathetic approach to the patient's mouth that von Breuner was a true revolutionary. The age would not have devoted so much attention to the odd rotting tooth or purulent gum. Prince Eugene, however, appreciated the intellectual significance of dentistry and clung to the Count with unrestrained affection. (There was also a more personal reason for this, but modesty prevents me from going into that here. Purely to prevent misunderstanding, I should add that it had nothing to do with sexually-motivated passion – yes, strange as it may sound, there is such a thing, allegedly – but that must suffice, for it only makes the whole thing, which has never ceased to seesaw between painfulness and broad-mindedness, still more terrible, humiliating and diabolical.) The two of them won many a battle together: fillings, bridges, dentures, roof-treatments and Vipla-teeth against the Ottoman! Christ help us! It is with a heavy heart that we are forced to concede that throughout history human reason has always reached the peak of its achievements in times of war, the degree of organization realized at such times far outstripping that of peacetime (*such* was the direction of human talent!). And wasn't linear programming, which may be seen as the cradle of computer science, created to satisfy the demands, desires and hobbies of the American military machine? Of course it was.

The manner in which von Breuner really stamped himself into the memory of all cultivated men, however, was through his curious, if insignificant, role in the development of Baroque mathematics. If Fermat was the prince of amateur math-ematicians, von Breuner was the nameless, provincial relative for whom they always lay a place at the banquet table. Riding the waves of the late Baroque, the Count arrived on the shores of his own narrow field. Von Breuner's contribution is so dis-armingly, so sympathetically and – most crucially of all – so *infinitesimally* small that this in itself constitutes a serious, positive statement about the structure of creation, a glorious silence about its magnificence, and this at the beginning of the eighteenth century – in other words: at the last possible moment.

Von Breuner had a confidential relationship with the Bernoul-lis. The whole family were zealous refiners of the Leibniz 'cal-culus'. One could have filled the Danube with Bernoullis, although I don't say it would be appropriate to do so, for even if it is true that the Danube is the alpha and omega of all things, the following question – which one would have to ask at Tulcea at the very latest – would still remain: what are the alpha and the omega? Von Breuner was particularly friendly with Jakob (Jakob I) and was devastated by the latter's death in 1705, above all because they were still on bad terms at the time. This is what happened. The younger Bernoulli, Johann, set his brother Jakob the task of determining the curve along which a body starting out from point A arrives most rapidly at the lower point B according to the forces of gravity. (More than two hundred years later, the prolific and delightful Simenon offered one of the wittiest applications of this in his whodunnit, *The Carpet of Khorasson*, where the question is whether a wife-murderer (that is, a husband) could etc., etc., within seventeen seconds. Inspector Maigret argued that the shortest path between two points was a straight line, forgetting that the idea was to find the shortest length of time. Brilliantly recognizing his mistake, he caught the murderer, who, apart from this one flaw, was a genuinely likeable, melancholic fellow.) Jakob – correctly – submitted the cycloid equation. From this curve it further became clear that at whatever point a falling body began, it would always reach the lowest point in exactly the same time, in other words the cycloid was also a tautochron. – Just think of Jesus and his parable about the vineyard workers. That is, as if the workers were sliding down a cycloid into the vines and were paid by the hour: *that's why* they all got the same. There was a time when this would have counted as proof of the existence of God . . .

Working on the principle of an eye for an eye, Jakob set his brother the central problem of isoperimetrics, that is: among geometric figures sharing the same circumference, which contain the greater area? This was later applied to the drawing up of borders during the French peace treaties at the end of the First World War, albeit in jest (Oh, French wit!), with reference to the barbed wire. And it was then too that Vyx first used the expression 'Iron Curtain' (*rideau de fer*) – an expression that met with great success – not realizing that he was speaking about the future. Only Count Apponyi remained silent, in four languages and with impeccable pronunciation. The nation's self-respect and confidence were injured, that was the real problem, not the monstrously enormous loss of territory. Count Czernin was in charge of common foreign policy. Queen Zita's sister acted as an intermediary between him and Clemenceau. We all remember the headline inspired by the latter: 'Count Czernin lied!' – Well it wasn't true !!!

Anyway, Johann came up with the wrong answer – decisions made in the vicinity of Versailles have been keeping the ruinous fires of nationalism alive ever since – for which Jakob criticized him publicly. This led to a fierce and highly unbrotherly debate in which von Breuner took the part of the younger Bernoulli, a mistake which sowed the seeds of dissent between him and his friend Jakob.

They went on meeting ... only somehow it just wasn't the same any more. They continued to respect and admire each other, but their embraces were somehow less passionate. That is to say, they respected each other's virtues, but were annoyed by each other's vices. And thus a good friendship withered away in Basel, at about the same time as Imre Thököly's uprising, and all because of a stupid maths problem ...

At any rate, among plane curves Jakob was especially attracted to the logarithmic spiral ($r = ae^{k\Phi}$), so much so that he had one such curve put on his gravestone with the epitaph: *eadem mutat resurgo*, albeit changed, yet I shall rise again, this being an allusion to the notion that all the new curves derived from the curve in question were also in part logarithmic spirals.

Von Breuner's horrible death does not seem to confirm this. It was the victoriously advancing Pálffy hussars who stumbled across his corpse, or rather, across those ghastly *remains*. The Count was tied to the trunk of an ancient tree that stood beside a small church not far from the hills of Pétervárad. They hobbled his neck and legs and drubbed him for a full five minutes before he died. Meanwhile Damad Ali stood before his magnificent tent – at which we have already marvelled – and looked on in satisfaction, with no idea that he too would end in a similar fashion. In fact this wasn't really how von Breuner met his still more horrible end. He didn't die from the beatings he took, but as the much later postmortem unequivocally revealed (*early discoloration of the skin, signs of suffocation*) – from the bites of a rare species of wild ant, which simply ate their way through the many-sided Count, the favourite of Prince Eugene of Savoy, the friend of a Bernoulli ... What a Danube bank!

Whichever way you look at it, Europe created a new mathematics.

Now, as regards the Peace of Karlowitz, January 1699, the only real losers were the – none the less gifted and heroic – Hungarian people, who fell out of the Turkish frying pan and into the Austrian fire ... And as for the grandiose dreams of Rákoczi (1676–1735), the less said the better ... The Sun King left us in the shit.

Today the boutiques of Budapest are selling little self-adhesive Hungarys. They would always have been popular. Stick, Hungarian ...

23

The continuation of the continuation of the continuation of the truth (travel diary)

From time to time a vague smell of onions wafts into the compartment. I look outside : Szolnok.

People chattering. Making my silence somehow disturbing. Perhaps I should speak.

'You say, young man, that you're heading east ? East and only east ? But where do you end up if you keep on going ? Well ? Well ? That's right, in the West ! In the westernmost West. Remarkable, isn't it, that the world is round ? Know what I mean ? The hope. That there's no such thing as easternmost !'

A pig stands in a field, its head held high. A proud pig, look.

I'm trying to read. Jonathan Harker (Bram Stoker: *Selected Atrocities of Count Dracula*) confirms my suspicion that we are now entering the East. I check the upper canines of my fellow-travellers. The male party of a married couple well-intentionedly suggests that I'd be better off addressing strangers in German rather than in Hungarian. 'Could be dicey.' But in Old Rumania, or in the region of the Danube Delta, I can, by all means, speak Hungarian. There it signifies nothing. Nothing. He wasn't trying to alarm me, only being helpful. 'Not a good idea.'

They tell me about their experiences in Budapest. The way they talk is the way we talked about Vienna in the seventies. The woman shakes her head, she can't understand how anyone could want more than Sunbeam, the department store, had to offer. 'To want more, it simply isn't normal.'

Later they drop off to sleep. Presumably they all have the same dream, for their hands fall into their laps at the same moment.

At Biharpüspöki I step out into the corridor. The station building stands in almost complete darkness, illuminated by a single, pale yellow light, a mood-lamp from the saloon. I look down at the track where the light from our window falls. Rubbish, bottles, paper, a drying turd-sausage. And then, on a sleeper, two objects, two perfect, natural forms, like in a photograph for *Vogue*: an egg leaning against a small Chanel bottle (eau de toilette, Egoïste, for men).

Bizarre still-life. The nocturnal station of Kolozsvár (Cluj, Klausenburg) is crawling with people. It conflicts so strongly with my mental picture that it almost corresponds to it again. The same state of fright. As if in a time of war. Everything is like the film *Brasil, Brasil* or the old, black-and-white Orwell *1984*. Behind the ruined façade a developed, hidden function. Developed, thus unknown. At first glance even the waiting-room seems immense, but shrinks the more I begin to find my way around.

All kinds of people. A man in an impeccable straw hat, as if straight from the beach. Thin as a reed, trembling from head to toe, reeking of sour alcohol. A girl in a mini-skirt. (Good.) A boy in the same. Pimps. A young girl, no more than a child, measures me with her eyes, and at once looks ten years older. (Or is she merely looking *back* at me?) Hawkers, lottery tickets, coffee, sandwiches. Wouldn't eat one if they paid me. Chatwin comes to my mind. Bruce Chatwin, who died from eating Chinese eggs. A great traveller. The vendors are ugly old she-devils, their lives have passed them by, they never sleep. It's two o'clock in the morning.

Bit by bit I find my way in the commotion: exit, information, W C. This way my fear diminishes. I'm like a finicky Westerner. I stop to ask myself: is there any feeling inside me other than *let's get the hell out of here*? No. Like Ulrich I'm not frightened, but everything is frightening here. Inspires fear.

From time to time the loudspeaker blares out. Then turmoil, people rushing in all directions. One corner empties, then fills again. Everything seems so fortuitous. Will I notice when the Kocsárd train – my train – arrives?

There are gypsies, one blonde, the classic 'eastern' type, in an inner-city denim suit. Counting money, changing money. In the embrasure of an alleyway a couple. *Hard porn.* As the witchlike cleaning woman passes, she lunges at them with her broomstick. They step out in silence and re-adjust their clothes, skirt down, zip up. Then they stroll back. I look into their faces and see nothing.

Wandering on the platform I peer into another waiting room. Bodies strewn over benches, fast asleep. Like the dead. Nothing moves. Pompeii. I watch them for some minutes. Nothing.

A black princess in a dark compartment. She's there whenever I open my eyes. Looking at me. Sometimes I dream the same. Night passes. As she gets off the train I can see them checking her papers in the distance. I can hear her laughing hoarsely. The policeman too.

★

I am in the home of Andris Tüske's brother, György, on the bank of the Maros. A quiet, severe house at the end of the world – with a natural, self-evident claim to wholeness. I look at the Maros and pretend it's the Danube. Costs nothing. György tells me that the electricity supply was cut off in December. Which meant they were without water too (electric pump). Even the nappies had to be washed in the Maros. 'The Maros devours its own banks.' They had to climb down a steep and shaky ladder. He shows me the spot. 'The river's changed beds. It used to lie over there.' The water is incredibly filthy. I dip my hand in. When I take it out again I can see the watermark. The river is heated by the nearby power station, pampering (spoiling!) the fish. 'Fisherman and hunter return empty-handed.'

The Outlines of a more severe view of life. – Yesterday I, the eternal papist, sat through two Calvinist services. A bit much. Mother Mary, help me, I whispered to Andras as we entered the second church. Ecumenical snigger.

'I kept quiet', says his grandmother the following morning. In the evenings they sing psalms together, the brothers and their wives, young women, young men. I share their silences. The thought I have now, I have had for ages: how good to be able to sing, to really want to. A memory from my altarboy days. To show willing, I sang a descant to the National Anthem. The priest thought I was simply out of tune. 'Superfluous, my child. We are plenty as it is.'

According to grandmother, cholera spreads through the air. (Hence the proverb: see a priest and die – he's probably just buried a choleric ...) For this reason we don't set off for the Danube. To be precise, we both do and don't set off. Time means something different here. Perhaps that's why I accidentally stepped on my watch this morning, the springs scrunching under my foot like a may-beetle. I sleep in the middle room. Now and then someone appears, as in a Mándy novel, and makes a discreet gesture, nods, shuts his eyes, or sighs, then disappears again. Here all is quiet and delicate. Unlike the roughness of the grim and distant mountains, the roughness of the muddy courtyard, the river, the village, the dark, cold night. (Approaching from Kocsárd station: a car sliding through the lifeless darkness, man-oeuvring between ditches and potholes, constantly braking as it winds its way past shabby houses and derelict factory walls. As if nothing were alive here, nothing but us.

At the crack of dawn, the children (3 + 2) come and trample all over me. Still half asleep, they establish that I am some sort of fish defying closer identification, which they, in accordance with our common hopes, will fish out from the Maros. (Undine-beginnings.) Yesterday I heard one of them praying (a tough little nut): 'Now, Lord, for the last time, *please make me good.*' The whole house is permeated by the presence of God – or rather, by allusions to His presence, which is not the same thing. I find all this at once disarming and thoroughly exasperating.

I leaf through a book (a Bible commentary of some sort) and find a sentence by Oscar Wilde: I can resist anything, but temptation. – Indeed, sir, indeed.

The flies crawl into my hair. As if they're building a nest.

Excursion to the Torda gorge. Again the *exasperating* beauty of nature, mountain brook, sky-high rocks plus ancient Hungarian legend. ('We are now standing at the mouth of the gorge. Words are powerless to describe the scene. As if a storm had rolled a thousand Egyptian pyramids into one; as if a host of burnt-out towers and churches stood before us; as if, under a narrow ribbon of sky, a mass of ruined temples and columns, burnt brown, red and white, towered up before our eyes. All is still. Only the gurgle of the brook disturbs the silence. The heart trembles at the sight of this almighty devastation.') I did, however, become familiar with the *mici*, the correct pronunciation of which is, I believe, 'mitch', but which I continue to pronounce 'mitzi' all the same – this is a region rich in *mici*, which are roasted far and wide, either on a grill or over an open fire, spicy minced meat, delicious. But no beer or wine. Only an improbably sticky, yellow soft drink, best described by the name horse-spittle. A dead fly in the neck of the bottle over which the liquid unavoidably gurgles. The Danube at the Iron Gate? Not *my* exaggeration. Horse-spittle in Romanian is : *suc.*

Scene: Fishermen on both sides of the Maros. Some have camped the night there in their tents. I fancy I can see their stubble. They call out to one another in Romanian. A kind of 'manly banter'. 'Wooden-hands!' 'Whale-hunter!' Then an argument begins. One gets undressed and prepares to swim over to the other side to demand satisfaction. By the time he reaches the other bank a young man has arrived, 'someone who commands respect'. As soon as the swimmer sees him, he backs down and, with excessive humility, begs forgiveness. 'I beg you. On my hands and knees I beg you to forgive me.' They throw stones at him as he withdraws. My hosts visibly enjoy my bafflement at this, for I simply can't understand how this passionate belligerence has turned so quickly into an equally passionate retreat. Hungarians, Romanians, the Maros.

Both Andris and György have offices, one facing the Szamos, the other facing the Maros. I could already do with an office myself (together with a wallet, the title of doctor, a nurse and a secretary – especially the latter, who'd handle my correspondence, do the typing and some of the smaller journeys; she could hire horses, get hold of carbon paper, do the vacuuming, secure new contracts, translate, and ask for loans from the bank; she wouldn't want an affair with me, but would rest a cool palm on my tormented, burning brow; she'd smoke cigars and be only a little bit cleverer than me and, discreetly, without so much as saying a word, she'd finish my novels about the Danube). My office would face – what else? – the Danube: a virtual, imaginary, ideal K-und-K, Habsburg, Central European, East European, postmodern, realist, okay, if you insist, *narcissistic* office. In us the experience of three rivers meets.

Let's go then. If there are too many problems, we can always turn back. I picture us cunningly avoiding quarantine. Gone without trace. – We see someone in a wooden hut in a bare beech grove, like an incredibly boring (and undubbed) scene from a low-budget Russian movie. An old fisherman in the process of dying a torturous death, suddenly springs up and rushes out of the hut, splashing through deep puddles, screaming, slapping and chopping the water as he approaches ... 'Listen, Andris, let's get out of here. I'll invent the Danube Delta for myself, just like I always do.'

In Vásárhely we run into their parents by chance. A small, bright thing, the mother. For a minute or two I can shamelessly indulge my mother-hunger. As if she notices this. Notices everything. Which is about as annoying as if she really were my mother. I introduce myself. She has heard my name, she says. A good name. But what about my heart? Is it good too? That's the question, I say with a cheerful grin. To this she replies, both teasingly and with severity: 'I don't like to meet people in the street. It's so much better at home, where I can take a good look at you and decide whether or not you need a good scolding.' 'I'm an eminently scoldable sort,' I reply proudly.

I had already heard much about their father. I listened with envy as they sang his praises. When he was released from prison, he'd spent all the money they'd saved over the years on a gramophone. Not on bread, or milk, but on a gramophone. And he put on Mozart's G Minor Symphony. 'Mozart to give us love of life, and the G Minor so as not to spare us anything.' My own fatherhood comes to mind. I'll never put on records for my children, and they'll never tell such stories of me. Whenever I think of the Tüskes' father, I can't help feeling that my own paltriness is a great mistake. No, not a mistake, but something which will have 'dire' consequences. The name of this something is tragedy.

We tell them where we're headed. Then mention the business of the cholera. At this the father extends his hand: 'Good luck, my boys.' As if I too were one of his sons. 'May the best man win.' The mother embraces us. 'You're mad, the lot of you. There's no point. Go on, then. Go.'

THE CHILD OF STATE SOCIALISM

The child of state socialism – which is what I am – took himself off one day to a neighbouring country, which shall for now remain unnamed. It was, at any rate, a country which had also just won its – so to speak – freedom. A country in which, to its eternal glory, the sun rises earlier than it does here.

Our man arrived in the tiniest of villages in the mountains, where he was met by two young men who would assist him in his travels. But it's not about them that I want to speak now, nor about their quiet home at the end of the world, nor about the energetic children who are left to play in the yard alone as there are no longer any other Hungarian (or Hungarian-speaking) children of their age in the village, nor about the delicate women-folk who float around the quiet house, nor even about that unexpected wholeness (wholeness is always unexpected) which our man experienced there during his two-day stay, as he saw with pleasure – because he was allowed to see – how, even under conditions so very different from his own, one could none the less strive towards the same ends. It is about something much less worthy and much more modest, yet at the same time equally instructive, that I shall speak.

This child of state socialism thought a great deal about himself – or rather, not so much a great deal, as many different things – but never in his dreams would he have imagined that he was a child of state socialism. Not that he thought himself free ; he was far too cautious for that. But – we are bound finally to admit – he did think that he had not been corrupted by the system (the system which no longer exists). Everything had its price, and this he had duly paid. And that, he thought, was that. He was very pleased when the whole thing fell to pieces, seeing it as a kind of liberation. A liberation of energy, above all, for he no longer had to be perpetually on the alert. Or at least no more than was natural.

The first thing he noticed in the foreign country was the lack of beer. Then the lack of wine. Then the lack of mineral water. Which, after three days, was no laughing matter. Without anything to drink, we don't feel like eating. Our lips start sticking together, and so on. After this, he suddenly noticed the poverty, which occurred to him, rather like an afterthought. The worn-ness, the shabbiness, the dust, the horrific and manifestly superfluous monstrosities of factories, the destruction of nature, the barrages for which the valleys had to be specially made, the senseless canals to which the water had to be brought by the glass, and poverty, *bitter* poverty, the like of which he'd never seen at home.

This confirmed the traveller in his suspicion that the self-image of his own country, as one treated cruelly by fate, was utterly mistaken, false, and no more than a form of self-pity. Offendedness and lamentation as Hungarian national charac-teristics. The endless whining. The terrible Turks, the awful Austrians, the trickery of Trianon, the indifference of the English, and to cap it all: the Russians. Oh, outrageous for-tune. But wasn't this really just an average European destiny? Now and again countries disappeared from the map, were shunted around like furniture and, sooner or later, along came the Russians. We have no special cause to feel sorry for ourselves.

But let's finally get to the point. The three men arrive at a hotel one evening, looking for a room for the night. It's dark, they're tired, and the choice is limited. The child of state social-ism has travelled relatively widely and, although hardly a man of the world, knows how to get by with the likes of porters and waiters. The hotel foyer was a cross between a Communist Party Headquarters and a railway station. Yet this did not in itself arouse our man's suspicion. But then the porter and the two young men entered into a series of peculiar negotiations. When-ever he interrupted with a question of his own, they gave him a dismissive wave of the hand, as if he were an interfering child. Suddenly his fear began to swell inside him. He could see that the porter was master here, master of time and space, and nothing could happen without his consent, unless some unfathomable intrigue were to bring change.

That was the first night. From then on he never gave the waiters orders, only requests. If they cheated him, he paid and said nothing. He was aware that he was in a strange land with strange laws, and was happy simply to be alive. Nothing dramatic happened, only that he began to speak more softly, grew more attentive, pricking up his ears, night and day, like an animal. And it was now that his defencelessness and subservience, his anxieties and inhibitions really made themselves felt, as qualities which he, the child of state socialism, had inherited from the system after all.

Then he went back home again, where he lived happily ever after.

HIRELING MAKES STEADY PROGRESS : FORWARDS

From the direction of Nándorfehérvár (Belgrade) he was pursued by the tolling of bells. This ringing of bells had once been ordered by Gyula II, even before Hunyadi's important battle, and, according to Aar, as a form of plea and pledge, and not, as popular belief has it, in commemoration of the (rare) victory. And anyone who has ever heard the bellowing of mechanical bells that sound on Hungarian Radio each day at noon may well have suspected that some kind of national compensation was involved.

We were in the land of Danilo Kiš.

One miserable autumn day, the Hireling received a telephone call from Paris. A hoarse voice laughed through the receiver:

'Listen here, you stupid Hungarian ...' The Hireling was very fond of the owner of this voice, whom many people said was a Serb, even though his mother was Crna Gorac and his father a Hungarian Jew. He himself was the only genuine Yugoslavian, the culmination of the absurd idea that is Yugoslavia, living proof of its existence, and also of the notion that the various peoples of Yugoslavia were capable not only of killing one another, but of enriching one another too. *Danilo Kiš was that richness.* He had the most beautiful adam's apple in the world, a real French adam's apple. And, at least in the Hireling's eyes, this East-Central-Hybrid-European was the incarnation of Frenchness as such: intelligence, eroticism, wit, rigour, manly dignity and manly self-irony, clownish, moral authority and – if you'll excuse the word – lightness. Weight and weightlessness, that was Danilo Kiš; death and immortality in one person.

They first met as follows. There was once a very distinguished conference, so illustrious indeed that when the Hireling stepped out of the splendidly gilded lift and looked around the reception hall, he saw to his amazement that all present were either Nobel Prize-winners or millionaires. Essentially, this is how he was able to identify himself, negatively. He looked into a Baroque mirror, and seeing that the person who stood before him was neither the one nor the other, he nodded: aha, that must be me. He stood at the edge of it all, watching the hustle and bustle, the champagne glasses, the dinner jackets, the earrings, American movie, ballroom, music: Tchaikovsky. He didn't recognize anyone, except perhaps from photographs.

Then a black whirlwind rose up on the other side of the hall, and a gangling apparition thundered through the crowd in a checked sports jacket. The hurricane appeared to flatten all who stood in his path, and yet in such a way as to pick them all up again with a graceful kiss of the hand ... no, not with a kiss of the hand, but with something more southern, less refined, grabbing the women by the arse, the men by the shirtfront, but with all the lightness, the heavy charm of a kiss of the hand. And there before the Hireling stood his elder brother (for the Hireling was a man deprived of elder brothers, who liked to familiarize his relationships, longing for sisters and mothers, inventing fathers and brothers, etc., etc., it was as easy as a sack-race). The stranger cried out, like the hero of an Ottlik novel, embracing, caressing and examining the Hireling: 'You! What! Well! So! Hungarian!' And at that moment everyone, the whole glittering gathering, knew who the Hireling was: the Hireling was the one of whom the hoarse fellow was, so to speak, fond.

'Listen you stupid Hungarian,' said the voice from Paris ('I'm hoarse, I got drunk in Dubrovnik'), explaining that there were apparently some kind of drops one could get in Hungary, and it would be good if the Hireling could send him some, but he shouldn't go to any trouble, it was mainly for the women's sake that he was asking, you know, to reassure them, well that was all, 'bye, you old fathead. The voice spoke polished Hungarian, not without an accent, but with a certain inner flexibility and invention. The Hireling was quite a good listener, and already at the conference the two of them went about together arm in arm, like a couple of girls, and the Hireling would listen to the man, excited and moved, as he spoke of 'internal', professional matters, of how he hadn't written anything for two years, and how valueless he now found his own values to be, and how he had grown bored of precisely the qualities for which he was praised, and then, at great length he'd speak about 'life', which was different from literature, and would end up saying: 'I'm only interested in form. Do you understand, in form?! You stupid Hungarian, can you grasp this?' Of course I can, you bloodsucking Serbian nationalist.

Just then you couldn't get those medicinal drops anywhere. The Hireling tried everything, he even went to see a film director who was making a film called *The Socialist Calvary of the Medicinal Drop*, about the trials and tribulations of its inventor. The director promised to help (and did help, too). And he went to see everyone he could possibly think of, phoning friends, organizations, chemists and sworn enemies, and then he went over to see a neighbour, then to a nearby school, after which he went home and slept like a corpse. Then suddenly the floodgates broke open and all kinds of strangers called, men, women, old and young: good morning, we've brought this for that Danilo you told us about, one after the other, with little half-filled bottles, leftovers, all of which they held up to the light and shook to show the Hireling that they were not empty. Coloured bottles, vials, mustard jars, beer bottles, in the name of the entire teaching staff, the football team, the church, for poor Daniel Kiss, as they put it, who is so very ill. They spoke as if they knew him well and loved him, as if each and every one of them had shaken his large, bony hand, had heard him laugh, and knew that baleful glint in his eye, that I had never seen in any other, as if, *horribile dictu*, they had read his books.

The last time they spoke on the phone, at the beginning of October, Danilo Kiš had said he couldn't understand the instructions that the Hireling had enclosed with the drops, and suspected, of course, that composition was not the Hireling's *forte* – he had already seen certain tell-tale *signs* of this ... He went on talking, frivolously, without shuddering at the thought of his own death, for what else were they talking about but whether, on the road to death, the ratio of drops to tea should be three to one, or one to three. But by then his voice had become so hoarse, so curdled, that it no longer seemed to come from Danilo's throat, and should no longer be heard as that of a worldly being.

The Hireling has a shelf (Ikea) where he keeps the leftover bottles, the drops, and he only has to glance at them to hear again all the voices of that enchanted afternoon, the voice of the tipsy cantor, the roadsweeper: good morning, here are the drops for Danilo, to help him get better, you'll see, he'll soon be well again, and everything will be fine.

Just imagine you have no other choice. Contractor (Hirer)

Please reply. Text of last telegram : Just imagine you have no other choice. Contractor (Hirer)

REPLY

I'm imagining. Sincerely, Hireling

We weren't really making steady progress at all. Our progress was most unsteady. Time split open like the rind of a melon, or rather like the Torda gorge, and Dalma burst in through the fissure. In vain had we sailed together for several days, talking, lounging about, nibbling, doing nothing, as was right and proper at such times ; we none the less remained under in the grip of the past. We called this past Roberto. His cabin always remained locked. But I couldn't help notice that Dalma stole in to see him at night. I wasn't jealous, simply a fool. And it would be a mistake to confuse foolishness with innocence.

Slowly, calm and dignified, the ship drifted through the starry summer night. Its ribs, its boards, its cabins, and all its iron, copper and oakum parts, indeed its whole body, shuddered continually, gently, almost imperceptibly. As if it wasn't the ship's shuddering we felt at all, but something inside us, the vibrating of our cells, or simply our thoughts, our desires, our memories, a living, eternal flickering, locked inside the safe, heavy hull of restlessness.

'My dear boy, I don't love you any more.'

'Why not ?' I asked blithely.

'Don't be so vulgar,' said Dalma, waxing serious. 'You know only too well. Because you don't want me.' She held onto the

222

handrail, gasping for breath. She stared at the dark water. 'Why aren't you honest with me? Tell me what you want. Is it me? Say something. Answer my question. Do you want me? ... Okay, I know the answer ... But what *do* you want? The Danube? Is that it, you want the Danube? Are you still hoping that the Danube is something more? What more? More than what?'

She began tugging at me. 'Is that what you want? To see him? Because you can, you know. You just have to spy on him. That's what you like doing anyway. You don't look at things, you just spy. You don't even have eyes ... You think you can go on doing that forever? How? Just spying into people's lives? That you just have to spy on me and see the streaks of blood on my hand? Or my legs? Or my calves? And for what are you spying on your uncle? For what? For whom? This spying of yours concerns you too, you know. And where is it all going to end? That you go on spying from the grave? Very poetic, I'm sure.'

She ran off in tears. 'What are you running away for?' She stopped a little further down. I can't stand her now. I look at her face, at that remote, yellow stain. To hit her as hard as I can. Yes. With my fist. Or to strangle her. She comes back, laughing between her tears, her face like a beautiful misty dawn.

'You wouldn't recognize your uncle. He's swollen up like a balloon.' Then, after a short pause: 'His body is revolting.' That couldn't be true. I could see his hat before me, and his manicured, sweetly fragrant hands. I could see the two of us standing by an iron fence at night. He reaches out towards me and I kiss his hand. 'Revolting. Rolls of flab dangle from his torso, like pieces of dead meat. He's buried in his own fat.' I once saw a girl in Amsterdam, buried in her own fat. She sat in a window by the Danube, and it was clear from her smile that she was waiting for me. Oh God.

'And what ...?' I couldn't bring myself to say it.

'What do you mean, what?!' the woman snapped back at me.

'What are we meant to do?'

We were both shouting.

'He thinks he is the Danube ... Look me in the eye!' she screamed. 'Who am I? What's my name? Not some false name, poetic name, code name, but my real name?!'

'Yes,' I mumbled, as if I had understood something. So Roberto is the Danube. That's his game. He imagines that he is the Danube, concretely, that this bit is Passau, that bit Eschingen, and every night he takes her wrist and leads her hand over his body. I see this hand, I spy on it, holding my breath, spying ... 'Now, tell me, what's this?' 'Szendrő Castle, perhaps?' 'No, my dear, that's my prick.' There is a bandage on that wrist, blood-soaked gauze, she sees that I see. An old hand, a tortured hand, a woman's hand, a traitor's hand, a gentle hand, a Jewish hand, a mother's hand, Mamma, the hand of centuries, the hand of delight, the hand of pain, the hand of memory, the hand of speechlessness, of silence, of self-sacrifice, of defencelessness, of selfishness, of humiliation, of defeat, of death, flying the whole length of the Danube, a male Danube, a body-Danube,

– up and away, above Molova Island, above the woollen pleats of the brow, which were once known as giant banks of shifting sand; farther back the Castle of Galambóc, perhaps the most shapely fortress of the southern Danube, sitting on the domelike hilltop, as deliberate and well-composed as a medieval coronet on the head of a handsome young earl. The exquisite youth was, in fact, Lady Mary Wortley Montagu's great-uncle. 'The Serbs allegedly,' and here the Lady casts a glance at me (it's not a very pleasant experience, glimpsing a whole empire in a pair of woman's eyes: English women have to live with this handicap), 'the Serbs, obviously according to the Slovenes, even speak Serbian with an accent.' In our embarrassment – which was the embarrassment of a whole civilization, the embarrassment of a Europe in the process of losing itself, just think of the general insanity that followed Yalta, and one is bound to ask whether the reserved West wasn't the more insane in failing to notice this, or the destitute East which noticed it to be sure, but immediately blamed it on the oppressor – in our embarrassment we suddenly burst out laughing. In this region there are many of those bloodsucking flies which, in the last century, wiped out whole herds of cattle and studs: Golubac flies, named after Galambóc (Golubac). And here too is the infamous Babakai Rock, its spearing head rising out from the whirlpools like some evil ice-age monster. This is the spot where Cicelle Rozgonyi leaped out of the fire – see István Kormos's poem 'Dame Rozgonyi' – and, her courage putting men to shame, saved the life of our bibulous King Zsigmond. At the same spot – which cannot be seen from the bank, and is only known to the initiated – there is a first-rate restaurant, the Chez-Babakai. This year the creations of the experienced Juszuf and his team were awarded seventeen points by the strict Gault-Millau. (A real secret favourite.) The nearby river Pek is rich in gold. According to popular legend, it was here that the Dessewffy family made their fortune, after a nugget the size of a fist hit Countess Tina on the thigh while she was paddling. She collapsed with a loud scream. Later she worked as a chorus girl between Los Angeles and Mexico City. She became famous for living strictly according to the European clock (her body too). Which is how it must have come about that, one hot afternoon beside the highway, the passersby could see a waltzing figure with a champagne glass in her hand. Inside the Countess's head it was midnight, New Year's Eve;

– approaching the Iron Gate, the hand hides behind the ear and the question inevitably arises: what would have happened had the Danube been forced at this point to turn back? Let's imagine the Danube shamefacedly winding its way back upstream, back into all the tributaries too – oh, I beg your pardon, where then would be that glorious Central European river which, in spite of bearing a sea of pain on its back, was still a *somebody*, only an utter Niemand would swing back at Esztergom, excuse me, I beg your pardon, – but we really can ask ourselves: which way has the Danube been flowing these past forty years . . . ;

– it was near the Iron Gate on 24 June 1830, that Count Széchenyi recognized the importance of regulating the Lower Danube. Then, after a modest lunch, he sailed the whole Danube on the wooden ship *Desdemona*. At Drenkova at the latest – where one can hear a loud humming and murmuring, and the base of a mountain that bows out of the bank, the Bosman, stretches across the riverbed, and where the water foams and bubbles as if it were being boiled in a cauldron, cutting about one hundred and twenty feet into the rock, where the two monsters, the rocks Kozla and Dojka, argue with each other incessantly as they drive the water onwards – and if not at Drenkova, then at the dreaded Gereben, which in Serb means crag, and in any other language means terror itself, and if we come from below towards Izmail, with a barge full of iron, or something more lasting than iron, and the whole hull begins to tremble at this point, this ugly stain on the neck, we are bound to ask the habitual question, which even the great Széchenyi was unable to answer: Have you prayed tonight, Desdemona?

– the woman's hand is flying, who knows where it will stop (it disappears into the swamp on an armpit). When the coffer-dam was being built, the beautiful Ada Kaleh Island ended up under water. The beheading of Agas, a customs-free zone as a hotbed of smuggling, winding Turkish alleyways, hairy nipples, on the other hand, at the Berlin Congress of 1878 they forgot to decide who actually owned the Island, Gyula Andrássy urged the Russians to withdraw and unfortunately won international approval for the occupation of Bosnia and Hercegovina, '*le beau pendu*' they called him good-humouredly, alluding to the fact that the Emperor – whom he now served as foreign minister – had, during the revolution of 1848–49, condemned him in effigy to the gallows. Count Gyula, who invented *fin-de-siècle* Budapest single-handed, often strolled down the corridors of Berlin arm in arm with the Russian foreign minister, Gorchakov (who, because of his protruding incisors, was less than popular, and was called by many, somewhat scornfully, 'the Wolf'; his life took a tragic turn in the first years of the century, when he lost his wife and children in the great Volga flood; even Lenin speaks of 'the poor Gorchakov', see *Letters to Tatyana Samolova*, Szikra, Budapest, 1951) and when – not without an ulterior motive – they asked the Hungarian statesman if he was really on such friendly terms with the Russian, he replied with a fine, masculine smile : If someone wants to push you into the abyss, it's as well to take him by the arm ;

– as we approached the massive sluice system, the commander of the sluice tower called out a greeting and the gigantic sluice gate at once began to close. We positioned ourselves behind the Soviet battleship 'as all good children should' . . . but at this the Soviet sailors – who, because of their uniformly cropped hair looked remarkably like the poet Mayakovsky, who was known to test the loyalty of his closest friend with his hysterical outbursts and was now approaching the end of his career – hurried to the bulwarks and with much shouting and waving (for this is what Soviet people are like, the homo sovieticus : in times of misery the true friend, in times of gaiety . . . there are no times of gaiety) started scattering their delightful sailors' gifts : souvenirs, photos, the odd romantic Kalashnikov, a T45 out of whose barrel a coconut rolled like a missile, filled with splendid Romanian *tuica* (plum brandy), desire and hatred in their fingers, then, once again, nothing. The sluicing commenced. As they let out the water, a wet and dirty eight-storey wall towered up before us. It felt like being in a mine shaft, the sluice gates slowly pulling apart and the sun warming the crypt-like air. What happened next, however, I wouldn't wish on my worst enemy. The massive diesel-powered propeller of the Soviet ship suddenly began to turn, churning up the water in the tight sluice chamber so violently that we went under. As the Soviet ship sailed off into the distance its captain, Mayakovsky, politely waved back at us, full of regret : before the laws of hydrodynamics even he was powerless, comrades, don't shoot ! And that is the authentic story of Mayakovsky's suicide ;

– the hand disguises its boredom through movement, crawling here, popping up there, sliding all the way out of the Carpathian Basin, that unrequested place of refuge and protection, and the Danube ambles along its bankless bed as smoothly, and calmly as the Tisza. The hand was left cold by the water-meadows on the left bank (build on a hill and the dog – i.e. the Danube – won't bite you, runs the Romanian proverb, itself building an untranslatable pun on 'hill'), and it was left equally cold by the even plain on the right, which evidenced the continuous development of Bulgarian agricultural irrigation. It hardly even touched Vidin, even though that town honours Lajos Kossuth with a commemorative plaque;

– in the same way that Svevo is the Joyce of Trieste, and Broch the Austrian Joyce, Hristo Botev is the Bulgarian Petőfi. On the occasion of the 1876 uprising, he threw himself into the crowd at Kozloduj, only to be struck at once on the brow by a stray Turkish bullet. A *stray* – of all things! The accounts (of Driault, Aar) tell of appalling atrocities. The irregular Turkish soldiers and Circassian groups led by the Porte set whole villages ablaze like night-lights. They violated the dignity of the men and the flesh of the women and cut the children into tiny pieces. They butchered two thousand people in the church of Batak alone. Here the whole village had fled to seek God's help, but God, to put it crudely, moves in mysterious ways. The church stood ankle-deep in blood. Their example, Aar notes, was followed by the German fascists in Oradour-sur-Glane some sixty years later. My friend in Komárom told me that he really had stood ankle-deep in blood in 1956 (it seeped in over the tops of his boots), so we are talking about actual wading here, not just about some metaphor. And it sticks, and it isn't even red! At Kozloduj, on the supposed site of Botev's footprint – hand in footprint – they built a cluster of modern buildings to house the first Bulgarian atomic power station, hence the saying 'the Botev has flown', after all, atoms can't be seen, they just exist;

– the hand was caressing its way towards Ruse – all caresses

228

lead to Ruse, all bodies will be one! The serrated lace-like contours of the Carpathians shimmered in the distance, an improbable mirage. But even the hills of Orjachov didn't cause the hand to tremble, even though the Romans had already recognized the significance of this capital observation post, and all the forays of the victorious Hungarians in the thirteenth century were in vain. And in spite of it being made clear again and again that French pride had played the decisive part in the defeat at Nikopol, they remained too greedy for glory. But they simply didn't understand the Turkish way of fighting, and didn't listen to the clever Hungarians. The Kaftan put his finger into the game sauce – for centuries they used this saying to characterize Zsigmond's undistinguished military leadership, alluding both to his misfortune and to his unscrupulous concessions to the ambitions of French cuisine;

– there is something attractive about the unbridled, tumultuous boredom of the untraceable jungle of Danube backwaters on the Romanian side. The hand is neither impatient nor aimless, but its aim is unnamable, even if we decide in retrospect to call 'things' by their names (cf. the legendary boredom of Flaubert's novels). Here the islands and sandbanks are always on the move, yet there is something internally permanent about them. For their insides have been knotted together once and for all by the lush vegetation, and are referred to in the vernacular simply as the cunt, the cunt of the island. It is interesting to note in this connection the etymology of the German word 'Inselfotze', which derives from the term 'Insel-futsch', that is to say the phut of the island, or the end of the island, thus the end for the Germans is precisely that which for us is the beginning of everything, although it's true it can also be the end, for that is where one ends, if one is a man, at least according to the workings of Bulgarian–German collective reason;

– for the proud title of being the most southerly point on the Danube, Svištov and Vardim fought as furiously as Kecskemét and Kiskőrös for the legacy of Petőfi. One might imagine that the question of being the most southerly point is simply a question of fact. If there are two numbers, either one is bigger than the other, or vice versa, or they are the same. *Quantum non datur*. But not so with the Danube. It won't allow itself to be arithmeticized, and just as Wittgenstein, according to the anecdote, refused to believe Russel when he said there was no crocodile in his study (he didn't know where to begin with such a sentence), the Danube refuses to believe anything at all. That, for a short time, Russel believed the eccentric Austrian to be mad was a different matter. It was only later that he changed his mind, and then again not on logical or philosophical grounds, but because he grew to love the man. And as for the question of whether it was of *this* love, or of love in general, that Wittgenstein said on his mysterious trip to Oslo : '*Unterseeboote blieben den Frauen weiterhin versperrt, da sie nicht entsprechend umgebaut werden könnten,*' is better left to the specialists to decide. The problem wasn't only that the Danube had changed beds, but also that the two towns had themselves taken an active part in nature's work. In one town, under the cloak of night, they had widened the riverbed, while in the other town they had earthed up the stretch in question. The battle got out of hand. A woman of Vardim would rather be left on the shelf than marry a man from Svistov. But, in a region where one was either from Svistov or from Vardim, they didn't even sleep with one another, preferring to swim over to the island of Belenski to get laid. (Even the progressive-thinking Pasha Midhat got caught up in this undignified wrangling.) It was only when both towns opened their dams at the time of the great flood in 1838, and were swept away by the furious current − with their inhabitants still screaming until they drowned that they were the first, the most southerly − that they finally came to their senses. Socialist Bulgaria's solution to the problem was to award the title − and the concomitant tax

"*Unterseeboote blieben . . .*" : Submarines continued to be closed to women because they could not be appropriately reconstructed.

relief – to Novograd, considering the river Jantra as part of the Danube. After the fall of Zhivkov, however, this decision was annulled ... God only knows what will happen now;

– Ruse, the body has its own distinctive paths, and the most circuitous of routes they are too. At Silistra, 3751 kilometres downstream, we waved goodbye to Bulgaria. The balls, the prick's two hills, the dark, the Cernavodă bridge.

Is it true that you call me your little one, and say that, for you, I am the sea? They had been at Brăila: incense and the smell of sheep. Do you know what your first sentence was, the first thing you said when we met? You said, let's start saying goodbye; that's what you said, in place of a greeting. That isn't what I said. I only replied;

– where the landscape grows wilder, the traveller grows wilder too;

– it is dark, oily darknesses drifting together. The Levantine mercenary spirit holds its molecular banquet. The water here is already massive. We have to get used to the idea of calling this too the Danube. Two bodies trembling. Before Galați: 'Poseidon, the burnt-out, three-storey shipwreck, lies like the corpse of a faithful dog.' Year precedes year, year follows year, says Eminescu, whom the Romanian lyric celebrates, like the Hungarians their János Arany. The sea recognizes its dead, doesn't it? Just like the proximity of Breg and Brigach, that of the sea poses unanswerable questions. Your movements are familar, not because I know them, but because they are never alien;

– you;

– the water of the delta is brackish. The sweet river-water and the salty sea-water mix. I shall never wash you off! Dirty my skin! Soil me! If I no longer love you, I can at least expect you to satisfy me! Don't talk so much. The splashing of oars breaks the silence. Waterfowl that nest in sedge and redwoods take flight in alarm. The dangling flab buries Tulcea. I look at Dalma's hand, at the bandage. The corner of her mouth quivers. Beside herself, she seems to bite the air, as if she were suffocating.

She keeps shutting her eyes, and all the while strokes, caresses, massages her belly and lap. As if she wanted to seize what was inside. As if she were surfacing from the water. This image of her I preserve. Her body heaves ever more passionately. The horizon suddenly opens out into infinity. Now. You silver seagull, black water – – –

Slowly, calm and dignified, the ship drifted through the starry summer night. Its ribs, its boards, its cabins, and all its iron copper and oakum parts, indeed its whole body, shuddered continually, gently, almost imperceptibly.

I bent down to kiss Dalma's hand, when all of a sudden she gave me such a slap that I immediately started to bleed.

24

The truth etcetera (travel diary)

In the morning I look out of my Brassó hotel window (cat. 1A, 500 Lei) and see into the courtyard of a barracks. Farther away, like some kind of mistake, the mountain is an ill-proportioned mass which seems set to slide onto the town, or into it. Snatches of fog, sheets fluttering in the wind – the confused, slovenly labour of a lazy, giant housewife.

Yesterday the hotel receptionist, the way she doesn't greet you, just files, copies, brings forward, corrects, enters, gives receipts. This machine is socialism. And joy? That for three times the proper price she lets you have the room after all. And gratitude? That she doesn't have you arrested. (In *that* film they also said: Porterland. Porterland – that was Central Europe.)

In the morning I hear the following sentence : How much clock, beziehungsweise, de time ? From my lips.

Without a watch : It's not seven o'clock, but dawn. Once again there is such a thing as dawn, morning, lunchtime, afternoon and evening, and one is tired. I am guided by signs, the signals of my body, of my surroundings, of nature. Let's go at once. That is, not now, not in five minutes, but : when we've finished

233

our coffee. We cannot stay, we have to leave immediately. This means that we accompany our hosts to work, and on returning to the house we don't in fact heat up the lamb stew, we simply drink wine and light gin and have a few sandwiches; and then we do set off, after all, we said (in the old days I'd have put it like this: we said two hours before) that we couldn't stay, we had to leave *at once*.

This doesn't mean a slower, calmer tempo; simply a different kind of measurement, involving different considerations.

★

Hotel variations. An old, heavily made-up woman in reception. On the table before her sits a haughty young man. Beside them an open bottle of wine, no glasses, a pack of cards, and passports. No vacancies, says the woman cheerfully. From farther away, from a corridor on the first floor, women's laughter. We look at one another, Andris, György and I. We would dearly like to sleep here. On.

Cabana Fîntîniţa Haiducului, by now we'd stay anywhere, all we want is a room. It is a chilly night. This motel really is 'anywhere'. The three of us sleep on two pushed-together beds, the blanket torn and stained. In the toilet, vomit and shit (and me). As we make our way up to the room on the third floor, there is a man sitting in the corner of the corridor asleep, his head tilting back, his brow covered in sweat, snoring. His hand in his lap, a knife in his hand. The Outlaw's Well? Spring? It's something like that, the name of the motel.

Törcsvár. We tire of the tourist attractions, and sit down in the Hanul Bran tavern. We eat *mici* with *mici*, there is no mustard, but there is wine (Murfatlar). The waiter is a tough guy from Bucharest. He is friendly and superior, loud-mouthed, helpful, handsome and has bad breath. Twilight, smoke, the painful murmur of people slightly drunk. Outside, farther up, a dark mass, Dracula's castle, dead. Cold moonlight sparkles on the waiter's canines, we keep saying to one another.

The Hireling's model is András Visky, a Transylvanian curiosity of the last century. He was nicknamed András Highsky because of his high forehead. He was a genuine traveller. He knew all a traveller should know – how to get from Manchester to Ulm via Berlin, off-season ... everything, that the shallows between Dévény and Szap were never less than fifteen metres deep, that in Budapest there are thirty-two icy days per year (according to a fifteen-year average), that the Kronenburg shipyard employs three hundred workers, whereas the one in Linz employs seven hundred, and also that the area of the winter docks in Újvidék is seven hectares. 'Oh brother, you have to live precisely,' he would often say. And he could achieve, organize absolutely anything without ever being in the least bit pushy. He would just have to utter the odd 'oh brother' and the problem would be solved. Dear old András Highsky!

*

Direction Tulcea; a whole day from Brassó.

Romania: a Tarkovsky paraphrase. The factory chimneys: the phalli of Satan – as the poet puts it. Vomiting yellow, blue, scarlet and pink clouds. Something very much at work, to be sure, and very much in vain. Thermal power stations, chemical plants, oil refineries. Ploeşti still-life: in the ubiquitous dust, the functioning monstrosity in the background, a jaded, staggeringly bow-legged old woman sits on a stool beside the factory gate, staring into space, her hand in her lap, while only inches away dumper trucks the size of houses swing to and fro. If you catch so much as a glimpse of this living being, this tiny crookedness, you know for certain that behind her Nothingness reigns, this second-class twentieth century.

We pass alongside the Ialomiţa, through a sluggish, dull terrain. We ourselves have grown boring: approaching, waiting, not existing. By the roadside they are selling cheap melon and grilled fish. No thank you. We're frightened of cholera. – A whirlwind tears across the fields. 'How hard it works!' shouts Andris. As if he felt sorry for the waltzing wind. Or envied it. – At the well, a cow. We have to queue up behind it. I haven't been this close up to a cow for ages. A curious creature, with its big eyes and rough tongue. Even the flies seem to be part of it. It is hot. – A foal lies in the shade, sweet, like a little child. – Someone crams two fistfuls of stuffed cabbage into his pockets.

At Slobozia we turn down towards Feteşti, where the Tüskes had served out their deportation. Ferdinand Saligny's iron bridge is indeed impressive. (I take down the details, the inscription, but lose the slip of paper.)

For the two others this is already familiar country. They keep nudging each other: 'Do you see? That's it! That's where we waited for Mother!' they say, pointing to a park in Feteşti. It was cold, dark and smelt of fish.

The Great Danube and the Borcea arm. Here the river begins to branch out, 'a crazy tangle of arms'. The road falls away from the Danube, then back again. After passing a hill we see a wide dried-out riverbed, filled with strangely arching rowing boats, festering mud and the smell of a nearby rubbish tip. We stand on the high, steep bank, facing the catchment area forests, the wide Danube bed before us. Empty. The river has disappeared. A moderate prank. (While writing these lines, the writer ran into Claudio Magris, who happened to be in Budapest giving a lecture on how he came to devote his life to the Danube, how he turned the Danube into a repository of cosmic conscience, as Joyce had done with Mr Virág (Bloom). Or was it about something else that he spoke? That the life of the individual has no weight, no authority, no tragedy. Time passes and that is life, the triumph of physical laws; and man is nothing more than the anaemic child of these laws. At the reception that evening, the present writer slyly asked his colleague, who seemed to bear the burden of a Danube book with such ease, how it was possible to bring such a book to a close. If one has already got as far as, say, Toplau. Finding the question hardly worthy of a reply, Magris smiled and said: 'You have to pump all the water out of the Danube.' And he grinned gleefully, like a child. The present writer remained sad and silent. No one ever seemed willing to help him, and he was already well beyond the pumping stage. He thought of the picture where the three of them stood in the stench, forest and barge, swallows in the high sand wall, stench forest barge, swallows and the past, with nothingness surging beneath them. – Nota bene, there is no truth to the rumour that the present writer and the great man of Trieste came to blows in public. (And it is not to this alleged duel that Magris refers in his *Illazioni su una sciabola*. Historical deductions based on a sword.)

We are sixty kilometres from Tomi, where the disgraced Ovid remained, even in exile, a loyal son of Rome. Sword in hand he defended the walls of Tomi against the barbarian invasion.

Hood of sweat, tulle of sweat, drying on my skin again and again. I lick my hand, salt. (Am I the sea? Erased.) The brothers tell me stories, sometimes repeating themselves, about how they played, swam, skated, and once again that everything revolves around the Danube, the Danube as totality, as tyrant, as despot, as petty monarch and king, patron, mother, and commissarial officer, and that Franciscans were deported here too, twenty friendly young men, who merrily built them a new thatched roof over their heads because the other one wasn't worth 'excrementum' any more, and one day they dug them out of six feet of snow, and one of them played football for Steaua in Bucharest and people were always trying to lure him away, but he never went, even though all he had to do was sign a scrap of paper, and it was from him they heard that Puskás was playing in Spain, but the Spaniards wouldn't let him kick with his right foot because they were frightened the shot would be deadly, and they even went as far as having his right foot stamped. And they knew an unmarried mother too, with two children. Why? It was very good with those two men.

Andris notices that the stories are not about what we see, that the stories are not *drawing closer* ... If you hear that they stood the Greek Orthodox priest on the slop pail and made him deliver his sermon from there – that was a story. But if you experience the darkness of a story taking place, that sense of being at something else's mercy, of being part of the darkness yourself – then the Danube bank will suddenly grow restless. 'Believe me, young man,' said the unmarried mother to the footballing Franciscan, 'believe me, there's more to this world than sentences.' And vice versa, continued Andris, that sense of security, that everything is as it should be – he interrogates, I keep silent, he is miserable in one way, I in another. It is dark, but the fear has passed. – Never had I heard anyone speak so discreetly and modestly about their suffering.

We hurried through tiny villages. Wattle houses, half-collapsed fences, dirt tracks. Spectacular poverty, never seen before. Suddenly a beautiful villa, roof in good repair, breezy verandah, orchard, great view of the Danube. Now here one could live. (To meet Dalma here? Who dies of cholera? And the soft-headed Roberto?)

Dobrudzha, Romania's pantry.

*

It was a terrible night, heat belched from the walls and I made the mistake of opening the window. The mosquitoes of Tulcea

238

are wicked, ruthless and thoroughly persistent. I woke up every half hour bathing in sweat. As if I were wrestling with cats, miaowing, growling, howling cats: such bloodcurdling mosquitoes were these.

Last night I became acquainted with a child. Or he became acquainted with me. Or perhaps we didn't get acquainted at all, simply ... Nice kid. Snow-white shirt, dirty face. Shining black hair like an Indian; whenever he shook it, it flickered like light, black light. We were staying at the Dunărea, that's when I noticed him. When he saw me he began to smile, and could hardly take his eyes off me as he went out of the room backwards, clowning.

Then out in the street too, as if he were following me. But there was nothing awkward in all this. He was just like a little dog, playful, faithful, unpredictable, light. I walked out to the Danube with the Tövises. We were silent, weary from the long day's journey. We sat down on the corridor-like terrace on the first floor of the Delta Hotel, in the company of 'light' white wines (Călugăreni). The Danube wound its oil-black way before us, and now and then I glanced at it so as my companions shouldn't notice – and then he popped up again, with two friends, playing guitars, singing and giggling. Once again I saw him staring at me with a broad smile as they went from table to table, sometimes not even waiting to be given money before dancing off again. When they reached our table, I smoothed his shiny hair. I almost played with his earlobes. He laughed again, and it was then I noticed he was a girl. They came back several times that mild summer evening. Finally she waved at me from below, and all three of them climbed into a rowing boat and disappeared into the darkness that swam above the Danube.

I scrape the dead mosquitoes from my skin. According to the woman at reception, there is no cholera and never has been. You don't have to go drinking from the Danube. My head aches.

25

The long day

The Hireling's head ached. A malevolent hand lay on his neck, another on top of his head and a third on his face. The three hands were trying to reach one another and the Hireling was resisting. Ever since his mother had died on 14 August ten years before, 14 August had always been a long day. Neither good nor bad, just long. He himself is not sad. He doesn't think of his mother or of his own motherlessness; he simply wishes that the day would come to an end, and the day simply refuses to oblige him. My mother died ten years ago: this is the sentence I shall not say to my travelling companions all day long.

He took out his notebook, his travel notebook, where, for example, he would jot down train connections, and looked at all the things he still had to do. He liked ordinary working days. He'd have to do some thinking about the sea, the great sea, the grandiose *mar*. He'd have to potter about in Sulina, inspect the pilots, take a look at the *Danube o kilometre* Sign, and, of course, the sea. The sea is not a goal, but an enemy. Death. The sea is not infinity, but, on the contrary, finiteness itself. The Danube is infinity. How could the end of something infinite be finite? Things like this he'd say to women. As if they were men; it makes no difference. And at such times he'd giggle too. Or to put it another way, can the infinite be anything but the cemetery of the finite? Talk. This is water, even if salty, and not a river.

(*Wenn man nicht weiter kann, hört man einfach auf,* said the Danube, whose mother tongue is German, before plunging into the sea they call Black.)

He will go to the main post office in Sulina. He will stand in the queue and look at his notebook. March has already been and gone this year. It can happen that there are two Marches in a single year, so one has to keep one's eyes open. Once he dreamed that the whole Danube had frozen over and he skated all the way down. All the judges gave him a perfect six, and the East Germans protested in vain. There was still such a thing as East Germany then. Once again, *everything* will occur to him: he really would have to hurry – back to Donaueschingen.

He will send three telegrams (when it is his turn in the queue).

TELEGRAM

I love you. Stop. Hireling

TELEGRAM

Stop. Stop. Hireling

TELEGRAM

I once had this uncle. Stop. Hireling

———————

This will do nicely, thought the Hireling, standing in the square outside the Tulcea Tourist Office. Just the place for an ending. It really is going to be a long day; a long day for a short farewell? – too much. The Hireling's headache was so visible that he was taken for a foreigner. Soon the dark little Lipovenian girl will appear, laughing and hurrying on towards Isaccea Street. Then

Wenn man. . .: When one can go no further, one simply stops. (Wittgenstein)

241

she'll come back with a group of youngsters. She'll glance expectantly at the man and he'll glance back just as before, grinning a little self-importantly for he sees on the little girl's face the pleasure he has caused.

On a ship called the *Pelican* (*Pelicanul*) they will sail down the Sulina arm to Crişani. They depart later than planned, apparently because they have to wait for a group of Italians who never turn up. When they finally set off, tourists are boarding the water-bus anchored beside them with cameras, video equipment and so on. The 'plebeian' audience on the *Pelican* whistle and catcall merrily. A woman in a coral-red blouse helps a fat, ungainly man in a white suit up the stairs.

They will see graceful rowing boats. On one of them the little Lipovenian girl. She studies the Hireling closely, then rows away with her friends. From another boat an old fisherman waves with a fish. They will eat at the Lebăda Hotel in Crişani, sour catfish soup (apparently you can only make good fish soup from Danube water, that is to say, there on the spot, and the fish must be so fresh that the odd longer bone still twitches in the warming water) with Murfatlar to drink. The Hireling imagined the catfish: it would be a little too fatty, but still very good: it would feel like bone marrow to cut, he thought. They will chat up a couple of Romanian girls, not impetuously, only as much as the menu requires. And just then, appearing quite out of the blue, his little girlfriend will be standing there before the table. She will secretly press a slip of paper into his hand, before running off again. On the little scrap of paper, torn from an exercise book, there will be numbers, a multiplication sum:

$$\begin{array}{r} 240.210 \\ \underline{48} \\ 50400 \end{array}$$

and the following words in capital letters: I AM A WOMAN. Later, the man will think to himself that this is the first sentence the girl ever addressed to him. Until now they had not spoken, only been glad of each other's presence. The Danube Countess, it is she. If I had three eyes I wouldn't even keep one on the paper, the girl will one day say saucily.

The dead fish is out of sorts, says the presumptuous, over-familiar waiter. Later they swing back to the Old Danube. The willow trees sweep the whole length of the deck. Increasingly more bird-life, lotus-islands, trees fallen to their knees on the hollow bank. An emerald-green sea of reeds sways in the wind, the sun is shining, strong, bright light. Once, somewhere in the Camargue, I saw a crucifix on which Christ lay so contentedly, so conceitedly, that he could have been sunbathing ... the sunbather ... The guide is a cheerful yellow-haired university student. She speaks good French, but is totally unsuited to her task and doesn't pass on a jot of information. I must entrust all my secrets to her. Water-lilies, water-marrow, Mila 23, here Patzaichin was born, the world-famous canoeist, the Lipovenian natural genius. An old woman rows alongside us in folk costume. A cry from our ship: Patzaichin's mother! The Hireling goes on laughing for some time. But later his laughter freezes on his lips, as, to his astonishment, he notices that there are not three arms of the Danube here, but almost as many as you please. And there is yet another Danube around every corner, or at least a sizable stretch of river that one could, or must, call the Danube. Or rather *Danube-like*. The Danube is no more, and becomes Danube-like. It hasn't grown old, but all the passion has gone out of it. Here it only flows because its bed slopes downwards. Perhaps, thinks the Hireling, it only really *lived* for the last time in the Kazan pass. Here there are no stakes – floods and the like – and the river has to do nothing but flow.

When they return to the main arm, the sudden wind will lift a woman's skirt and practically blow it into the Hireling's face. Merci Madame, the Hireling will say out loud. Again they leave 'the three rusty sisters', the three old fossils (Jeser, Mîndra and Costila). Time passes slowly, you can already smell the approaching fish-meal factory, the stench, when they are overtaken by the water-bus with the Italians on board, HALT, SONNE! the Hireling will hear, and the fat man in the white suit stands in the middle of the deck, a pistol in his hand, great commotion, people scatter left and right, only Dalma stands beside him, behind him, waiting for all that will happen to happen, *Halt, Sonne!* Roberto will shout once more, aiming at the setting sun which topples above the town behind a bend in the river, Roberto's tortured, snarling face begins to burn, meanwhile he sways as if searching for his balance, as if reaching out to clutch at the sun. The Hireling follows the path of the bullets with his gaze, as they head directly towards the sun. Roberto sprawls, burning, his face glistening with perspiration. He pants. Dalma is silent. *Halt, Sonne!*

On the square the Hireling saw the little girl again. He was a little frightened of this meeting. I am ... What was he to do now? But he didn't have to do anything: the girl sat down on the bench beside him, he thrust his aching head in her lap and tried to sleep. The sun shone brightly, in spite of having just been shot dead. The end. On the girl's face a sharp, cruel line. She stares at the Danube without expression, and softly runs her fingers through the man's hair. The Hireling decided that when he woke up he'd find his slip of paper and copy down into his notebook the names of all the ships he'd seen that day, 14 August: Razelm, Istria, Salvator, Bucureni, Polar, Malnaş, Izer, Mîndra, Costila, Tîrnava, Someş, Caraiman, Topliţa, Polar XI, Cincaş, Snagov, Mizil, Lupeni, Rîureni, Athanassios D, Tîrgu Jiu, Braşov, Vîrsan, Călimăneşti, Gheorgheni, Voiajor, Leopard, Cardon, Cocora, Dorobanţi, Cormoran, Pontica, Căciulata, Grădina, Armug, Colina, Zheica, Semnal.

Specialist Literature (not) Consulted

Gyula Antalffy: *Thus We Travelled in Days of Old*
Antos, Berényi, Vígh: *Danube Fishing Guide*
Autrement BP Danube Blues Octobre 1988
Adolf Ágai: *A Jouney from Pest to Budapest, 1843–1907*
Ingeborg Bachman: *Simultan*
Jean Bart: *Europolis*
Iván Bedó: *Pirates on the Danube*
Berinkey, Farkas: *Investigation of Fish Nutriens in the Soroksár Arm of the Danube*
István Bogdán: *Old Hungarian Tales*
Bokody, Hábl, Susoczky: *Water Tours*
Richard Brautigan: *Not Blown by the Wind*
Elias Canetti: *The Voices of Marrakesh*
R. Chandler: *The Lady in the Lake*
Bruce Chatwin: *The Songlines*
Columbus: Ship's Log
The Courtly Culture of the Hungarian Renaissance (edited by Ágnes R. Várkonyi)
Ana Clavel: *Fuera de escena*
F. Cramer: *Chaos und Ordnung*
Hans Dernschwam: *Transylvania, Beszterecebánya, Turkish Diary Danube* (Guidebook series: Panorama)
Hans Magnus Enzensberger: *Europe, Europe*
Geo Special, Budapest 1989/4
Franz Grillparzer: *Tagebuch auf der Reise nach . . .*

Gault-Millau Guide
Hubert Hegedűs: *On the Danube, On the Sea*
Heinrich Heine: *Deutschland: Ein Wintermärchen*
Otto Herman: *Lives of Fishermen and Shepherds*
Panait Istrati: *Thistles of the Plain*
Botond J. Kis: *The Book of the Delta* (from the library of Júlia Sigmond)
Joszef Kőrösi: *The Land of the Capital*
László Kőváry: *Landscapes, Travel Sketches*
Milan Kundera: *The Art of the Novel*
István Lázár: *Travellers and Observers of the World*
Claudio Magris: *The Habsburg Myth*
G.G. Marquez: *Love in the Time of Cholera*
Daphne du Maurier: *Rebecca*
Dr Béla Mátéka: *Penny Guide to Budapest*
Andor Medriczky: *Old Baths of Budapest*
Old Pest–Buda (edited by Imre Trecsényi-Waldapfel)
Géza Ottlik: *School on the Frontier*
Palotás, Balázs: *General Bridge Building* (technical college textbook)
O. Pastior: *Der Krimgotische Facher*
Christoph Ransmayr: *The Last World*
Dezső Rexa: *Holiday Resorts by the Danube*
Nat Roid (Deszo Tandőri): *Looks Too Good Dead*
Russian and Ukranian Travellers in Old Hungary (edited by Lajos Tardy)
The Siege of Buda (Hungarian Archive, edited by Katalin Péter)
Laurence Sterne: *A Sentimental Journey*
Bram Stoker: *Dracula*
Laszló Székely: *My Viennese Travels*
György Szerémi: *The Twilight of Hungary*
Jenő Sz. Farkas: *The Story of Voivode Dracula*
Lajos Tardy: *Our Old Renown in the World*
Theory of Order (from the library of István Mányoki)
György Timár: *The Secrets of the Danube*
Kálmán Tolnai: *From the Danube to the Nile*
Antal Váradi: *Memories of Old Pest*
Jules Verne: *The Danube Pilot*
Edgar Wind: *Art and Anarchy*